Lestrade and the gift of the prince

Sholto Lestrade had never smelt the tangle o' the Isles before Arthur, Duke of Connaught, put him on the trail to the Highlands. Murder is afoot among the footmen of the Royal Household: a servant girl, Amy Macpherson, has been brutally slaughtered.

Ineptly disguised as a schoolmaster in his bowler and Donegal, with his battered old Gladstone, the intrepid Superintendent is impelled by a villainous web of conspiracy northwards to the Isle of Skye by way of Balmoral.

With the skirl of the pipes in his ears and more than a dram of a certain medicinal compound inside him, Lestrade, following the most baffling clues he has yet unravelled, takes the low road alone, save for the trusty but mysterious Alistair Sphagnum in his twin-engined, bright red boneshaker. Narrowly escaping the inferno of Room 13 in the North British Hotel, Lestrade falls foul of The McNab of That Ilk and The Mackinnon of *That* Ilk, and plays a very odd game of 'Find the Lady' in Glamis Castle.

Coming from *Scotland* Yard is no help at all to a Sassenach in trews and everyone is convinced it's a job for the Leith Police. Threatened by ghoulies, ghosties and wee, sleekit beasties, Lestrade hears things go bump in the night before solving the case of Drambuie.

Wit as sharp as a skean-dhu distinguishes this ninth adventure of the Yard's most famous flatfoot.

LESTRADE
AND THE GIFT
OF THE PRINCE

M. J. Trow

Constable · London

First published in Great Britain 1991
by Constable & Company Limited
3 The Lanchesters, 162 Fulham Palace Road
London W6 9ER
Copyright © 1991 by M. J. Trow
The right of M. J. Trow to be
identified as the author of this Work
has been asserted by him in accordance
with the Copyright, Designs and Patents Act 1988
ISBN 0 09 470530 5
Set in Linotron Palatino 10pt by
CentraCet, Cambridge
Printed in Great Britain by
St Edmundsbury Press Limited
Bury St Edmunds, Suffolk

A CIP catalogue record for this book
is available from the British Library

'And he that will this health deny,
Down among the dead men let him lie.'
                                John Dyer

1

The rain set in early that night. She listened to it throbbing on the tear-streaked windows at Windsor, splashing in the gutters that had killed him. But she would not accept that. She would never accept that. It was Bertie. Bertie the disappointment. All his appalling peccadilloes. At the Curragh. At Cambridge. It was that that had broken her darling's heart.

'Indeed, Mama,' the reprobate had said, 'I will be all I can to you.' And she had kissed him.

But that was earlier. In the Red Room where Phipps and Leiningen had half carried her. Her *liebchen* had only just gone and a stunned Household whispered in corners of the passing of Albert the Good. Now, in the early hours with only the December rain for company, she had had time to think. She forced herself to stand, away from the sofa, alone. She looked at Dr Watson's draught of brandy-and-something-to-make-her-sleep. She could not sleep. She would not sleep. She was a widow. And a mother. And a Queen. And she found herself wishing, suddenly, that she was none of these. That one of her ghastly old uncles had sired a boy who would have ruled in her place. And that she and Albert had been allowed to skip away, hand in hand, across the primroses at Osborne or the heather at Balmoral . . . Balmoral. And the scent of the Highlands was on the air.

'Ma'am.' There was a guttural cough behind her and she turned to see the kilted nether limbs of her dead husband's ghillie, standing like a Douglas fir in the doorway, with the light at his back.

'Brown,' she said, without emotion.

'I came as soon as I heard he was ill,' he growled, sweeping off the tam-o'-shanter with its familiar bunch of pheasant feathers. 'Ye have ma condolences, Ma'am.'

She crossed the room to him. And they stood, the Queen and her servant for a long time, listening to the rain.

'Hold me, John,' she whispered.

He reached out a tweedy arm and took her gently by the shoulder, cradling the glossy head and placing it against his chest. She looked up at the tangle of beard, for all the world like the *chevaux de frise* those awful Americans used in their entrenchments, and breathed in the smell of the Highlands – the waft of the heather, the scent of the glens, the hint of the haggis.

'Oh, John, John,' she whispered.

'I know.' He bent to kiss her parting, grateful she was not wearing her tiara. Many was the mouthful of rubies he'd had in the months past. 'I want you to remember,' he said, in the broad Scots he used just for her, 'that yon Prince's death changes nothing. I love you now as I always have and always will.'

She looked up again, her eyes swimming with tears. 'Can a woman love two men?' she asked him. But John Brown's experience did not run to such things. He had once read of the possibility, in a naughty bookshop in London, but he was a Highlander. He shared his bed with no one. Except that sheep that time.

'Nay, lassie,' he told her, 'dinna let his going cloud your judgement.'

She sniffed with the ferocity of an Ironclad and broke free of him. 'You're right,' she said. 'But . . .' and the voice was hard again, in command, 'there must be no hint of . . . us . . . to the outside world. The great and small vulgar, as Mr Peel used to say, must never know.'

'So your journal, Vicky . . .'

'Will contain no word of it. I will, I must, be the dutiful wife. And the dutiful widow.'

He nodded, chewing his heavy moustache.

'There will be a time,' she said, 'when I must observe the niceties.' She turned to the window again and saw through its tears and her own the outline of the trees in the park, tossing their heads in the winter gale that roared along the Royal Mile

8

and the darker speck in the distance that was her bronzed grandfather, George III, riding to nowhere for ever.

'Full mourning is for one year,' she said. 'Black, like the colours of the night. I shall wear it for the rest of my life.' She whipped round, as though sensing the sneer at her back. 'And I'll have no talk of hypocrisy, John Brown.' Her eyes flashed with the fire that had reduced court officials and visiting dignitaries. God help Mr Gladstone if the unthinkable should happen and he should become Prime Minister.

'Indeed not, Ma'am,' Brown assured her with the old look she knew so well. 'Nothing is further from my thoughts.'

'I *did* love him . . . once. But he changed. He became maudlin. Self-absorbed. I can't . . . *We* can't love someone like that. And besides, his jokes were excruciating. He had no sense of humour. And you know, Brown,' she was Queen again, 'I do like a laugh.'

'Indeed, Ma'am,' and as the careful positioner of countless banana skins on the polished floors of Balmoral, he knew that only too well. 'So you dinna want to see what a Scotsman wears under his kilt?'

She looked at the strong face, the powerful legs. Yes, dammit, she would use the term 'legs' again. It was only Albert, with his Teutonic obsessions, who insisted on the proprieties. And such euphemisms were so horribly middle-class, weren't they? Nether limbs, indeed. She shuddered, wrestling inwardly with the sensuality which, for all her nine confinements, smouldered beneath her bombazine surface.

'Not tonight, John,' she said softly. 'It . . . wouldn't be right.'

'Aye,' he sighed. 'Well, I must be awa'. Oh, tell me . . .' He paused in mid-bow. 'Ma tincture. The one I sent by post-boy. It did no good, then?'

Victoria, by the grace of God, blinked. 'Oh, no,' she said suddenly recalling it, 'he was too far gone.'

'Did . . . er . . . the doctors mention it?'

'No.' She shook her head. 'I think Dr Watson would have tried anything towards the . . . end. But he did think the Prince looked a little brighter some days ago. That's when he administered your tincture. Alas, thereafter, dear Albert failed. What was it, by the way?'

'Ma'am?' Brown was nearly at the door.

'Your tincture. What was it?'

'Oh, a medicinal compound, Ma'am. Known only to a wee few. A dram or two o' that would be like to get Queen Anne back on her feet. In some cases.'

She nodded. 'We thank you, John,' she said. 'When next we are in Balmoral . . .' and she smiled at him.

He winked at her and took his leave.

He padded along the silent passageway, lit fitfully by the unreliable emissions of the Windsor Gas Company. For a man so large, he moved like a cat, twisting along the corridors he knew almost as well as those at Balmoral, and he entered the room.

Albert the Good lay in the uniform of a Field Marshal, with his Garter cloak in velvet splendour across his shoulders. Brown looked at the Prince, realizing for the first time how bald he'd become. He clicked his teeth at the gentle face, Teutonically composed, the lips blue, the cheeks grey.

'Well,' he muttered, 'we'll chase no more capercaillie together . . .' He bent over the body. 'You sanctimonious bastard!'

He looked about him at the bedside clutter. As he'd hoped, it lay undisturbed in the hysteria and chaos of the day. He saw a small bottle, the one that said 'A Present From The Highlands' on it, and he snatched it up. He sniffed it gently, careful not to inhale too deeply. He drew back quickly and replaced the stopper.

'Tsk, tsk, Albert laddie,' he said, 'I dinna know how you can drink this stuff,' and he bent over the master again. 'It's a good thing the Royal Physician isnae acquainted with wood spirit, isn't it? This stuff'll strip wallpaper at thirty yards.'

He turned the bottle round and smiled at the apt legend written on the label, 'Afore Ye Go'. He tucked it into his sporran, patting it with pride in the knowledge that it was the biggest in Scotland, and left the mausoleum that was already a shrine. Tired already of southern comfort, he would go north.

The clock ticked with a deafening thud. Or so it seemed to the little boy standing before the huge desk. He faced a man of vast proportions who scowled at him through the bottoms of bottles that passed for pince-nez.

'I want to make it quite clear to you, Master Lestrade,' the huge man said, 'that here at my Academy for the Sons of Nearly Respectable Gentlefolk, we do not tolerate such behaviour.'

'No, sir,' the little boy said, staring fixedly ahead, determined not to cry.

'Your father is in the police, is he not?'

'Yes, sir.'

'And your mother?'

The little boy frowned. 'No, sir, she isn't.'

For all his immense girth, Ranulph Poulson was an athlete of the first water when it came to child abuse and his right hand snaked out to catch the policeman's son a nasty one around the side of the head.

'Don't be flippant with me, boy,' the Headmaster snarled. 'You forget I've seen your Latin Grammar book. It's not very edifying and it leads me to suppose that you will never amount to very much at all. How old are you?'

'Seven, sir.'

'Quite. And if you wish to be eight in some distant future, you will not respond to every question with what the lower orders call cheek. Wit it couldn't possibly be.' He paused in his own rhetoric and leaned back in the chair. 'What I meant,' he said, whipping out a handkerchief that appeared to have been picked up in Rotten Row and wiping his spectacles with it, 'as you well know, Lestrade, is what does your mother do for a living?'

'She is a laundress, sir,' the little boy told him.

Mr Poulson dropped his spectacles. 'You mean she takes in washing?'

'Yes, sir.'

'Other people's washing?'

'Yes, sir.'

'Good God.'

Now Poulson sat on the horns of a dilemma. Mrs Lestrade was a washer-woman. He could just picture her red hands and smell the suds. He shuddered at the thought of one eternal, life-long Monday and it filled him with dread. Some of his parents were bank clerks, under-underwriters, proof-readers and artificial limb manufacturers. What if they were to discover this terrible truth? On the other hand, the Lestrades' money

11

folded as well as anybody else's and he *did* have overheads. On the other hand, it was bad enough that Lestrade's father was a policeman. He knew it was a mistake to allow his secretary, Miss Minute, to enrol pupils on his day off. On the other hand, he had run out of hands. For a moment, he toyed with summoning her, calling her to account. 'Come here, Miss Minute,' he would have shouted. But he thought better of it.

'Well, Lestrade,' he said, when the shock had subsided a little, 'when a man of the eminence of Mr Mountfitchett tells you to stand for the Queen and to put your hand down your trousers, what do you do?'

Silence.

'What you do not do, young Lestrade, is to take him literally. He clearly meant,' and he stood up to emphasize the point, 'that you place your thumbs down the outward seam of your nether garments. Not . . .' and he blanched, 'what you did. And in the chapel, too. Sister Chippenham fainted. And she's had medical training.'

Poulson lumbered across his study and glowered down at the boy. 'Your parents pay good money for your education, Lestrade. And this is how you repay them.' He held up a hand black with finger-stalls. 'Luckily for you, my old trouble has recurred or I'd beat you to within an inch of your not-very-promising young life. Understand?'

'Yes, sir.' Even now, the boy's lip refused to quiver.

Poulson leaned over him. 'Dirty little boys like you', he hissed, 'do not go to heaven, Lestrade. They go to the Asylum. And on the way there, they go blind. Blind from looking for the hairs that form on the palms of their hands.'

Lestrade's fingers twitched behind his back. He fought down the urge to rush to the window to check for himself.

'Which is your bed in the dormitory?' Poulson asked.

'Bed Number Thirty-six, sir,' Lestrade told him.

'Right. You will see Sister Chippenham this morning – and approach her with care, you degenerate. I want no more vapours. You will tell her to give you Bed Number Thirteen.'

'Aahh!' An involuntary cry burst from the seven-year-old.

'Yes, Thirteen, you deviant. The one by the open window and the drains. Now,' he returned to the chair, 'because I am a reasonable man, we will say no more about this morning's little

12

fiasco. Let me see.' He turned to the window overlooking the driving sleet that blew horizontally across the wilderness of Blackheath. 'Peasants once behaved revoltingly out there, Lestrade. Mr Taylor, your history master, will no doubt be teaching you that this term. It is fitting therefore that for revolting behaviour, you will put on the full marching pack kindly lent to us by the City of London Fusiliers and you will run around the heath for the rest of the day. Fine, bracing December weather. No problems at all.' And he flashed his teeth at the boy. 'All right?'

'Yes, sir.' Lestrade swallowed hard.

'And tomorrow is a holiday on the occasion of the funeral of His Royal Highness Prince Albert. When the other boys are having their outing, you will tackle the second declension. Do I make myself clear?'

'Yes, sir.'

'Good. Now, get out.'

And the little boy left. For a while, he stood shivering by the door, then he controlled the lip and hauled the copy of Summers's *Latin For Idiots* out of his trousers, the same pair into which his hands had innocently strayed during morning prayers.

'Well?' a voice whispered around a corner.

Lestrade held out a hand. 'That's threepence, Derbyshire,' he said.

'No beating?' Derbyshire was incredulous.

Lestrade shook his head.

Derbyshire fumbled in his pockets to find the change.

'You, boy!' came a roar from the lungs of Mr Mountfitchett, alert now to an appallingly early contagion of self-abuse that seemed to be sweeping the school. 'Come here this instant – if you can see your way along the corridor, that is.'

Derbyshire, as innocent in these matters as Lestrade, looked round for his young friend in desperation. But Lestrade had gone in search of Sister Chippenham, checking Derbyshire's pennies with his teeth as he went. As the cricket results were to prove for the rest of the century, Derbyshire had no chance at all.

2

For all he spent the day in close confinement in the little room under the eaves where all recalcitrants were sent, Lestrade never did master the second declension. Even forty-two years later, he was hazy on it. And gerundives had eluded him for ever.

Even so, he was able to find his way to the Horse and Collar that morning in another December, eternities later. All in all, it was the close of a very eventful year. Everyone was whistling the Kashmiri Song as they went about their windy business off the Strand. They had given some Frenchwoman a Nobel prize for something her husband had done and every woman you passed in the street was trying to look like a Gibson Girl. A maniac called Ebenezer Howard was building something he called a Garden City in the lovely, unspoiled fields of Hertfordshire. No one knew why.

And the Yard? Well, the Yard was the Yard. Nimrod Frost, Assistant Commissioner, had led the Criminal Investigation Department with his usual horizontal verve. Rumour had it that he had been dismissed from command from one of Kitchener's concentration camps in the late, Great War, for being too unpleasant. 'His Nims' had continued to rule with a nimrod of iron until he suddenly keeled over in the summer of 1901, a martyr to Miss Featherstonehaugh's cream cakes. And in his place came a little nut-brown man from India with a thing about the little patterns on the ends of people's fingers. Walter Dew had made Inspector by being in the right place at the right time. And the cases were knee-deep in Norman Shaw's Opera House. From the sergeants' stews in the basement, where the rats came out of the river in search of tripe sandwiches, to those weird

14

attic rooms where the seventeen men of the Special Branch went about their paranoid trade, the building positively groaned with overwork.

Lestrade had received the telegram the previous day: SUPT LESTRADE STOP MEET ME TOMORROW TWELVE SHARP STOP HORSE AND COLLAR STOP HUSH HUSH STOP NOT A WORD TO ANYONE STOP ESPECIALLY TOP BRASS STOP

It was unsigned and as Lestrade had missed the lecture on Heraldry for Policemen, he was stumped by both monogram and telegram.

'Connaught,' Detective Constable Jones had assured him, 'Arthur William Patrick Albert, Duke of.'

'Tell me more,' Lestrade had insisted, dunking his Bath Oliver for the requisite number of seconds.

'Son of the late Queen-Empress,' the encyclopaedic minion had told him, polishing the shoe-boxes of depositions to left and right. 'Born the first of May, 1850. Named Arthur after his godfather, the Duke of Wellington. And William Patrick Albert after Arthur. Entered Royal Engineers 1868, made Duke of Connaught and Strathearn 1874. Served with the Seventh Hussars and Rifle Brigade. Commanded Brigade of Guards in Egypt 1882 and held field command in India 1886 to 1890. General 1893. Became a Field Marshal last year.'

'Hmm,' Lestrade had mused. 'A military man, then.'

'You could say that, sir.' Jones had wondered again how his guv'nor had risen so far.

'I wonder what he wants with me?'

'There *is* talk on the ground floor, sir.' Jones had risked a hernia by hauling the Remington into position

'There's *always* talk on the ground floor, Jones,' Lestrade had assured the lad. 'What is it this time in particular?'

Jones looked about him. Only the fire crackled and spat in the corner. And in the distance the click of outsize number elevens wandering the corridors. Chief Inspector Walter Dew looked over his pince-nez at the young detective and paused in mid-stir, the spoon looking ever more runcible in the centre of his Darjeeling.

'It's all right,' Lestrade had said. 'We're alone. Inspector Dew is deaf, aren't you, Walter?'

15

The inspector had looked at his watch. 'It must be nearly half-past ten, sir,' he had said.

'Quite. Well, Jones?'

'There's talk of the introduction of an officer-class in the Metropolitan, sir. Bringing in army men.'

Lestrade and Dew exploded with laughter simultaneously. 'There was talk of that when I was in the City Force, lad,' the superintendent told him. 'Mr Gladstone was Prime Minister and this place hadn't even been built. Young Walter here was a twinkle in his father's eye. Your father's eyes never twinkled, did they? The great Athelney Jones of the River Police?'

Jones had looked oddly at him.

'No, well, it's all those years bobbing up and down on the Thames. That's why we're called Bobbies, you know.'

'No, sir,' Jones had had the effrontery to correct him, 'we're called Bobbies because . . .'

Lestrade had held up his hand. 'It's what passes for humour at the Yard, lad. Remember, *I* do the jokes,' he had said. 'No, mark my words. Whatever his lordship wants, he doesn't intend to take over the Force . . . does he?'

Well, now he would find out. The Horse and Collar stood in those days on the corner of William IV Street, one of the few houses in London where it was reputed Dr Johnson had *not* lived. You entered it by the side door if you were in the know – a legacy of the old days when the Press Gang had come up river from Greenwich Reaches in search of likely lads. And Lestrade took up his position in the snug, his Donegalled back to the wall. From here, he could see all three doors at a glance. He hoped he'd know his man. The only one of Victoria's sons not to have inherited to *too* great a degree his mother's poppy eyes and impressive girth. He also stood head and shoulders above his mother – God Bless Her – but then, that was to be expected. The British Army was not so degenerate yet as to rank midgets among its Field Marshals.

Lestrade was embarking on his second pint of mine host's excellent brew – the one with Tincture of Thames Water – when he sensed a hush fall over the place and, slowly, he saw the caps come off. He saw a black plume, nodding upright, move above the heads at the bar, coming from the main door to his left.

'God bless you, sir,' a rough voice shouted.

And another, 'Three cheers for his Grace the Duke of Connaught!' and the huzzas drowned the drone of conversation and the metallic clang of the spittoons. The crowd broke, frozen in an instant of astonishment, and a tall gent with a clipped military moustache emerged, looking at Lestrade. He wore the full dress uniform and astrakhan busby of a colonel of the Rifle Brigade, complete with sword and spurs.

'Lestrade?' he asked.

The superintendent of that name rose dumbly.

'Connaught,' and the Field Marshal extended a gloved hand. Lestrade bowed and extended his, when suddenly, Connaught nodded sharply, swerved his hand past Lestrade's and nudged elbows with him. He winked his left eye, then lifted his right leg before sitting down with arms folded on the table. 'Oh,' he said in surprise and a little disappointment, 'you are not of the Order.'

'Er . . . oh, no, my lord, please. I'll get the orders.' He clicked his fingers and mine host bustled forward proudly, Mrs Mine Host beaming at his elbow.

'No, my dear fellow.' Connaught unlaced his cap. 'I mean . . .' and he leaned forward so that busby and bowler brushed together, 'you are not of the Brotherhood?'

'Ah.' Lestrade understood. 'No, sir. Church of England.'

Connaught sighed. 'Pint of your best, landlord,' he said, 'and a small one for this gentleman.'

'Very good, my lord.' Mrs Mine Host bobbed and seemed to freeze in mid-curtsey, grinning like a maniac at the Duke until her husband shepherded her away. Connaught noted the crowd at his back, staring in stunned silence.

'Carry on,' he waved at them. 'You're all doing a marvellous job. Well done. You've never had it so good.'

Slowly, they shifted back to their former conversations and the air rang with the rattle of spittoons and the scraping of sawdust. Connaught leaned forward to Lestrade again and both men placed their respective titfers on the table beside them. 'Thought I'd be as unobtrusive as possible, Lestrade,' he said. 'Nothing showy. Delicate matter, you see.'

'I see, sir.' Lestrade took in the patent-leather cross-belt with its silver chains and whistle, the dark green tunic with its elaborate black frogging and the gleaming honeysuckle hilt of the sword. Comforting at least that Field Marshals and people of their kidney carried the same whatsits as the humble copper on the beat.

'After all,' Connaught went on, 'could have worn my togs of the Seventh Hussars with all that gold braid or the scarlet of a Field Marshal. Didn't though. Didn't want to arouse suspicion, you see.'

'Of course not,' agreed Lestrade who had lived with the arousal of suspicion all his working life.

A pint and a half of best bitter appeared on a silver salver, carried by mine host. In the background, Lestrade noted that the publican's wife was being restrained by burly publican's arms and another member of the family was already painting 'By Appointment' above the bar.

'Your good health!' Connaught sipped the froth. 'So that's what beer tastes like.'

'Er . . . no, sir,' Lestrade assured him. 'Now, your telegram . . .'

'Ah yes. Well, it's not generally known, Lestrade. And all this is of course in the utmost secrecy . . .'

Lestrade glanced over the Duke's shoulders at the dozens of gaping faces. 'Quite,' he said.

'I could have come to Scotland Yard, but that would have drawn too much attention.'

'Yes, of course.'

'It's not generally known that I am to be made Inspector General of the Army next year. Bertie's New Year Honours list and so forth.'

'Congratulations, sir.'

'Yes, indeed, but you see, the point is that I shan't be in the country all that often. I've just got back from Ireland now and I'm off to South Africa in a few weeks.'

'I see,' bluffed Lestrade, who actually saw nothing at all.

'But there's this little problem. I was at Balmoral last week – you know, Mama and Papa's holiday retreat up . . . there.'

'Ah yes,' nodded Lestrade sagely with the worldly-wiseness of a man who had never been further north than Macclesfield.

'Well, the damnedest thing has happened.'

'Oh?'

18

Connaught eased himself closer so that prince and superintendent were eyeball to eyeball. 'One of the servant gels was killed.'

'Really?' Lestrade's eyes narrowed. 'Accident?'

'Well, her head was driven in by a heavy object. Fourteen blows to the skull, they say.'

'Not likely, then,' Lestrade muttered. 'What do the local police make of it?'

'Ah well, there you have it.' Connaught continued to whisper. 'If it doesn't involve illicit whisky or sheep, they're at a loss. Their official view is suicide.'

Lestrade sat bolt upright. Fourteen blows to the skull was the most determined suicide he'd ever heard of. 'Why are you telling me this, my lord?'

'Bertie thinks highly of you, Lestrade. Since that business at the coronation. He doesn't go to Balmoral much, of course, not any more. Too many painful memories, I think. Not to mention the tartan linoleum. But I mentioned it to him at the Palace and he suggested I call you in.'

'I am flattered, sir, but the problem is that I have no jurisdiction in Scotland. My powers end at the border.'

'Tosh and fiddlesticks,' said Connaught. 'Can't you take some leave or something?'

'Leave?'

'Yes. Look, Lestrade, I don't suppose you chappies make very much, do you? I'll cover all that. Expenses and so on. No problem. But I don't want the Scottish Constabulary thundering all over Balmoral. It's not decent. It's not done. Look here . . .' and he leaned even closer so that he was whispering in Lestrade's ear and his moustache tickled. 'Since Mama's day, and indeed before, there've been some unfortunate goings-on going on. I don't have to tell you about Bertie, do I? He's my brother and the King-Emperor, I know, but his behaviour leaves much to be desired. There was that Lady Mordaunt, you know, the incontinent one; Mrs Keppel; Mrs Langtry; Mrs . . . Oh, no.' He coloured crimson. 'She's . . . somebody else's. Tranby Croft; The Grange; Kimber; well, practically every country house on the map. Then there was Eddie, my nephew . . .'

Lestrade had met him before.

19

'. . . Some nonsense with a flower girl in the East End; that Cleveland Street thing with those choirboys . . .'

'Errand boys,' Lestrade corrected him.

'Yes, well. Some of us in the family want all that played down. There are international implications, you see. I shouldn't be telling you this, I know, but Bertie's been in Paris this year, coming to an arrangement with the French. We don't have many friends in the world, Lestrade. We're too damned powerful, that's why. But we can't be splendidly isolated for ever. Especially now that old bugger Salisbury's gone. There is anarchy wherever you look. The thrones of Europe aren't safe, Lestrade. Imagine how it would look in the *Anarchist Review* – 'Servant Slaughtered in Royal Palace.' There'd be some eyebrows raised in the Wilhelmstrasse, I can tell you. It won't do. It won't do at all. That's why I've called you in. And that's why I want no one – no one at all – to be involved. This is absolutely hush hush. Clear?'

'I may need some help, sir,' Lestrade ventured.

'Constables, you mean?'

Lestrade nodded.

'Keep them to an absolute minimum, then,' Connaught said. 'And I mean that. Well,' he leaned back, 'the man to deal with is Ramsay. He's Steward of the Household at Balmoral. He'll be your eyes and ears. And your interpreter.'

'Interpreter?' Lestrade's jaw fell slack.

'Not literally.' Connaught took up his cap. 'They mostly speak English on the estates. But,' he fitted the chin-chain under his lip, 'they're a clannish lot, Lestrade. You'll have to tread carefully.'

Lestrade smiled. It was the story of his life.

'Name?'

'Snellgrove, sir. Peter Wimsey.'

Lestrade's tired old eyes narrowed on the sheet before him. 'Peter Wimsey Snellgrove,' he repeated. 'Service?'

'Four years with the Post Office, sir.'

'Yes, well, that doesn't count, does it? Service?'

'Er . . . six months at Rotherhithe with Mr Jones.'

Lestrade leaned back in the chair. 'Oh dear,' he said. 'I can see why you put in for the Detective Branch. Well, Snellgrove, I have to say it doesn't look very promising. Can you read and write?'

'Of course, sir.' The young constable was rather affronted.

'And use one of those telegraph things?'

'I can send a telegram, sir,' Snellgrove assured him.

'Well. We shall see . . . I'll give you two weeks' trial., After that, Athelney Jones can have you back.'

'Very good, sir. Thank you, sir.'

'So you must be . . .?' Lestrade turned to the other young man.

'Next, sir,' the lad said.

'No, I mean, what is your name?'

'Marshall, sir, Edward Tacitus.'

Lestrade looked him up and down. He ususally did that a few times with rookies. With this one, once was enough. 'Service?'

'Three years Number Four Dog Handler at Walthamstow, sir.'

'Is that it?' Lestrade asked after a pause.

'Yes, sir.' Marshall shrugged.

'So be it,' the superintendent sighed. 'You, I take it, have the usual skills.'

'Indeed, sir. I went to Mr Poulson's Academy.'

Lestrade's pen dropped from disbelieving fingers. 'In Blackheath?'

'Yes, sir.' Marshall's face brightened. 'Do you know it?'

'Know it, laddie? Apart from Mr Disraeli, I am its *only* famous old boy. Well, well, well. Of course, the staff will have changed. Old Poulson's dead, I know.'

'You wouldn't have known a Mr Mountfitchett, I suppose, sir?'

'Well, yes, as a matter of fact . . . I would have thought he'd have retired years ago.'

'Ah, well, he has now, sir.'

'Ah.'

'Something about being found with his hand down a boy's trousers. Nothing to it, I'm sure. Though of course if it happened today, I'd have to feel his collar.'

'Yes,' mused Lestrade. 'He'd probably enjoy that. Well,

gentlemen; a few orders of the day – rules for the road, so to speak. That gentleman over there, the one buried in paperwork, is Chief Inspector Dew. He's a hard man, but a fair one. Cross him and you'll go down, I promise you. Those two in the corridor we call an outer office are Detective Constables Dickens and Jones. You'll do well to immolate them. Although I'd never say it to their faces, they're what coppers ought to be – intelligent. Which brings me to Chief Superintendent Abberline, who isn't. Yes, it's bloody unprofessional of me to say so, but this is the Yard, gentlemen. The most public institution in the world. Put a foot wrong here today and everybody will know about it tomorrow. You take orders from everybody for the first five years, but if there's ever a conflict of orders or you ever need advice, then you come to me. Now, your first assignment. Snellgrove?'

'Sir?'

'We're low on tea. Nip to Hip Hop's Chinese Emporium in Richmond Terrace. Tell them Mr Dew sent you. He speaks the language like a native. You'll need three green forms and eight white ones – all available from Sergeant Major in Accounts, third floor back. Clear?'

'As a bell, sir.'

'Good. Marshall?'

'Sir?'

'Bath Olivers. They're round, biscuity things with little dents in them. It's a fair step, but the best ones come from Harrods Confectionery Department, in Knightsbridge. Same number of forms, but be sure and tell them to put it on Mr Abberline's bill. Got it?'

'Perfectly, sir.'

Lestrade winked. 'Good lad. Nice to see the old school doing so well.'

The constables took their leave and made for Accounts on the third floor.

'Fancy you being at the guv'nor's old school, then, Tass,' grinned Snellgrove.

'Old school be buggered,' said Marshall. 'Never been near the place.'

'But how . . .'

'When I was at Walthamstow, Number One Dog Handler

22

was an old bastard called Derbyshire. Now he *had* been to Lestrade's old school. Better than that, he'd been there with Lestrade.'

'Get away!'

'I just got a few names as soon as I knew I was being posted here. You never know when it's going to come in useful.'

'You old reprobate.' Snellgrove slapped him round the head.

'Stick with me, son. We'll be running this place inside a month.'

The policeman's policeman – 'Lord Love Us' to anybody below the rank of sergeant – sat by the crackling fire in his palatial office, slowly roasting his nuts. In the end he had to move back for the heat was oppressive. There was a knock on the frosted glass panel.

'Come!' he called.

A rather battered, yellow face appeared round the door, the eyes brighter than usual. But there was something of the impermanent in the Donegal draped over the arm and the bulging Gladstone bag.

'Coming or going, Lestrade?' Mr Edward Henry demanded.

'I wish I knew, sir,' the superintendent admitted. 'It's about leave.'

'*Leave*, Lestrade?' Henry crossed to his leather-topped desk. It gave him comfort in moments like these to feel the walnut burr barrier between himself and his underlings. He had known Lestrade, man and man, for nearly three years. He was a maverick, a blithe spirit, and he had a knack of getting up people's noses. But he got results. And there, for the Yard, the story began and ended.

'It's nearly Christmas, sir,' Lestrade reminded him.

The Assistant Commissioner checked the date gadget on his desk: 14 December. So it was. 'So it is,' he said. 'I thought you were working over Christmas?'

'Ah, it's my aged aunt,' said Lestrade.

'What is?'

'She's ailing. Picture, if you will, a frail, silver-haired old lady, living alone in the autumn of her years, no sound but the endless clack-clack of her knitting.' He produced a relatively clean handkerchief and trumpeted into it. Way across the river, a lighter called back in the fog.

'Don't tell me,' said Henry. 'You're all she's got and you must spend Christmas with her.'

Lestrade's lip quivered, probably the first time it had since he was seven. 'It may be her last, Mr Henry.'

'Yes, and I'm the Akond of Swat.'

'Really, sir? Congratulations.'

Henry ignored this. 'You have two calendar weeks, Lestrade. After that, I stop your pay. Merry Christmas,' and he returned to his nuts by the fire.

'Thank you, sir.' Lestrade's smile froze. 'And complaints of the season to you too.'

Lestrade had never smelt the tangle o' the isles. But he'd often caught a blast of Billingsgate borne on the river. It was probably much the same. Two over-dressed recruits of the Detective Department met him in the bustling concourse of Euston Station, snorting and hissing along with the engines as they struggled along the platform carrying their own baggage and Lestrade's.

'"Stick with me," he says,' quoted Snellgrove. '"We'll be running this place within a month." All I'm running is a temperature.'

'Stop moaning, Snellgrove,' Marshall gasped. 'We're going on our hols. That's not bad after one day at work.'

They rattled north through the iron grey of that mid-December and, as dusk settled like a winter carpet over the land, they found the twilit Saracen's Head in Lincoln. Great Tom tolled the hour as the trio of policemen crossed the cobbles, Lestrade's ankles ricking in all directions as he did his best to keep his dignity and his footing. They spent a cosy night on the expenses of the Duke of Connaught, whose chit Lestrade carried, and set off in a foggy dawn to the armpit of the North-east, Sunderland.

Here, the quaint little rustic of the Fenlands became the incomprehensible Geordie of the Tyne and the Wear. The whole place was black with coal and grey with the dust of grindstones. The bustle of the docks in the evening had lessened to the lonely wail of lighters trailing the harbour. The lighthouse winked at them from the pier where the great, grey North Sea roared and bellowed. They found warm comfort in the Saddle, where the Southerners faced their first taste of the brown substance called Newcastle Ale. They tasted some more. After all, the Duke of Connaught was paying.

From here they crossed the Pennines, the backbone of England, and the locomotives of the North-western line took them to that confluence of the Calder called Carlisle. Here, the townsfolk they met glowered at them. No one wore bowlers this far north and Lestrade's Donegal had an altogether London air about it. Perhaps they had not forgotten the unspeakable atrocities committed by 'Stinking Billy', the Butcher of Culloden. True, that was in 1745, but to the men of Carlisle, that was yesterday. For that reason, the London three ventured no further than the Coffee House and slept upright with their backs to the wall.

Lestrade waved goodbye to his lads at Coldstream the next day as they crossed the Tweed. So this was Scotland, he mused to himself as the purple mountains of the Lowlands broke above the groundmist. Snellgrove dumped the baggage on the little platform while the train took on more water.

'Here we are, then,' beamed Marshall. 'The parting of the ways, guv'nor.'

'That's right,' Lestrade said. 'Now, remember. You two are my anchors here on the border. You find a hotel – a cheap one, mind – and you never stray more than a few feet from the Post Office. If I get into trouble up . . . there, I may need to whistle pretty sharpish.'

'We'll be waiting, sir,' Marshall assured him.

'Good. Well, get on with it, men.'

'Goodbye, sir.' Marshall thrust out a hand. 'You'll forgive me for saying this, I know, but . . . well, travelling with you these last three days has been . . . Well, I feel I know so much more about policing. More than I ever learned before. It's been an honour, Mr Lestrade, sir, a real honour.'

'Yes, quite. Quite.' Lestrade shifted uneasily. The last person to pay him a compliment had been his mother.

'Mind how you go, guv'nor.' Marshall gripped the superintendent's shoulder firmly and held his lower lip with the rather

25

stiffer upper one. Then the whistle blew, the green flag came up and Lestrade and locomotive lurched into the mist.

'Do you think people will talk about us, Tass?' Snellgrove asked, hauling up his Gladstone.

'What do you mean?' Marshall hailed a passing porter.

'Well, this place is like Gretna Green, isn't it? Famous for . . . irregular marriages. You don't think people will think . . .?'

Marshall looked appalled. 'I am appalled, Detective Constable,' he said. 'This is Britain, albeit a repulsively northern part of it. There's irregular and irregular. It'll be all right as long as we both keep one foot on the floor all right. Now, where's that chit?'

'What chit?' Snellgrove packed the back of the little, grunting, groaning porter.

'This one,' and Marshall produced the note with the crest of the Duke of Connaught.

'That's Lestrade's,' Snellgrove said.

'Is it?' Marshall looked closely. 'Oh dear, so it is,' and he held it up feebly as though to attract the attention of the superintendent, rattling on to the North-east again. 'Never mind, he'll have to put his hand in his own pocket for a change. Still, he'll meet his match up . . . there. The Scots are as mean as he is.'

'Excuse me,' a border voice hailed them both. 'Is this baggage yours?'

The policemen turned to face the grey-whiskered man in the railway livery and peaked cap.

'It is,' they admitted, looking at the little beast of burden who struggled under it.

'Aye, well, you'll need to get somebody else to carry it for ye.'

'Why?' asked Marshall.

'This man's duties only extend to carrying forms of fuel. That man over there carries baggage. It's more than ma job's worth to allow it to be otherwise.'

'I see.' Marshall fumed at the pettiness of it all, but he too was a slave to tape, most of it red. 'So that man . . .'

'Aye, he's the luggage porter. This un's the coal porter.'

*

26

Lestrade had already signed the register of the North British Hotel when he realized that the Duke of Connaught's chit was not in his pocket. Neither was it in that secret place of his on which no mortal being had ever set eyes, namely his wallet. The desk clerk, a shrivelled prune of a man whose impeccable Lowland Scots accent could pierce whalebone at forty yards, gave him the disdainful look he reserved for all down-at-heel Sassenachs and shamed Lestrade into staying.

'Room Twelve,' the man had shrilled. 'I'll have your bags taken up presently, Mr . . . Lestrade, is it?'

'Thank you,' said the superintendent. 'I'll find my own way up.'

'I'm afraid you'll have to, sir. It being the festive season, we're a little undermanned just at the moment. Getting staff to work over Hogmanay is well nigh impossible, these days.'

Lestrade wondered to himself who this Hogmanay chappie was that people found it so distasteful to give orders to, but he felt it wasn't his place to ask. He toyed with the lift, but it reminded him of the one at the Yard and, as his mother had once been frightened by one, he took the plush-carpeted stairs, determined to send a telegram to Coldstream in the morning to get his lads to search the station there for his lost chit. The room was pleasant with a magnificent view along the arrow-shaft of Princes Street. He didn't know it, but the rooms to the south-east that looked up to the great, grey granite of the castle and the castle rock cost nearly twice as much. He had been let off lightly.

It was about nine in the evening, by the chimes of the Gothic clock overhead, that he heard a knock on the door. He wasn't much enjoying *The Lustful Turk* anyway. The whole concept of eunuchs and their doings was rather alien to a man born in Pimlico. A rather florid gentleman with the unmistakable air of a single-glazing salesman stood there.

'Ah, would you be Mr Lestrade?' he asked, doffing his hat.

'If you asked me very nicely,' Lestrade concurred.

'I see. Well, I wonder if I might ask you a very big favour.'

'You might, Mr . . . er . . .'

'Acheson,' the salesman said.

'Bless you,' said Lestrade. 'What favour?'

'Well, I'm in ladies' netherwear . . .' Acheson confessed.

27

Instinctively, Lestrade drew back. He was nearly fifty years old – an impressionable age. However, he had to admit that Acheson carried it all very well. There was hardly a trace of make-up or so much as a fol-de-rol to betray him.

'I mean, I sell what the French will insist on calling lingerie.'

'Ah, well, no thank you,' said Lestrade. 'I think I'm all right just at the moment. Perhaps next month,' and he tried to close the door.

'No, Mr Lestrade, I don't think you understand. You see, I'm next door. In Number Thirteen.'

'Bad luck,' beamed Lestrade and tried again. But Acheson had all the angles of the itinerant pedlar and his boot was firmly in the door.

'Precisely.' The man seemed quite desperate. 'It is. It's a phobia of mine, Mr Lestrade. Oh, I'm not normally super-stitious,' and he twisted his fingers together behind his back. 'It's just that I have this thing about thirteen. It was the number at the Last Supper, you see. And if I stay in that room I fear tonight will be mine.'

'Ah, the night your number came up.' Lestrade understood.

'Would you, dear Mr Lestrade, consent to swapping rooms? It's only for one night. I shall be away in the morning. And it will be my pleasure to buy you breakfast in return.'

'Well, I . . .'

'Please. I have tried the young man in Number Fourteen, but he's out. You would be doing me a great kindness, sir.'

Lestrade hesitated. 'Oh, very well,' he said. 'As long as the breakfast has nothing like porridge in it.'

Acheson looked very relieved. 'Kidneys à la urinoir?'

'Mouthwatering,' Lestrade agreed and began to repack his bags.

It was accomplished in a moment and no harm done. If anything, Acheson's four-poster was more comfortable than Lestrade's, and after the umpteenth act of bestiality by the Bey, somewhere on the Moroccan coast, Lestrade's battered old eyelids closed.

He awoke to a sensation of heat. When he had dozed over his late-night cocoa, brought to him by an incredibly surly Scot who lacked nearly all the rudiments of humanity, his fire had been all but out in the grate. Now, he was positively sweating, and the bedclothes lay on the floor in an untidy heap. He sat bolt upright in bed, clouting his head on the headboard as he did so. Immediately, he began to cough. He hadn't done it so heartily since he had joined the City Force back in '73 and old Doc Watsupp had grabbed his testicles with the finesse of a bargee. Come to think of it, his eyes were watering then as well. The room was full of smoke, acrid, pungent. Like . . . like lots of ladies' underwear on fire.

He heard thumps and bangs, punctuated by shouts, and from somewhere the manic clanging of a bell. He scrambled off the platform that was the four-poster and ran for the door. The handle felt hot, but he wrenched it open and a sheet of flame drove him back into the room.

'Come on, man,' he heard a voice call. 'Jump now, when I tell you.'

Lestrade shielded his eyes. He couldn't see a thing and his lungs roared and strained in his chest.

'Now!'

He threw himself forward, blindly trusting the voice that came from somewhere beyond the wall of fire. He felt the flames lick and crackle at the hem of his nightshirt and he collided with the flock of the corridor wallpaper so that the little bristly bits went right up his nose. He was aware of somebody spanking him soundly, and for half a second expected to turn and see the cadaverous form of Mr Mountfitchett. Instead, a blond young man in a dressing-gown stood there, a huge aspidistra leaf in his hand. Had it been a lily, Lestrade would have known that here was an Aesthete of the Wilde School, but that great card-player was dead. And he was the only queen in the pack. The joke was on him.

'Sorry,' the young man said. 'But you were smouldering somewhat.'

'You saved my life,' wheezed Lestrade.

'Time for the adulation I deserve later,' said the man. 'Now, there's a wee problem in Number Twelve.'

'Number Twelve?' Lestrade blinked desperately, trying to focus in the smoke.

'That's where the fire's coming from, but the door's locked. I can't get in.'

Lestrade looked up and down the passageway. 'Where is everybody?' he choked.

'I think we must be the only ones on this floor. The night clerk has gone for the Fire Brigade. I thought I heard the bell earlier.'

'So did I,' said Lestrade. He touched the panel. It was red hot. 'Shoulder job, then.'

'I've tried that,' the young man said. 'It won't budge.'

'It might with two of us. Ready?'

'Aye, ready,' and they both hurled themselves at the door. It crashed down, driving the air in and upwards as it went. They fell with it, Lestrade's nose thumping painfully into the brass numbers on the central panel. As they lay there, the flames billowed out into the passageway, sending showers of sparks to the ceiling.

'There,' coughed the young man. 'I can see his feet.'

They inched forward through the acrid black smoke, blind with tears and wilting in the heat. Lestrade's hand felt a stockinged foot and they began hauling together, dragging the body to the door and beyond.

'Right, lads!' There was a general shout and Lestrade felt himself being thrust backwards along the corridor by a jet of water that stung and nipped. 'Oh, Christ. Sorry, man,' he heard a gruff voice say and the next thing he knew, several brass-helmeted firemen were jostling him along the corridor to safety.

In the hotel foyer, all was chaos. The night clerk was dabbing hopelessly at the plush carpet where dirty great firemen's boots had trampled in the Edinburgh mud. Guests revived each other with smelling salts or hostile talk of suing, depending on their sex and inclination. Lestrade was surprised to find so many men carrying smelling salts.

'Well,' he heard a voice at his shoulder, 'we tried.'

Someone had thrown a blanket over him and he stood there, numb and soaked through, his eyes red-rimmed, his nose bleeding. 'We did,' he said to the young Scot.

'I'm Alistair Sphagnum.' He extended a hand.

'Sholto Lestrade. And thanks again. If it weren't for you, I'd have been well and truly cured by now.'

'Oh, it's nothing that any extraordinarily brave man wouldn't

30

do. That's what comes of Sassenachs – oh, saving your presence, of course, Lestrade – coming this far north. They canna live without a fire. And our friend in Room Twelve canna live with one.'

'You're sure he's dead, then?' Lestrade asked.

Sphagnum nodded to where two burly firemen in sooty uniforms tramped down the stairs carrying a stretcher. 'It looks like it,' he said.

'Does anybody know this gentleman?' The Fire Chief unbuckled his helmet straps.

'We do,' chorused Lestrade and Sphagnum.

'I met him as he changed rooms,' the Scotsman said.

'Changed rooms?' The Fire Chief's eyes narrowed. 'Now, why would he want to do that?'

'He was superstitious,' said Lestrade. 'He was in Thirteen. Asked me to change with him.'

'You were in Fourteen?'

'No,' said Sphagnum, 'I was in Fourteen.'

'I was in Twelve,' said Lestrade.

'Were you now?'

Lestrade knew hostility when it got up and hit him. 'Yes,' he said, slowly and firmly.

'And are you sure you didn't ask to change rooms with him?' the Fire Chief asked.

'Why should I?' Lestrade asked.

'That's what the Procurator Fiscal might like to know,' he said.

'Who?' asked Lestrade.

'Come off it, Chief,' said Sphagnum. 'There's nothing unlucky about the number twelve, you know. You've just heard the man explain it to you.'

'Aye, well, we only have his word for that, don't we?'

Lestrade squinted at the man. For a Chief of the Fire Brigade, he'd have made a damn good copper. 'You wanted us to identify him?' Lestrade asked.

'Aye.' The Chief flicked aside the blanket and a woman screamed.

'It's not a pretty sight, madam, I agree,' the Chief called.

'It's not that,' the woman called, being steadied by various adjacent males. 'It's . . . that . . . man.' Her enfeebled finger

31

pointed to Lestrade whose blanket had slipped off his shoulder to reveal his nightshirt plastered to his buttocks so that the material was stretched across them, outlined in the lurid gas-light of the foyer. He hastily covered himself up. Arson *and* indecent exposure in one night did not bode well.

'My God.' Sphagnum drew back from the blackened head of the corpse, the teeth bared and yellow, the lips stretched and bloodied.

'One moment.' Lestrade took the corner of his nightshirt from under the blanket, careful that the fainting lady did not see and read too much into it, and he dabbed at the face.

'Well?' growled the Chief. 'Is it him?'

'Oh yes,' said Lestrade when his mouth had closed. 'It's him all right. He told me his name was Acheson. He was a travelling salesman.'

'Well, his travelling days are over,' nodded the Chief.

There was a commotion at the double doors and an army of uniformed men strode in.

'Oh, God,' Sphagnum groaned. 'I hope you hadn't planned to catch up on your beauty sleep, Lestrade. We're in for another grilling, so to speak. It's the Leith Police.'

'That's easy for you to say,' Lestrade murmured. 'Mr Sphagnum . . .' He motioned the young man away from the centre of activity.

'Aye?'

'What woke you up? The fire?'

'No. It was a thump. Or rather, a series of thumps.'

'From Room Twelve?'

'I couldn't tell. But you were between me and Acheson. Didn't you hear anything?'

Lestrade shook his head.

'Why do you ask?' Sphagnum said.

'Oh, no reason,' shrugged Lestrade. 'It's just that I've seen what fire can do to people before.'

'And?' Sphagnum waited.

'And I've never known it batter a man around the head before.'

'Good God.'

'At least, not several times.'

32

3

Inspector Thaddeus McFarlane of the Leith Police was as suspicious of Lestrade as the Chief of the Edinburgh Fire Brigade had been. He drank almost constantly from a small, leather-bound hip flask and between coping with the rumblings and gurglings which gave witness to the fact that he was a martyr to dyspepsia, kept threatening Lestrade with a night in the Tollbooth. If guarding a tollroad was the most the Leith Police could throw at a murder suspect, he had absolutely nothing to worry about.

It was dawn over the city when they let the superintendent go. Someone had salvaged his bowler and his Donegal and his battered old Gladstone, although his copy of *The Lustful Turk* seemed to have gone up in the inferno. That was as far as Lestrade knew. In fact it was now in the possession of the flatulence-prone McFarlane who read it avidly between sips of whatever the hip flask contained, toying with charging Lestrade with the possession of pornographic literature. If he saw him again, he vowed to throw the book at him.

McFarlane's surmise was correct. Lestrade was disturbed. But not by *The Lustful Turk*. Something did not sit right about the whole business of the late Mr Acheson. First, the coincidence of his changing rooms with Lestrade. Who but Lestrade and the dead man knew of this switch? Not the desk clerk, certainly. Lestrade had gathered that much before he left the hotel flanked by policemen in the wee small hours. And then there were Acheson's wounds. Blows to the head. Had Acheson fallen, overcome by the flames and smoke? Or had those wounds been administered *before* the fire was started? And was that fire started deliberately, to conceal the fact? The fact of murder. One

33

thing was certain. There was no chance of Lestrade seeing the corpse again. He couldn't find a mortuary in a city this size and he sensed that asking a policeman would not elicit the most positive response. Perhaps, however, the dead man's room would still yield a clue, burnt out though it must be. On the pretext of retrieving more of his belongings, he trudged back to the North British Hotel. And as he turned the corner, past the little stone statue of a sickeningly cute dog and over the Waverley Bridge past the station, he suddenly realized that there *was* one man who knew of the last-minute change of rooms – the young Scot, Alistair Sphagnum.

'Morning, Lestrade,' a voice hailed him in the lobby. 'Returning to the scene of the crime, eh?'

'Mr Sphagnum,' said Lestrade. 'I might say the same of you.'

'Ah,' the young man smiled, 'but I at least have an excuse. I didn't have the chance last night to introduce myself properly. I am an undergraduate in the law faculty at the University.'

'The University?' Lestrade was none the wiser. 'Which one?'

Sphagnum stopped in his tracks. '*The* University,' he explained. 'And even if I say so myself, I am probably the only student to have read all four thousand three hundred and eight books in the Playfair Library – two of which, I might add, were written by my grandfather, Sphagnum of That Ilk. Now, tell me, what is your reason for returning?'

'Call it a morbid curiosity. That and the fact that I left my smoking cap here.'

'Well, if it wasn't smoking before, I'll wager it is now,' a thin reedy voice piped up.

Lestrade looked round him and noticed, hovering at Sphagnum's tweedy elbow, a white-haired, pince-nezed individual with the look of a rather miffed ibex. It struck Lestrade particularly because not long since, in the case of the Tax-Evading Taxidermist, he had collided with the mounted head of just such a beast on his way down the main staircase at the Museum of South Kensington. Altogether, the mounted version looked rather more alive than this one.

'Ah, forgive me.' Sphagnum led the little old man forward. 'May I introduce Dr Spittal of Glenshee? He's an honorary lecturer at the University – and what he doesn't know about fire isn't worth knowing, believe me. Shall we? I've acquired the late Acheson's bag from that morose bugger on the desk for a trifling sum. It's a good thing I'm of immense private means and the only generous Scotsman north of the Wall.'

This time they took the lift, largely on account of Dr Spittal's inability to raise his feet far off the ground. The blue cordon of the Leith Police had been replaced at the earliest opportunity by a tasteful panel with Highland scenes placed across the corridor by the management, anxious that news of the fire at the North British should reach as few ears and eyes as possible. Together, Sphagnum and Lestrade heaved it aside and wheeled the little old professor between them. Sphagnum motioned to Lestrade to stand aside and the little old boy tottered alone through the blackened doorway of the room that had once been Lestrade's. He sniffed, adjusted his pince-nez and scratched his head, peering from left to right.

'This fellow,' he suddenly said, turning to the men at the door, 'what did he do?'

Sphagnum looked blank.

'He told me he sold ladies' unmentionables,' said Lestrade.

'Aha,' the old man crowed. 'I knew it. Flannelette. Worst curse known to man after tertiary syphilis and a damn sight more inflammable.'

'So what happened?' Lestrade asked after a suitable pause had elapsed.

'Ssh!' Spittal and Sphagnum silenced him simultaneously. Lestrade stood back, a little shamefaced. Spittal glanced upward, poked the grate with the brass poker which had bent in the flames to the shape of a sickle and began to draw a wetted index finger along the window-sill. A board had been placed over the melted glass and the whole room resembled some dank-smelling dungeon.

'Right.' Spittal staggered back to the door. 'What happened is this, gentlemen. The fire started in the grate, due to an over-abundance of flannelette material. It spread quickly. Rather like most of my colleagues' lectures, hot air rises. Black, acrid smoke would have filled the ceiling and the flames then billowed sideways, probably fanned by the draughts at almost all orifices of the room.'

'So the water closet would have been of no help?' Lestrade asked.

'None whatever. I take it the body was found by the left side of the bed?'

'It was,' said Sphagnum. 'At least, that's where Lestrade and I dragged it from.'

'Right. He probably awoke because of the heat and fumes. He possibly tried to rise, but the carbonic acid and carbon monoxide would have stopped him in his tracks. It was that that caused his death, without a doubt.'

'Not the blows to the head?' Lestrade quizzed his man.

'Eh? What blows to the head is that, Lestrade?' Spittal peered at him over the pince-nez.

'Mr Sphagnum and I both clearly saw under the charring the impact of several blows.'

'Well, you may have, Lestrade,' Sphagnum said. 'God knows, I'm pretty well versed on lots of things, but I confess, I didn't see that.'

'No, no.' Spittal was adamant. 'In cases of fire, people die from shock, suffocation, or stupor. In the case of scalding, of course, oedema glottidis or broncho-pneumonia. Wait a minute.' He glanced at the blackened, peeling ceiling again. 'That's very peculiar.' He clicked his teeth – clearly a mistake, because they suddenly fell out of his mouth. 'Oh, Dashielham-mit!' he said. It was the worst profanity Mrs Spittal would allow under her roof or anyone else's.

'What is?' Lestrade gingerly lifted the dentures from the sooty carpet.

'Och, well.' Spittal accepted them. 'I always cleaned my own teeth with soot when I was a boy. What "what is"? What?'

'You said', Lestrade reminded him, 'that something was very peculiar.'

'Aye, right enough. Well, the only way blows to the head could have killed him would have been if the ceiling had caved in. But it hasn't. How about the tester?'

'You've got a method of testing this?' Lestrade was impressed.

'It's the bit over the bed, Lestrade,' Sphagnum explained.

'No.' Spittal tottered over there. 'Only one plank gone. Could that have done the damage?'

Lestrade shook his head, half-talking to himself. 'Not the

damage I saw,' he said. 'Dr Spittal, could you tell if the blows had been delivered before or after death?'

'Of course,' said the old man. 'But I'd have to see the cadaver.'

'Not possible,' said Lestrade.

'Well, it works like this. If I were to drop burning material – as it might be a flannelette fol-de-rol – on your arm, it would leave a tell-tale red blister. If I then removed the raised cuticle, your papillae would stand out as swollen and red. If I were to take scrapings then and heat them over a bunsen burner, the whole gubbins would solidify and they'd exude – positively exude, mind you – serum albumin and chlorides. Now, if you were dead, the stuff would go milky all right, but it wouldn't solidify – and the contents are usually bloody.'

'I was afraid they would be,' sighed Lestrade.

'Of course, the other way is to carry out a post-mortem. If there's no soot in the larynx and trachea, then our wee friend died *before* the fire. Then again, the blood spectrum is that of carboxy-haemoglobin if the person was alive when the burns were received, because blood only unites with carbon monoxide during respiration. D'ye ken?'

'Er . . . oh, I haven't for ages,' bluffed Lestrade, assuming that the old man had changed the subject. Spittal looked at him rather oddly.

'Well, doctor.' Sphagnum suddenly shook the old lecturer's hand. 'I really appreciate your rising so early and giving so freely of your expert advice. Let me see you to a cab. Mr Lestrade?' And they helped the old man back down to street level.

At the doors he stopped. 'Man,' he said to Lestrade, 'you didn't find your smoking cap.'

'As you surmised, doctor,' Lestrade said, 'a pile of ashes now. Never mind. Thanks once again.'

Spittal shook their hands and Sphagnum lifted the frail little body into the hansom. 'He's a nice old boy,' he said on his return and winked at Lestrade on the hotel steps. 'Wouldn't think he'd done thirteen years in Barlinnie for arson, would you?'

*

Breakfast, it transpired, was on Alistair Sphagnum. Not literally, for his table manners were perfect. Somehow the North British Hotel had lost its appeal, even though it promised a free anything to the inconvenienced gentlemen. So they went to a little place Sphagnum knew on Carlton Hill, past the memorials of the ancient dead – Nelson, whose graven image here seemed to resemble a telescope 108 feet high – and, even less accountably, Abraham Lincoln. Perhaps he once had an Edinburgh address as well as the one at Gettysburg.

'Powsowdie or Cullen Skink?' Sphagnum asked Lestrade as they perused the menu. 'I'm afraid the Stoved Howtowdie wi' Drappit Eggs is off.'

Lestrade didn't need Sphagnum to tell him that. 'Do they serve tea?'

'Tea?' Sphagnum cocked a Lowland eyebrow. 'Aye.'

'That'll do nicely,' said Lestrade, assuming that bacon and eggs was probably served no further north than Watford.

'A pot of tea, hen,' Sphagnum said to the aproned, dolly-mopped floozie whose soured countenance could have turned milk. 'And may I say how utterly charming you're looking today?'

She sneered at him and bustled about her business.

'Rum do, eh?'

'No, I'll have the tea straight thanks,' smiled Lestrade.

'No, I mean this business about old Acheson. It's a peculiar thing.'

'Indeed,' Lestrade nodded.

'A pity we couldn't take another peek at the wee cadaver, though.' Sphagnum began to crush some indescribable brown peat into the bowl of an elegant meerschaum.

'Hmm,' agreed Lestrade, who was just thinking along the same lines himself.

'I do have a bunsen burner in my rooms.'

'I was going to ask about that,' Lestrade said. Morbid curiosity was a way of life with him.

'What? The bunsen burner?'

'No. Your rooms. Do I take it from an earlier conversation that you are a student at Edinburgh University?'

Sphagnum sat upright. 'I am unaware of any other,' he said.

'Quite. So why were you staying last night at Room Fourteen of the North British Hotel?'

'My, but aren't you the suspicious one,' grinned Sphagnum. 'If I didn't know better, I'd say you were the pol's.'

'The what?'

'Och, I'm sorry. That's what comes of spending too long among the low-life of Glasgow on my vacations. The police.'

'As a matter of fact . . .'

The tea arrived and the tray was thumped down.

'Thank you, hen, gracious as ever.' Sphagnum jerked his head in the floozie's direction. 'A graduate of the John Knox Charm School if ever I saw one. You were saying . . .'

'I was saying', said Lestrade, 'that I did once toy with being a policeman. Sadly, I failed the physical.'

'Oh?'

'I had a brain.'

'Ah,' smiled Sphagnum. 'I know what you mean. So what is it you do, Lestrade?'

'Er . . . I'm a teacher,' the superintendent said.

'Of what?'

'Children,' he answered.

'Och, I see. Here in Scotland, where we have real schools, our domini specialize, y'see. In subjects.'

'Ah, yes,' said Lestrade. 'Well, the classics, I suppose. You know, Latin and . . . the other one.'

'Shall I be mother?' Sphagnum asked, raising the china pot.

It didn't seem likely, looking at the man's broad shoulders and fuzzy chin. But then, it was still relatively early in the day.

'So what brings you to Scotland, then, on your salary?'

'An aged aunt.' Lestrade kept up at least part of the story. 'She died recently and I'm taking a few weeks' holiday.'

'You've not chosen the best time,' said Sphagnum, 'or place. Christmas is a family time, Lestrade. Do you have any family?'

He thought of Sarah, his wife, whom death had taken years ago. He thought of Emma, the living mirror of her mother, whom he hadn't seen in over a year. She'd be ten now. He'd sent her a card and a doll with golden hair.

'No,' he said. 'None.'

'And Hogmanay?' Sphagnum said.

'No, none of that either.'

'No, Hogmanay is what we in Scotland call the New Year. If you're still north of the border by then, you will find it rather strange, as an Englishman an' a'.'

'Well, we'll see.'

'Now, about this Acheson thing.' Sphagnum leaned closer over his tea. It was surprisingly good and safer, surely, than Cullen Skink.

'You were telling me why you were staying at the hotel,' said Lestrade, who recognized a neatly sidestepped answer when he didn't hear one.

'Was I? Och, aye. My rooms at the University are in the process of being redecorated. The mess . . . you wouldn't believe. You can't get the staff these days. So I left. I said to the chappie in charge, "One day, matey," I said to him, "one day is all you've got. Then I'm cancelling the order." Well, you've got to keep the working class in their place, haven't you?'

'Quite,' said Lestrade.

'I know where they've put him.'

'Who?'

'Acheson.'

'Where?'

'Aha. Oh no, you don't. I don't know why, Mr Lestrade,' said Sphagnum, 'but I suspect that for a classics master, you know rather a lot about *corpus delicti*. Am I right?'

Lestrade had no idea. He just smiled.

'I thought so,' said Sphagnum. 'Now, I must confess that, encyclopaedic though my knowledge is, I am not too *au fait* with post-mortem appearances. So, I think we sort of need each other on this one.'

'This one?' Lestrade cocked an eyebrow.

'Och, come off it, Lestrade, you're as intrigued as I am. This is really exciting. All I had to look forward to was a rather boring Christmas in the faculty. Well, when you've been paralytic with drink from Advent to Lent once, you've nothing left to experience. *This* is a real adventure. Of course, it'll mean a wee spot of breaking and entering.'

Lestrade's other eyebrow joined the first. 'Isn't that illegal north of the border?' he asked.

'Well, I've only been studying law for three years,' said Sphagnum, 'but I believe it's illegal anywhere.'

40

'And how do you propose to do it?' Lestrade asked.

'Well, I've got a jemmy in my rooms.'

'As well as a bunsen burner.'

'I've got a lot of rooms. But we'll have to wait until dark.'

'I'll drink to that,' Lestrade raised his cup. 'What do we say if we're caught?'

'Caught? Och, I've studied the career of Daft Jamie McWhorter, the cat burglar of Holyrood. I don't intend to get caught. And in the mean time,' Sphagnum clicked his fingers in order to extract the bill from the surly floozie, 'we've a day to kill, so to speak. Shall I show you the sights? Oh dear, I appear to have left ma wallet in ma rooms.'

'I take you to be a student of the arcane, Lestrade,' said Sphagnum.

Lestrade would have denied it. Flagellation did little for him. Not even the contortions of Mimi La Whipp of Carnaby Street could rouse his passions. But before he could deny it, Sphagnum swept on. 'So I'll spare you the usual nonsense. We've got the first floral clock in the world at Princes Street Gardens, complete with cuckoo, though I fancy at this time of the year, it's probably the world's first weed clock. Ah, but this'll tickle your palate.'

He pointed upwards to the corner of a quaint old house. 'See yon cannonball?'

Lestrade did. It protruded from below an upstairs window-sill.

'When the Young Pretender a few years back took the city, he couldn't take the castle. There was some argy-bargy and a shot landed there.'

'Did no one think to remove it?' Lestrade asked innocently.

'Remove it, man? Are you mad? It's all that's holding the house together. Now, I know you're a man interested in murder.'

Lestrade tried to look casual as a drayhorse broke wind near his elbow.

'Over there's the Netherbow, the ancient gateway to the city where Burke and Hare sold bodies to Dr Knox, the surgeon. I was a medical student, you know, for three or four days.'

41

'You didn't take to it?'

'No adventure. All I ever saw was photographs of people's duodenums. That's no way for a grown man to make a living.'

Bearing in mind some of the medical men he'd known, Lestrade agreed.

'Now.' Sphagnum stopped at another corner, even greyer, windier and quainter than the last. 'This is the West Bar and over there is the house of Major Weir. Have ye heard of Major Weir?'

Lestrade confessed he had not.

'Well, if you're standing comfortably, I'll begin. Thomas Weir was the commander of the City Guard some time ago. He it was who officiated at the execution of Montrose, the only other great Scots hero, beside myself and the Bruce. Anyway, Major Weir shared that hoose with his sister, Grizel – a lady, I fancy, much of the same mien as that fragrant soul who served us tea this morning. He confessed at the age of sixty-nine that they had both been up to no good for years and had been indulging in revolting practices.'

'Really?' Lestrade's bored ears pricked up. 'How revolting?'

'On a scale of one to ten, thirteen,' Sphagnum told him. 'Necromancy, incest, production of phenomenal quantities of yarn, that sort of thing.'

'Yes,' Lestrade agreed, 'that's pretty revolting.'

'Anyway, it seems the old Major was a servant of the Devil and his familiar was his staff of office. The story goes that they burnt the staff along with the Major and the thing turned in the fire, twisting and writhing in its death throes.'

'So that's why you can't get the staff any more,' Lestrade observed shrewdly.

'Aha, but you can,' beamed Sphagnum. 'The brand was plucked from the burning, which is not generally known. And I just happen to have it in my rooms.'

'Of course,' said Lestrade, not at all surprised. 'And does it have magical properties?'

Sphagnum smiled. 'That's for me to know and you to find out,' he said. 'They do say of course that the hoose is haunted. It glows of a night with eerie lights and the creak of old Grizel's wheel can be heard a-spinning. And the spectre of a ten-foot woman, shaking with laughter, walks the Stinking-Closs over there, surrounded by other phantoms, gaping with tahies of laughter.'

'Well, well,' was Lestrade's profound observation.

'Oh, it's true, Lestrade,' Sphagnum assured him. 'I've heard the tap-tap of the old Major's staff on the cobbles myself.'

'But you said it was in your rooms,' Lestrade reminded him.

'Och, man, allow me some poetic licence, will ye? As Rabbie Burns said to the Procurator Fiscal. Now, over here . . .'

And so it went on for most of the day, until Lestrade's head was spinning with stories and Lestrade's feet were throbbing with the miles covered. At least, lunch and dinner were quite edible and the most generous man in Scotland went Dutch with Lestrade for both. After dinner, Sphagnum disappeared, like the ghost of old Grizel and her unlikely brother, for it was dark and time to fetch various things from his rooms.

All day Lestrade had tried to wheedle out of Sphagnum where the body of the late Acheson might be, and all day the canny Scot had kept uncannily silent on that score. So they went together, a little after midnight, creeping out from the new rooms they'd been given with grovelling apologies from the management of the North British Hotel. Past St Giles the High Kirk, its spire silent in the cold, staring night, past the twisted walls of Gledstone's Land, through the very Heart of Midlothian and beyond the Cannongate to Parliament Square. Here, at a side door, Sphagnum suddenly pulled Lestrade into the shadows and flicked out a key.

'Is this it?' Lestrade whispered.

'No,' said Sphagnum. 'This is the Signet Library. The Writers to the Signet are what you would call solicitors.'

'Soliciting is an offence in England,' Lestrade observed.

'Aye, well, most solicitors I know are fairly offensive too. But nevertheless, their library is quite useful.'

'Ah, yes.' Lestrade followed his man up a winding staircase. 'Their books must be useful to you as a law student.'

'Bugger their books, man. Here.'

Sphagnum suddenly crouched on a half-landing and pressed his shoulder to the wall. A panel creaked back to reveal utter blackness. 'Lucky I had a bull's-eye in my rooms. Now, follow me close and watch your . . .'

But it was too late. Lestrade's bowler and the head beneath it crunched into the stone lintel and, as he reeled back, he saw more stars than those studding the Edinburgh sky.

Sphagnum steadied him. 'Man, man,' he whispered, 'keep your head, now. Remember, we need you for this post-mortem work.'

'Where does this lead?' Lestrade asked when his vision stopped swimming.

'A wee flight of steps takes you down to the cellar of the house next door.'

'The morgue?'

'You know, you're pretty bright for a classics master.' Sphagnum winked, though in the darkness, Lestrade missed it. The Scotsman lit his lantern and it threw manic, darting shadows on the roof of the stairway as they went. It seemed to have been hewn out of solid rock – just how solid Lestrade could already testify.

'It's an old Covenanters' passage,' Sphagnum explained in answer to Lestrade's unspoken question. 'The things men'll do in the name of religion. Now, here we are.'

They faced a brick wall, green with mildew and hanging with cobwebs. The rats nosed upwards, outraged at this intrusion into their lair. They squeaked their annoyance at Lestrade and scuttled away, dragging their tails behind them.

'It's here somewhere, I know it is.' Sphagnum was tapping the bricks with his iron crowbar.

'Let me try.' Lestrade was on home ground now. It was not the first time he had jemmied his way into premises under lock and key. It would probably not be the last. He tapped, he pressed, he tinkered. 'There *is* another panel here?' he checked with Sphagnum. That wall looked two feet thick. If he had to break through, he'd be drawing his pension before he got to the other side.

'Here, let me try the Major's staff.' Sphagnum produced a curious gnarled stick with a finial carved in the shape of a horned goat. He placed the tip against a brick and the wall slid back with a jarring scream.

'Well, there you are.' He beamed at Lestrade. 'Magical properties. Walk this way.'

It was probably an old Edingburgh custom, so Lestrade did. They emerged into a basement room, less damp and rat-infested than the one they had just left. Silent sleepers lay on slab marble, wrapped in white linen and cold as the clay.

'Here's the gas supply,' Sphagnum called from the far corner. Lestrade winced as his groin collided with a newly dead toe. He'd experienced this before. He knew of old the punch packed by the dead, the mortal blow.

'Is that him?' Sphagnum produced his bunsen burner from his little canvas bag of tricks.

'Not unless burning changes your generative organs,' whispered Lestrade. 'This one's a woman. Aha.'

'Got him?'

'Got him. Bring your bull's-eye.'

By the flickering shafts of light, Lestrade set to work. He placed his bowler on the chest of the deceased woman to his right and hauled aside the linen shroud. Acheson's body was virtually black from head to foot. It had clearly been washed and the tell-tale signs were there on the left temple. Lestrade rummaged in his pocket and Sphagnum saw him take out a set of brass knuckles which he proceeded to put on. There was a click in the half-light and a murderous blade appeared out of the superintendent's fist.

'What's a teacher of classics doing with one of those?' Sphagnum asked.

Lestrade did not look up. 'I have some rather unruly pupils,' he said, and began to scrape away the flaked skin. He counted eight separate blows across the side of the skull. Any one of them could have caused death. Then he flicked the blade under a large blister on the forearm and sliced it off. He dropped it, pus and all, on to a handkerchief and made a mental note not to use it again; not at least while the blister was still in it. Carefully, he popped the viscera into Sphagnum's test tube.

'You look a little grey, Mr Sphagnum,' he observed.

'Ah, it's the December air,' the Scotsman bluffed. 'Ready?'

Lestrade switched on the gas and struck a match. Sphagnum steadied the blue flame and held the tube over it. Both men crouched to watch the reaction. After a minute or so, Lestrade nodded grimly. 'Milky,' he said. 'Your old professor was right.'

'Which means?'

'Which means that our neighbour Mr Acheson was beaten to death, I'd say with a hammer, *before* being burned.'

45

'So it *is* murder?'

Lestrade nodded. 'The fire was designed to cover up that fact. The question is, who wanted Acheson dead and why disguise the murder with fire?'

'That's two questions,' the lawyer felt bound to comment.

'Hey, yous!' A thunderous Scottish accent intruded on their whispers.

Lestrade switched off the gas tap while Sphagnum grabbed the lantern and extinguished it. For a second they stood in total blackness, then another bull's-eye threw its light from the top of the staircase.

'What d'ye think yer doing?' The voice behind the lantern came again.

Lestrade backed towards the entrance behind him, but the wall had slid shut with a crunch and not even Sphagnum's staff had enough magic in it to open it quickly enough.

'Over here!' the law student shouted and hurtled into an adjacent room, Lestrade hard on his heels. There was a clatter of hob-nailed boots on the stairs and Lestrade recognized the flatulent tones of Thaddeus McFarlane bawling out.

'Stop. This is the Leith Police. You are surrounded. You cannot possibly get away!'

That seemed to be true. Sphagnum tried door after door and all seemed to be locked. None would give to his frantic wrenchings.

McFarlane could be heard bawling at his constables. 'Come on, they're over here.'

Heads bobbed into the minimal light from the solitary window at pavement level and the single bull's-eye threw crazy rays that danced off the institutional green of the walls.

'I've got 'em, Inspector,' an aggressive voice called.

'That's a corpse you're dancing with, Taggart, you dunderhead. Put her down this minute.'

And there was a thud as the cadaver hit the floor.

'Over here, Lestrade.' Sphagnum had reached his last door.

'Lestrade!' McFarlane belched. 'Give it up, man. You haven't a chance.'

There was a sickening crunch as constable collided with constable in the darkness.

'Thanks for that nifty piece of gratuitous identification,' Lestrade hissed as he reached Sphagnum's side.

'Sorry. I wasn't thinking. What about this door? Shoulder to shoulder and bolder and bolder?'

Lestrade shrugged. 'After three,' he said.

'Three!' shouted Sphagnum and the two men launched themselves as they had in the hotel and the blazing inferno of Room Twelve. This time, the thing merely swung open, dangling on a single hinge, and both men tumbled through it.

'This way!' yelled McFarlane as the light broke in and his constables scrabbled after him. Lestrade and Sphagnum rattled up the stone steps to another door. Sphagnum's staff shattered the glass and Lestrade's shoulder bounced uselessly off the frame.

'Agghh!' he screamed. 'The hinges are on the other side.'

'Aye,' muttered Sphagnum, 'that's a McAlpine building for you. This way, man.'

He ducked sideways, skidding down a polished corridor where long-dead policemen in dundrearies and helmets glared down at them. Whistles blew and dogs barked as they flew around interminable corridors, scurrying upwards, ever upwards, with constables snapping at their heels.

'What *is* this place?' gasped Lestrade as they began to reach corridors where gas lights still burned.

'Didn't I tell you?' asked Sphagnum. 'It's the Edinburgh Central Police Station.'

He put his shoulder to a door and he and Lestrade hurtled through it. Sphagnum gave a startled shriek and Lestrade grabbed him just in time, his white knuckles buried deep in the Harris tweed overcoat. Sphagnum clutched the superintendent, feeling his heels slipping on wet lead.

'Jesus Christ!' the Scotsman hissed and glanced down. Below them lay Blackfriars Street: forty feet below them.

'What now?' asked Lestrade, fighting to regain his breath.

'You tell me.' Sphagnum's heart was still descending from his mouth.

'I thought you had studied the career of Daft Jamie McWhorter, the cat burglar of Holyrood?'

'So I have, man, but he used to steal cats. What possible use is that to us now?'

There was a pause. 'He used to steal cats?' Lestrade repeated.

'Well, why d'you think he was called Daft Jamie?' Sphagnum pointed out.

They heard the crunch of hobnails on the stairs below them. 'All right, then,' said Lestrade. 'This way.'

This time he took the lead, hurtling along the narrow parapet that skirted the roof. He reached the edge, took a deep breath and leapt in the darkness. He'd dropped on to another parapet about ten feet lower and turned to watch Sphagnum do the same. Together, they cut sideways, out of reach of the braying constables, who, on McFarlane's orders, were doubling back down the more conventional way. It was the last ten feet, ironically, that defeated Lestrade. Holding his bowler on his head, his Donegal billowing like a flying squirrel, he sailed into another black drop, only to twist his ankle with sickening pain as he reached the ground. He cursed Mr Cobblestone anew for his murderous invention and was hauled into an alley by the trusty Sphagnum.

'Two bobbies,' the Scotsman whispered. 'Coming up on our tail. Sit there and put your leg out.'

'What?'

'Do it!' Sphagnum hissed. He sat opposite Lestrade, each man with his leg out straight like a pair of rather unusual bookends. The two constables clattered round the corner into the alley and stepped neatly over them both before hurrying on into the darkness. But no sooner had they gone than a second pair followed and this time, they both went sprawling over the outstretched legs, causing Lestrade to howl anew as a size twelve boot crashed into his ankle.

In the darkness, Sphagnum's staff came up and caught one bobby a nasty one on the temple. He rolled over, groaning. The other one was already sitting upright, clawing for his truncheon. Unable to reach his brass knuckles in time, Lestrade relied on his own and drove them into the constable's nose. The man's eyes rolled upwards and he lolled back.

'Come on, then,' hissed Sphagnum. 'No time for false modesty,' and he began unbuttoning his constable's tunic.

In record time, two constables emerged from the alley, one carrying a Donegal and a slightly battered bowler. He swung his leg rather. The other, taller, his trousers flapping around his calves, carried a coat of Harris tweed. They collided with a red-faced inspector and a clutch of constables. Mass salutings followed.

'Any sign?' McFarlane burped, taking solace from his hip flask.

'None, sir. McTroon here has twisted his ankle. I'm taking him to the Infirmary.'

'Right you are. This way, men!' And they hurried away.

It wasn't until they got to Thistle Street that McFarlane suddenly stopped, holding back his rushing bobbies. 'Wait a minute,' he said, dropping his hip flask in the moment of realization, 'we haven't got a McTroon at the station. Lestrade!'

The superintendent of that name changed as quickly as he could out of the borrowed uniform. After all, he was in trouble enough without the charge of impersonation of a police officer. Rather than risk any more awkward questions from suspicious hoteliers, Lestrade slept along with a quarter of Edinburgh's inhabitants, in the street. He awoke, numb with the bitter cold of impending Christmas, with his head resting on that nasty little stone dog again. It was a little after dawn. Sphagnum had split up from him (there was, this time, no safety in numbers) and had agreed to lie low for a while. After all, as Lestrade pointed out with some acidity, it was not Sphagnum's name that had been bawled out with such clarity in the basement morgue of Edinburgh Central Police Station.

And in the mean time, he had places to be. He daren't risk returning to the hotel for his Gladstone, which left him with only one suit of clothes to his name, and without the chit of the Duke of Connaught he'd be hard put to it to replace them. He hobbled north in the slowly gathering light, watchful of any bobbies, whether from Greyfriars or elsewhere, who should still be hunting him. He had just crossed the Waters of Leith with the pain in his leg making his eyes cross, when he saw a familiar face.

'Morning,' waved Alistair Sphagnum. 'I didn't think you'd get far with that foot of yours. So be my guest.'

He was dressed rather oddly, in a long buff coat and a cycling deerstalker, complete with goggles. Fur gauntlets reached to his elbows. 'Welcome aboard!' he beamed.

Lestrade could not believe his red-rimmed old eyes. Behind

the Scotsman throbbed an outlandish vehicle the superintendent had never seen before. It was bright red with yellow trim and appeared to be a boneshaker with an engine.

'What is it?' he asked.

'Well, I suppose you'd call it a boneshaker with an engine,' said Sphagnum. 'Its makers call it a twin-engined Quadrant – one of only six in the world.'

'What does it do?'

'Well, in your case, Lestrade, I should think it's the answer to a maiden's prayer. Sit here.' Sphagnum helped him to climb into what was in fact a sidecar, positioned to the right front of the bicycle itself. 'Put your feet in these stirrups.' Lestrade did, so that he was sitting as though in an armchair with his legs splayed out in front of him.

'Right.' Sphagnum climbed astride the saddle beside Lestrade. 'Where to?'

Lestrade looked perplexed. The springing of the contraption didn't strike him as at all safe, but that was not his problem. His foot throbbed more than the Quadrant's engines.

'This'll do twenty-three miles an hour with a prevailing wind,' Sphagnum told him proudly. 'And I think it's time we shook the dust of Edinburgh, don't you? The question is – in which direction?'

'All right, Mr Sphagnum,' sighed Lestrade. 'You win. I can't get far on foot like this, I'll grant you. I'm going to have to trust you, though I'm damned if I believe I can.'

'Oh, ye of little faith,' tutted Sphagnum.

'I'm not a teacher – of classics or anything else.'

'No!' Sphagnum gasped, a difficult feat with his tongue firmly in his cheek. 'Tell me it isn't so!'

'I'm a superintendent of Scotland Yard.'

'Get away!'

'It's a fact.'

'Well, I'll be . . .'

'Probably. I have some urgent business at Balmoral. Will this thing get us there?'

'In a trice,' Sphagnum smiled. 'In the mean time, there's a venison patty and some bannocks in that hamper. Oh, and a flask of whisky. It'll be pretty chilly on the moors.'

'On the moors?' Lestrade's eyes widened. 'I thought we were going by road.'

And his bowler bounced away as the Quadrant roared into life, snarling down sleeping Fettes Road on its way to the north.

Inspector Thaddeus McFarlane bounced his hand on the hotel bell.

'Ah, Inspector, you're back,' said the desk clerk.

'Yes, but it'll heal. I walked into a bunsen burner last night.'

'Tsk, tsk.'

'This man Lestrade, the guest in Number Twelve who ended up in Number Thirteen. What do you know about him?'

'No more than is in the register.'

McFarlane checked it. A false address if ever he'd seen one. Scotland Yard, indeed. Very droll. That was obviously what passed for humour down . . . there.

'Oh, there was a friend of his who called,' the desk man remembered.

'When?' McFarlane belched.

'Er . . . let me see, an hour or so after Lestrade arrived. He said he was a friend and asked for his room number.'

'What did you tell him?'

'What it says there,' explained the clerk. 'Room Twelve.'

4

Constable Marshall opened his copy of the *Coldstream Examiner*.

'Do you always use a gold-plated lorgnette for close work, Tass?' Snellgrove asked him.

'No,' murmured Marshall. 'Not before the Duke of Connaught's chit fell off the back of Mr Lestrade's lorry. Tell me, Wim, do you think they'd have caviare up here or will we have to have it trained in?'

'It's funny we haven't heard from Lestrade though.' Snellgrove sipped his morning tea. 'This stuff tastes better in the Spode, doesn't it?'

'We'll hear from Lestrade soon enough,' said Marshall. 'And in the mean time,' he waited while the hotel flunkey placed his footstool a fraction nearer to the fire, 'we'll just have to rough it out.'

North of the border. Down Braemar way. Sphagnum's Quadrant rattled up what passed for a road through Gleann Beag, hurtling round the Devil's Elbow with Lestrade's part of the machine off the ground entirely, and on up misty Glen Clunie. The forest of Ballochbuie hemmed them round and above the roar of the engines, Alistair Sphagnum lovingly painted a picture of the Cairngorms which lay ahead. A picture Lestrade could not see at all because of the swirling green vapours.

They alighted, or rather Sphagnum did (Lestrade had to be carried by two ghillies), and signed the book at the Deoch and Doris Hotel. Sphagnum became Mr Jones, an unlikely prospect for a Scotsman, and Lestrade relied on his old alias as Mr Lister. Then he sent two telegrams by way of an errand boy, when the blood had returned to his fingers: one to his constables waiting like greyhounds in the slips at Coldstream, the other ahead to Mr Ramsay, Steward of the Royal Estate at Balmoral.

Lestrade's room was tiny and painted white. Glazed stags with rampant moth stared down at him, sensing Sassenach intrusion under the patchwork quilt below them. Electricity effectively stopped at Kirriemuir, where the balls came from, and so Lestrade hobbled through the little hostelry with a candle dripping wax painfully on to his hand. Mine host, who seemed to be covered in hair from head to foot, had asked the superintendent if he wanted a skirlie, but Lestrade had told him he could manage and the man had retreated into the kitchen, a little perplexed.

Sphagnum and Lestrade spent the next morning in the sitting-room, Lestrade wrapped in several layers of tartan against the cold, and they watched the rain pound the window panes. Lestrade endeavoured to read a paper, but the light in the room was appalling and, anyway, he couldn't really raise much interest in the fact that the Boer War had just broken out. After all, that was five years ago.

'Mr . . . Lister, is it?'

They looked up at the new arrival.

'No, I'm Jones,' said Sphagnum. 'This is Lister.'

'Allan Ramsay.' The man extended a hand. 'I'm pleased to know ye.'

He pulled up a chair that seemed to be made from stags' antlers and unbuttoned his voluminous Ulster. 'Mr Lestrade,' he whispered, 'I'm glad you're here. But who . . .?'

'Inspector Sphagnum,' said Sphagnum, equally *sotto voce*, 'Leith Police. I'm helping the superintendent with his enquiries.'

Lestrade's jaw opened slightly.

Ramsay looked a little put out. 'I understood the Scottish police were not to be involved,' he said, flicking the freezing rain out of his nostril hairs.

'Ah,' smiled Sphagnum. 'Who did you deal with before?'

'Inspector McNab.'

'Well, there y'are. The man's an acknowledged idiot.'

'Is he?' asked Ramsay.

'Och, that's well known. Unprofessional of me to say so, of

course. But his rank comes from having something on the Chief Constable; no more, no less.'

'I see.' Ramsay raised a sandy eyebrow.

'Er . . . Inspector,' said Lestrade, his teeth a little gritted, 'would you walk this way for a moment?'

Sphagnum did, though he drew the line at hobbling, and they reached the bar.

'What do you think you're doing?' Lestrade hissed.

'Watching out for your interests.'

'Thank you, I can manage.'

'Can ye?' Sphagnum's voice rose, then he beamed at Ramsay. 'I think we'll try a single malt,' he said loudly. 'You've a gammy leg, you don't know the area and the Leith Police almost certainly have a warrant for your arrest. Now, I don't know what you're about, Lestrade, but it's my guess it something hush-hush. I happened to notice your telegram to Balmoral. And yon Ramsay, I would guess, is the recipient of that. You need friends, Lestrade, believe me.'

There wasn't a reason in the world why Lestrade should, but the alternative to trusting Sphagnum a little further was to cause a scene and blow his cover. No doubt the moors outside were littered with the corpses of ptarmigans whose fate that had been.

'Right then,' said Sphagnum, 'the single malt it is,' and he rang the brass bell to order it.

'Can we talk here?' Ramsay asked when Lestrade had returned to the log fire.

'As long as we whisper, Mr Ramsay,' Lestrade said. 'I expect you are as aware of the need for diplomacy in this matter as I am.'

'More so, Mr Lestrade,' Ramsay said. 'The honour of the greatest monarchy in the world is at stake, no less.'

Sphagnum brought a tray with a bottle and three crystals. The first sip seared through Lestrade's lip, the second hit his tonsils. By the third, he'd lost all feeling between his head and his waist. Ramsay took up the tale.

'I don't know how much his Grace the Duke of Connaught will have told you,' he began.

'Assume I know nothing,' Lestrade told him. Most people did.

'Very well. The deceased's name was Amy Macpherson.'

'A most superior person?' Sphagnum could not help interjecting.

'No,' said Ramsay, rather pompously. Lestrade knew the Steward of the Royal Household reminded him of someone. Now he'd placed it. It was that deer in *The Monarch of the Glen* by Landseer – it had the same smell under its nose, the same disapproving nostrils. 'As a matter of fact, rather inferior. She had less intellect, I suppose, than this glass of malt. She was a little on the slow side. A few mickles short of a muckle, if you ask me. Folks in these parts called her Amy Simple Macpherson.'

'How old was she?' Lestrade asked.

'Seventeen. She was a maid of all work.'

'With you long?'

'A little less than a year. Before that she'd skivvied for Angus Laidlaw over at Abergeldie.'

'Who's he?'

'Head ghillie on all the Royal Estates north of the Tay. A legend in his own lifetime. Landowners the length and breadth of Scotland consult him on all matters venerial. He was beside himself when he heard the news.'

'He was?' Sphagnum asked.

'Looked upon the wee girl as his own, y'ken. Mind you, he's fierce and proud that one. When he heard he just raised an eyebrow. His left.'

'That's beside himself?' Lestrade checked.

Ramsay gave him a withering look. 'Angus Laidlaw is as broa' a Scot as you're ever likely to meet. Descended from the Lennoxes of Argyll and the Blairs of Atholl – and that's just on his mother's side. Why, man, when the old Queen was alive, I've seen him toss telegraph poles at the Braemar Games.' He leaned forward to resume his whisper. 'Personally, I find it all a little sweaty.'

'Quite,' Lestrade said. 'Now, about Amy Macpherson . . .'

'Aye?'

'When did she die?'

'Have you not seen the police report?' Ramsay asked. He turned to Sphagnum. 'You being attached to the constabulary and a'.'

55

'That's McNab for you,' Sphagnum bluffed. 'Plays his cards very close to his chest. What can you expect from the Grampian Constabulary?'

'McNab's with the Forfar Police,' Ramsay corrected him.

'Well, that's just my point,' said Sphagnum.

'Well, then, let me see. It was three weeks ago come Thursday.'

'That would make it . . . the fourth of December,' Lestrade computed. He had a brain like an almanac.

'No. November the thirtieth,' Ramsay put him right.

'The Feast of St Andrew,' said Sphagnum.

'Go on,' said Lestrade.

'St Andrew,' said Sphagnum, 'the patron saint of Scotland . . .'

'Not you,' Lestrade interrupted, 'somebody else. Who found her?'

'Miss Pringle, the governess.'

'Whose governess?' Lestrade frowned.

'Little Elizabeth Bowes-Lyon,' Ramsay explained. 'She'd come to spend Christmas, what with the family at St Paul's Walden Bury.'

'Did you see the body yourself?'

'I did,' Ramsay shuddered. 'Miss Pringle was carried in a dead faint to me as head of the Household. She was deadly pale. She'd gone into the cellar in search of a candle and found the poor wee girl at the foot of the stairs, in a pool of her own blood.'

Sphagnum swigged his glass.

'Did she expectorate as to the cause of death?' Lestrade asked.

Ramsay shrugged. 'She was hardly in a fit state. I don't mind telling you, Mr Lestrade, I had to loosen her stays.'

'Miss Macpherson?'

'Miss Pringle. Well, I'm a married man. God alone knows what Her-In-The-Hoose would have said had she walked in at that moment.'

'When you saw the body,' Lestrade went on, 'did you form any opinion?'

'Miss Pringle's or the dead girl's?'

'The dead girl's.' Lestrade's eyebrow followed that of Angus Laidlaw.

'I've never seen anything like it,' the steward said. 'Her head, man, it was all but gone.'

'Gone?' Lestrade and Sphagnum chorused.

'Unrecognizable. A mass of blood. Sort of . . . congealed . . .' and he reached for his glass again, taking refuge in its power.

'Did Miss Macpherson have any enemies?' Lestrade asked.

'Och, no,' Ramsay said. 'She was a sweet, harmless thing. Och, she broke wind now and again, but not so bad you'd want to stave in her head.'

'Quite.' Lestrade too had never known wind-breaking so provocative. 'How many servants have you at the castle?'

'Thirty-eight, including myself.'

'And groundsmen?'

'Och, aye, we have groundsmen.'

'No.' Lestrade found it easier to be patient after the umpteenth sip of the amber nectar. 'I mean, how many groundsmen?'

'Oh, sixteen. And twelve ghillies.'

'Yes,' ventured Lestrade. 'You'll excuse my southern lack of . . .'

'Servants,' explained Sphagnum, reading what was left of Lestrade's mind. 'Especially a man who attends a Highland chief. The sort who carries your shotgun and loads for you and guts venison and so on. All rather sweaty, Mr Ramsay, I expect you'd agree?'

Ramsay would.

'And guests?' asked Lestrade.

'At the time of the wee girl's death, six.'

'Any of those still there?'

'All of them,' Ramsay told him, 'except Mr McAlpine. He's gone to Glamis to carry out some repairs.'

'May I know who they are?' Lestrade asked.

'For reasons of discretion,' Ramsay whispered, 'I've taken the trouble to write them down. Walls have ears, y'ken, even at the Deoch and Doris. It's written on rice paper so you can eat it when you've digested the names.'

Sphagnum craned his neck to read them, but Lestrade was faster. Years of work at the Yard, hundreds of shoe-boxes containing depositions, miles of pavement walked, in and out of season. It all added up to one thing – never share all your secrets with a civilian. You might as well show the list to the late Sherlock Holmes.

'Thank you,' he said, popping it into his breast pocket. 'I think I'll save it for later. I didn't come direct to the castle,' he explained, 'because I wasn't sure how the land lay. But my time is precious. I will have to come tomorrow.'

Ramsay nodded. 'We'll be ready. There's no possibility of you gentlemen pretending not to be policemen, is there?' the steward asked. 'The scandal and all?'

'I'd thought of that,' said Lestrade, 'but it makes it doubly difficult to ask questions. When's Christmas?'

'I believe it falls on the twenty-fifth this year,' Sphagnum told him, face like a poker.

'I mean, what is today's date?'

'The eighteenth. All those on the list are spending Christmas with . . . the incumbent.'

Lestrade looked at Sphagnum. Sphagnum looked at Lestrade.

'Expect us at ten tomorrow,' Lestrade said. 'And be so good as to assemble those guests in the library, will you? I shall need to allay any rumours.'

'And lay a few ghosts, eh, Superintendent?' Sphagnum winked, tapping the goat's head of Major Weir's staff which Lestrade noticed was never very far from his grasp.

'That too,' he murmured.

'Superintendent Lestrade?'

He turned in the sharp light through the leaded window, where the flurries of snow already splashed the morning, turning to rain in their indecision.

'Ma'am.' He bowed as low as a man with a badly sprained ankle could.

There swept into the room before him a poppy-eyed figure, somewhat loose of jowl. She was probably his own age or a little older, but the years had not been kind and she only had one ear.

'What?' she shrilled. 'I'm afraid you'll have to speak up. I only have one ear.'

'Ma'am,' Lestrade repeated. On another case, in another

58

time, he had had the exquisite pleasure of bowing before Queen Alexandra. Why was the whole family, in-laws and outlaws, profoundly deaf?

'What?' the lady repeated.

'Ma'am.'

'Yes, yes,' the lady tutted, sweeping past him to take a chair by the fire, 'I heard all that. I am waiting for the rest of the sentence.'

Lestrade smiled but it appeared as more of a wince.

'Sit there,' she said imperiously, pointing to a stool that looked savagely uncomfortable. 'Up-wind of me. I should be able to hear you from there.'

'You are the Duchess of Argyll, ma'am?' Lestrade desperately looked for somewhere to put his bowler.

'I know that,' the lady assured him. 'What is it you want?'

'Your brother, the Duke of Connaught, asked me to make a few discreet enquiries, ma'am,' he told her, 'concerning the death of the maid, Amy Macpherson.'

'Deaf?' the Duchess trilled, leaning forward by the crackling logs.

'Murder, ma'am.' Lestrade thought it best to vary the number of syllables.

'Oh, dear me, yes.' The Duchess leaned back, clutching her pearls convulsively. 'A shocking thing. Shocking. That poor wretch.'

'I understand the local police have already been?'

'Indeed they have. Not exactly Scotland's finest. Tell me, have you ever got your hair caught in a horse-drawn sleigh and been dragged, literally dragged, for several hundred yards?'

'Er . . . no, ma'am.' Lestrade felt somehow inadequate.

'Well, there you are.' She rocked backwards. 'Now, about this girl. How may I help? My God, you don't think Arthur did it, do you? Because I should think his many public engagements give him a water-tight abilone.'

'No, ma'am, I don't think that. I should like to interview your guests . . .'

She sat bolt upright, blinking in the firelight. 'Superintendent, please. My mother was the Queen-Empress, my husband – God rot him – was Liberal-Unionist Member of Parliament for

Manchester South. He is now the Duke of Argyll. Kindly do not speak to me of breasts.'

'Visitors, ma'am.' Lestrade leaned a little nearer, although the heat from the fire was already mottling his cheek and causing his moustache to droop. 'May I talk to them?'

'Be my guest,' she said, leaning back.

'May I use the library?'

'I'm not sure we have any books on detection,' she frowned, 'but you're welcome to look, of course.'

'Thank you, Ma'am. Am I to understand that you spend every Christmas here at Balmoral?'

'Good Lord, no,' she said, 'but I cannot abide spending what is supposed to be a festive season with the Duke. It's rather akin to chronic toothache when one is at the brandy snaps.'

Lestrade nodded sagely.

'It's one's birth, you see.' The Duchess rose and the superintendent rose with her. 'I was born without aetherial aid,' she explained, whirling towards the door which opened mysteriously before her. 'Mama always said I'd be "something peculiar". Well, you don't come more peculiar than being the Duchess of Argyll, I can tell you. Oh, my God.' She suddenly slumped sideways against the door frame. Lestrade caught her, steadying her weight on his good leg.

'Your Royal Highness, are you all right?'

'Er . . . yes, yes.' He helped her to her chair again and the opener of the door leapt to the Duchess's feet, with smelling salts in hand.

'One of her turns,' the flunkey growled.

'Does she have them often?' Lestrade didn't like the colour of the Duchess of Argyll at all. She clashed violently with the tartan wallpaper.

'I have second sight,' she moaned.

Well, that clearly made up for her shortage of ears, Lestrade mused.

'I see it,' she whispered, batting aside the flunkey's phial so that it smashed to pieces in the grate.

'What, ma'am?' Lestrade asked.

'Fire,' she said, looking down at him. Not surprising, Lestrade reassured himself. There was one two feet away. 'You, dear superintendent,' and she clutched his sleeve. 'My poor man, you're in mortal danger.'

'I am?' Lestrade's eyebrows rose simultaneously.

'Promise me,' she said earnestly, 'promise me you'll stay away from waterfalls.'

'Er . . . I promise,' said Lestrade.

'And please,' she shuddered, 'don't accept lifts from strange men.'

Only the other day, Lestrade had done just that from Alistair Sphagnum. Still, it was too late now.

'Come along, ma'am,' said the flunkey. 'Time you were awa' to your bed,' and he helped her out.

Unusually for Lestrade, he interviewed the outdoor men first. He had called all the guests together in the library under the watchful stewardly eye of Allan Ramsay and had explained the situation. He had apologized for dampening their Christmas, although the weather itself was already having a fair crack at that, but a girl was dead and he'd a job to do. Mercifully, the omnipresent Sphagnum was mending a puncture on his machine and Lestrade positively refused permission for him to be there during his interviews.

He stationed himself with his back to the wall and his head under that of a stag whose glazed expression indicated that he had been at Balmoral a long time. A giant of a man bowed his head in order to enter the doorway and stood there in the rough-checked cut-away jacket well-known in the island of Harris. Beneath the swinging kilt of a thousand pleats stood two stalwart legs that appeared to have been hewn from solid granite.

'Angus Laidlaw?'

'The same,' the Highlander said, 'man and boy this forty-five years.'

'Please,' Lestrade gestured, 'have a seat.'

'Nay, mister, I've been gutting venison. Best keep up-wind o' me and I can't be accused of leaving entrails all over Her Late Majesty's chintz. Man, I didna ken what a chair was until I was eighteen. It came as a shock, I can tell ye. I'll stand.'

'Very well. Mr Laidlaw. Er . . . who is this?'

A small replica of the giant had crept in at Laidlaw's elbow.

'It's ma eldest son. Wee Fingal.'

Lestrade took the lad in. There was something rather odd about him. As though Laidlaw read his mind, he said, 'Aye, I ken. There's something disturbing in his gait. Well, he's not as other ghillies and in his case, I'm not at all sure a man's a man for a' that. Writing to bloody pen pals in France, indeed! Still, there it is. The rood I have tae bear.'

'You are the head gamekeeper, I understand,' Lestrade said.

'Then you don't understand very much.' Laidlaw tugged off his glengarry and stuffed it into his shoulder strap. 'I'm a ghillie. That's a head-and-a-half taller than any soft Sassenach gamekeeper saving your presence.'

'How long have you worked on the estate?'

'Here at Balmoral? Let's see. I took over from old Hamish Laidlaw of the Minch who in turn took over from McAvity Laidlaw, known throughout the Isles for his Up and Under.'

'So that would be?'

'Eighteen ninety-four.'

'And I gather you look after the other estates as well?'

Laidlaw nodded. 'All ye can see from the park of Lochnagar, which for about ten months of the year is bugger all.'

'And I understand from Mr Ramsay that the dead girl, Amy Macpherson, was in your employ?'

Laidlaw's face turned grey, as though he had just munched a lemon, and his lips pursed. 'Yon ashtray.' He pointed to the brass receptacle by Lestrade's arm. 'Would you pass it?'

Lestrade did so.

'They wouldn't have had these in the Old Queen's day,' the ghillie told him and spat volubly into it. '*That's* my view of Allan Ramsay,' he said. 'Thank ye. You can put it back now.'

Lestrade wasn't sure he should, but in lieu of anywhere else to put it, balanced it back on the bamboo whatnot. 'I'm sure Mr Ramsay meant well,' he said.

'Och, aye, his heart's in the right place. But then, come to think o'it, it's not. *My* heart's in the Heelands. He's a bloody Lowlander. They're renowned for the worship of the pound note, y'ken.'

Lestrade kenned, but he had thought that was true of all Scotsmen. 'Tell me about Amy,' he said.

The Highlander shifted so that the firelight flashed on the cairngorm in the pommel of the skean-dhu stuffed into his sock. Wee Fingal stood to one side. 'She was a fine girl.' His voice was soft, melodic even. It had lost the edge of steel and crag. 'I took her into ma household at Abergeldie when she was a tiny wee bairn. Before I realized how much young Fingal enjoyed wearing a kilt. Her mother died at her birth, y'ken. Her father was a regular soldier. And a regular bastard. He buggered off as soon as he saw Amy's mother putting on weight.'

'So you raised her?'

'In a manner of speaking. Actually, it was the hoosekeeper there, old Mrs Abernethy; she became mother to the child – as she was tae this one, his own mother having had one look at him and expired an a'. I just saw that she was clothed and fed.'

'How long had she been a servant?'

'Here at the castle? Aboot a year. Everybody loved her, that's what I canna understand.'

As Allan Ramsay said it would, Laidlaw's eyebrow rose, just a little. It was the only emotion he ever allowed to show. The only emotion he'd ever been taught.

'She had no enemies, then, among the servants?'

'Like one o' the family,' Laidlaw said.

'What about the guests?'

'Aye, well, that's not for me to say. I load their guns for 'em and drag back their deer. I even have to shoot for 'em on occasions and then congratulate *them* on their marksmanship. But pass a judgement on any of 'em? No, sir, that I will not do.'

Lestrade nodded. He'd interviewed more servants than the Duchess of Argyll had had sleigh rides. He understood the loyalty below stairs. He wouldn't break this man. Suddenly, Laidlaw closed to him and stooped a little. 'But I would just watch out for the one who dresses like some damned nigger. Come, Fingal. Time for claymore practice, you bloody little nance.'

They bowed stiffly and were gone.

The one who dresses like a nigger. Lestrade expected perhaps an officer of the Black Watch. What he got, as the early Hebridean night closed in, was Sir Harry Aubrey de Vere

Maclean KCMB. He'd been told that Sir Harry was dressing for dinner and several glances at his half-hunter didn't seem to be hurrying him up. So the superintendent left the library annexe and made his way haltingly to the turreted room in the East Wing where Maclean had his accommodation. More dead stags watched him go, interspersed now and then with haughty, turbaned Indians who eyed him shiftily. But they kept their place among the canvas and the paint. At least they hadn't been stuffed.

He knocked on the door that Allan Ramsay had indicated. He looked up and down the gloomy corridor. Silence. Only the spluttering of his candle flame kept him company. He touched the door. It gave under his fingers and he gave the passageway a final check before slipping inside. There was a whirring thump and he felt something rip across his waist. His candle fell sideways, the brass holder tumbling from his grip and rolling across the carpet. He stood stock still, aware that something taut and dangerous was stretched across his waistcoat, resting and vibrating on his watch chain.

A bull's-eye shone full into his face out of the total darkness.

'Good God,' a voice said. 'Don't move.'

Lestrade saw moving about in the dark what he could only describe as a Lascar. It was bearded and turbaned and the sharp shafts of the bull's-eye flashed on the hilt of an oriental dagger stuffed into its flowing robes. Not the full dress uniform of the Black Watch, surely? Then blackness.

'Bugger Balmoral!' the voice hissed. 'You can never find a match when you want one. Ah!'

There was a clunk, followed by a thud and the scrape of sulphur. 'Never trust these new-fangled lantern johnnies.' The match-flame glowed under a lamp cover and the strange, Eastern-looking character with sandy hair stood in the light. Lestrade glanced down. A length of copper wire hummed tautly inches from his groin. A threat lower and it would have made a new man of him.

'My dear fellow,' the Berber said, 'how can you ever forgive me? That was a damn close shave. Allow me,' and he extricated one end from the door frame so that the wire trailed harmlessly along the floor.

'I was trying out my new camel castrator. I never dreamt

anyone would come in. To tell the truth, I got so carried away with my inventions, I hadn't noticed how dark it's got.'

'Camel castrator?' Lestrade swallowed hard, his worst fears confirmed.

'Yes, I know,' the Berber sighed. 'It does have some way to go, doesn't it? Ah, well, back to the drawing board.'

'Sir Harry Maclean?' Lestrade checked.

'McLane,' he said, thrusting a hand out of his robes. 'It's pronounced McLane. Actually, it's all a bit of a farce, really. I was born in Cheltenham. I'm about as Scottish as you are, Mr . . . er . . .?'

'Lestrade. Superintendent Sholto Lestrade.'

'Ah, yes, the Yard chappie. Sorry I missed your little speech in the library this morning. Working on the castrator. It still pings a little to the right.'

Lestrade thanked God it did. 'Have you been at Balmoral long, Sir Harry?'

'Well, between you and me, Lestrade, it seems like years. Actually, it's only been a week. I don't really know why HRH invited me. Perhaps she thought I was Scotch or something.'

'Would I be right in assuming you're itching to be back in Cheltenham, sir?' Lestrade sensed a certain transience about this man.

'Cheltenham?' Maclean blinked. 'Have you been there?'

Lestrade nodded, recalling his murky past. A distinctly strange family who lived in Parabola Road. All in all, not the happiest of memories.

'Well, there you are,' Maclean shrugged. 'There's only one thing worse than Cheltenham, Lestrade, and that's an evening in Galashiels. No, I itch, as you put it, to be off to Tangier.'

'Tangier?'

'Morocco. Do you know it?'

'It's a little off my beat, sir,' Lestrade confessed.

'Quite. Quite. My dear fellow, where *are* my manners? Do have a seat.'

Lestrade accepted gratefully as his foot was killing him. He stood up again almost immediately however as the hilt of a Tuareg sword seemed to be embedded in his bottom.

'Ah, thank you,' said Maclean. 'I've been looking for that. A present from the Sultan. I carry it everywhere.'

'The Sultan of . . . er . . .?'

'Morocco. I'm his military adviser. Well, actually, bodyguard, inventor and official piper.'

'Ah.' Lestrade knew the opium dens off Seven Dials. He too was a man of the world. 'That would be one of those hookah things with the many hoses.'

'Allah bless you, no. Bagpipes, man. The Sultan adores the skirl of the pipes.'

'Indeed?'

'Actually, it's a damned nuisance being invited to spend Christmas here. I'm in the middle of protracted negotiations with the Raisuli.'

'The Rice . . . er . . .'

'The blighter's the Sherif of the Riffs. Thinks he ought to be Sultan. In fact he's a brigand. Quite a nice chap though. Nice enough to be a Scotsman.'

That didn't say much as far as Lestrade was concerned.

'Unfortunately, the fellow has a penchant for kidnapping people. Something to do with potty-training, I expect. Now, how can I help, Superintendent? I'll be Morocco-bound again in a few days.'

Looking at him, Lestrade didn't doubt it.

'The death of this girl, Amy Macpherson . . .'

'Ah yes. Rum, that, wasn't it? Saw a girl slaughtered in Marrakesh once.'

'Really?'

'Yes. Run over by the Express. Ghastly business.'

'Did you know the girl?'

'Lord no. Some nigger.'

'Amy Macpherson?'

'Nigger? Was she? Surely not.'

'No, I believe she was fairly Caucasian, sir.' Lestrade thought it best to clarify the matter. 'Did you know her?'

'I'd probably passed her in the corridor. You know, like Shi'ites that pass in the night.'

'Quite. This may seem rather an impertinent question, sir, but did you notice any of the other guests behaving oddly, either before or after the incident?'

'Well, they all did, Lestrade. There's none so queer as folk, as we say in Outat Oulad. And that McAlpine chappie *did* leave shortly afterwards, you know. Now . . .' Sir Henry stood up. 'I'm sorry to say I can't be of much help. I wonder if you'd mind buggering off for a bit? I've got to face Mecca and you're in my light. See you at dinner?'

For a fleeting moment, while Lestrade wondered how he could face the castle's guests wearing the same brown check he had worn for a week, there was a tap on the door. Fleeting it was, for when he opened it, there was no one there. His room at Balmoral was not much grander than the bothy they'd given him at the Deoch and Doris. Her Royal Highness, the Princess Louise, Duchess of Argyll, had clearly overbooked. But then, essentially, he was an uninvited guest.

He turned back to the rows of stuffed salmon that graced his boudoir and found himself opening and closing his mouth in sympathy. The tap came again. This time he was faster and with a twirl acrobatic in a man twenty years his junior he snatched the knob. It came off in his hand it is true, but the door opened anyway and Alistair Sphagnum stood there.

'Mr Lestrade,' he beamed, 'I hope I'm not intruding.'

'Mr Sphagnum,' Lestrade beamed back, 'has it been my imagination or have you not been glued to my person all day today?'

'Och, come on Lestrade, admit it. You missed me a teensy-weensy wee bit, didn't you? Tell me,' he flopped into the nearest chair, 'any joy with the suspects?'

'Mr Sphagnum,' Lestrade found his tie, draped over a salmon, 'you know that as a police officer I cannot divulge . . .'

'Yes, yes, I know all that. Just as well I've got some information for you then, isn't it?'

He threw a buff envelope down on the table. Lestrade read the stamp at the top: 'Forfar Police'.

'With Inspector McNab's compliments,' said Sphagnum.

'He gave this to you?' Lestrade was open-mouthed.

'Not exactly. He was rather busy, I didna want to bother him, so I helped myself.'

'You mean it was lying around in the police station?'

'In a manner of speaking,' admitted Sphagnum. 'It was lying around in a Rix and Westerby Impregnable Safe.'

'Which was open?' Lestrade didn't care for the way this conversation was going.

'Eventually,' Sphagnum smiled. 'The desk sergeant had gone to look for a particularly obscure form issued by the Procurator Fiscal. Had he found it, it would have allowed me to keep parrots, macaque monkeys and three-banded armadillos in my rooms, until hell freezes over. As it was, he couldn't find said form, so I am naturally disadvantaged. While he was gone, however . . .'

'. . . You rifled his safe.'

'Rifled is a rather strong word. It smacks of deliberate aim. I just happened upon this.'

'Well, what is it? I hope your petty larceny was worthwhile.'

'That's for you to judge.'

Lestrade looked at the gummed envelope edge. 'This has been opened. And resealed,' he said.

'If you're asking, "Did it happen to fall against the spout of a boiling kettle?" the unimpeachable answer must be, "Maybe."'

Lestrade was less careful. After all, he'd forged constabulary envelope headings before. He turned it first one way, then the other. 'It's in Greek,' he said.

'Not exactly,' said Sphagnum, 'but it might as well be. Actually, it's Gaelic. Man, but it's a broa' bricht moonlicht nicht tonight.' He stretched his blue hands before Lestrade's fire.

'Is that usual?' Lestrade asked.

'Aye, at various times of the year. It depends on the cloud cover, of course.'

'No, I mean police reports in Gaelic. Is that usual?'

Sphagnum shook his head. 'Emphatically not. Whatever the Antiquarian Society of Scotland might like to think, Lestrade, the tongue is dying out. You do need to have a certain intelligence quotient to master Gaelic these days and it's way above that of any policeman known to man – oh, saving your own guid presence, of course.'

'And of course, it just so happens that you can read it,' Lestrade nodded knowingly.

'Och, a word here, a sub-paragraph there. I get by.'

Lestrade wrestled with the paper once more. He wasn't even sure which way up it went. 'All right,' he said. 'What do you want?'

'Aha!' Sphagnum cackled, rubbing his hands together. 'A wee peek at that Sassenach brain of yours. Your thoughts on yon guests. Who's your money on?'

'This isn't a game of chance, Mr Sphagnum,' Lestrade frowned.

'Och, isn't it? See you, Jimmy, every criminal case I've ever read about contains a vast amount of that particular commodity. I won't bore you with my vast and superior knowledge.'

'So this is just . . . academic interest?' Lestrade asked, narrowing his eyes at the tall, curly-haired Scot.

Sphagnum opened his arms in all innocence. 'Criminal curiosity,' he said, wide-eyed. 'Nothing more.'

Lestrade looked at him. The Scot was as inscrutable as old Mr Foo who laundered the shirts of Chief Inspector Dew. In this light, he was almost as yellow. Perhaps he could post the document to Marshall and Snellgrove waiting hotfoot at the border. They could send it on discreetly to . . . whom? The boffin at the Yard could probably translate it, given time. But then, the gaffe was blown. He knew Sub-Inspector Hill of old. Had a mouth on him like a Thames foghorn. He might as well send it to George Robey. And the two weeks granted to him by Mr Edward Henry were nearly up. And yet. And yet.

'No,' he said, 'I can't.'

'Ah, well,' Sphagnum said. 'I'll just get this detailed account of Amy Macpherson's death back to Abergeldie.'

'All right.' Lestrade stopped him. 'But this is *very* unorthodox, Sphagnum. I want your word – your word, mind – that what passes in this room will go no further.'

'Cross my heart and hope to die in England,' Sphagnum grinned.

'Very well. But first, the report.'

'Uh-uh,' Sphagnum smiled. 'First, your theories.'

Lestrade screwed up his lips and with them, his moustache went right up his nose. 'No,' he said. 'In any case, not before dinner. If I told you my innermost thoughts, you'd be staring at people throughout the meal.'

A gong groaned below to summon the faithful to eat.

'I'll just be awa' and put my tails on,' Sphagnum said, pocketing the envelope. 'Best not leave this lying around.' He glanced about him. 'I wouldn't trust some of yon fish further

69

than I could throw them. See you back here at . . . what? Midnight?'

Dinner was indescribable. Something greasy, grey and swimming in liquid under a silver tureen cover was brought in between two pipers. The first was Angus Laidlaw, tall, square, immaculate in his tartan and doublet, the ptarmigan cockade nodding proudly in his beret. The second was altogether smaller, padding on silken feet, his head swathed in a turban, a long, ornate sword protruding at right angles from a gold chain sash – the unlikely figure of Sir Harry Maclean KCMG, piping in the haggis.

The Duchess smiled on them benignly and, judging from the row, they must have come up on her on her bad side. Everybody else seemed to be enjoying it however and the whisky flowed like water and the pipes played on. And on. And on. When they broke into 'A Hundred Pipers an' a', an' a'', Lestrade was eternally grateful they were only two. In accordance with the Old Queen's rituals, no one spoke to anyone else throughout the meal. The only welcome break was when Angus Laidlaw paused to wet his whistle (which was, after all, an old police custom too) and Sir Harry dropped to his knees on a prayer mat in the corner, his arms outstretched. Clearly, mused Lestrade, the haggis hadn't agreed with him either.

Lestrade had never lost a hand of whist in his life, largely because he'd never played the game before. Until, that is, the night he played with Alistair Sphagnum. He could, it is true, have gone Misere of Ayr, but that didn't quite seem cricket. Scotch whist remained a mystery to him and so it was that Lestrade voiced his theories first, having failed to gain a single trick. He bounced his ideas off Alistair Sphagnum as he was wont to do off Walter Dew. He noticed immediately that there was less of an echo.

'First,' Lestrade leaned back and lit a cigar, which the thoughtful hostess had provided in her guests' rooms, 'Hamish McCrum.'

70

'Ah, yes, that little weasel with the foul eating habits. What did you make of him?'

'You mean apart from the fact you could hear his lips smacking over the noise of the pipes? Well, like all of them, he had the opportunity.'

'Ah yes,' Sphagnum said, 'that applies to everybody connected with the household. Anything *particular* about him?'

'He's a musician.'

'Really?'

'Plays cor anglais in the Glasgow Philharmonia.'

'A merry band,' mused Sphagnum. 'But shouldn't that be cor écossais?'

'Probably,' said Lestrade, but he didn't know a Stradivarius from his elbow and he let it pass. 'On the Night in Question, he played for the assembled guests and retired early.'

'Aha!'

'His room is in the West Wing, so he would have had to travel the length of the castle to reach the cellar where the girl was found. If, that is, she died where she was found.'

Sphagnum smiled. In that room full of glass-eyed salmon, Lestrade was fishing. 'She did,' he leaked.

'Of course,' Lestrade trawled deeper, 'if I only knew what time she died . . .'

'All in good time,' said Sphagnum. 'Go on.'

'There again,' said Lestrade, 'the *cause* of death. If I had an inkling . . .'

'You *have* an inkling,' Sphagnum assured him.

'All right, then,' said Lestrade, 'if I had *more* of an inkling as to how many blows, the spacing on the skull, the force required . . .'

'What point are you making?' Having cheated at cards, Sphagnum was not going to give way now.

'Mr McCrum is a slight man. From the side he'd pass as a stick insect. You don't play the cor anglais with your arm, do you?'

'No, with your lungs, I think.'

'Then unless Mr McCrum battered the girl to death with his lungs, I'd say he probably didn't have the strength. Tell me, was she . . . disturbed?'

'Simple, didn't Allan Ramsay say?'

'No,' Lestrade explained, 'I mean, molested, interfered with.'

'No sign of that,' Sphagnum was willing to concede. 'Although there was one word in the Gaelic I couldna' understand.'

'Oh?'

'Och, no, I ken *all* the words in Gaelic associated with that sort of thing. When I was at school we'd write them on the blackboard of Monsieur Bête, the French teacher. He was none the wiser, of course.'

'Well, I think that's another reason to rule out Mr McCrum.'

'Oh? Why?'

'Because for most of the dinner, he had his hand on my knee.'

'Did he?' Sphagnum's face was a picture as he poured himself another single malt. 'Thank God. I thought it was just my knee he was fondling.'

'Ah,' said Lestrade, 'with both hands occupied, it does tend to explain his eating habits, doesn't it?'

'Ruling out Mr McCrum, then, who's next on your wee black list?'

'Mr McAlpine I have yet to meet. By a happy coincidence, if that's what it is, he and Miss Pringle who found the body are at Glarms. Where is that, by the way?'

'South-west as the osprey flies. Nice little hoose. Haunted.'

'Oh, good. Which leaves among the remaining guests Sir Harry Maclean, the McIndoe sisters and Canon McColl.'

'Ah, yes, the boring old fart.' Sphagnum rummaged for his briar. 'Strange, really, Maclean is so much larger than life, McColl relatively dead. Of these two, who's your money on?'

'Well.' Lestrade was warming to his theme now. The amber nectar had something to do with it. 'Let's see what we have. Canon McColl was educated, he tells me, at Glenalmond and Naples.'

'Ah.' Sphagnum raised an intellectual eyebrow. 'You know what they say, "See Naples and die."'

'Indeed they do,' nodded Lestrade, totally unaware of the fact. 'He's a long way from Ripon. I wonder if any young girls have been beaten to death in his patch?'

'Er . . . that's parish, I believe,' Sphagnum interjected. 'You think he might make a habit of it?'

'It had crossed my mind. He was, after all, an intimate friend of Gladstone's.'

'Ah, you've lost me there, Superintendent. I don't go back as far as you, remember.'

'Mr Gladstone, our late Prime Minister, had a predirection for nipping out from Downing Street late at night to save fallen women.'

'Did he now? Not called the People's William for nothing, then?'

'Indeed not. What if there was something more sinister in it? What if his motives were interior? What if the good canon was a party to his little peccadilloes?'

Sphagnum raised an eyebrow. 'So he had little peccadilloes, did he? But I watched McColl at dinner, as a good student of law should. I didn't notice a raging passion beating under his smock.'

'You never do,' Lestrade told him. 'Look at Felix Waddington, the axe murderer of Penge; Humphrey McCumfey, the mad scyther of Biggleswade; Padraig Kellogg.'

'Who was he?'

'Ireland's only serial killer.'

'I don't entirely follow your spoor, Lestrade.'

'Quiet, mousy men. Men with rimless glasses, small feet and stoops. They give freely to charity, fear God and honour the King. But if you're of a female bent and you meet 'em under a bright moon, wallop! It's the slab for you, my girl.'

'So Canon McColl?'

'All I'm saying is still waters run deep. Like all of them, he had the opportunity.'

'Motive?' Sphagnum asked.

Lestrade paused. 'If he's mad, that's motive enough.'

'You think he's mad?'

'He *is* a canon of the Church of England.'

Sphagnum smiled. 'I'm getting to know you, Lestrade. You're a sly old mudiewarp and no mistake. You don't really think it's him, do you? What of the McIndoe sisters?'

'Spinsters.' Lestrade ran a finger around the rim of his glass. 'At that funny age when some women become decidedly unstable.'

'Ah, yes, ma aunt did that. Fell off some library steps at forty-six and was never the same again.'

'In what way?'

'She was dead.'

'Oh, I'm sorry.'

'Don't be. It's Ould Reekie I feel sorry for.'

'Her husband?'

'Her dog. She fell on him, y'see.'

'Ah, so she crushed the animal?'

'Och, no. But he was a little peeved to say the least. Went for her in no uncertain terms. But it did give Auntie a unique place in Scottish history.'

'Oh?'

'The only leading member of the Kirk of Scotland to be savaged to death by a Pitcairn terrier. Poor Ould Reekie died of shock. Either that or the taste. Could it be the McIndoe sisters, then?'

Lestrade shook his head. 'Unlikely,' he said. 'Women kill with poison, a pistol or occasionally a garotte. I've never known one, let alone two, use a blunt instrument.'

'What about Lizzie Borden?' Sphagnum had done his homework in the University law library.

'Ah, she was American,' Lestrade explained.

'What of Maclean?'

'Yes. Now, he's interesting, isn't he?'

'He is that. The only Presbyterian Moslem I've ever met. Could that sword of his have cracked the girl's skull, d'ye think?'

'You tell me,' said Lestrade, archly.

'In the fullness of time,' Sphagnum promised.

'Very well. No, it couldn't. I've seen a few of those things in my time. Your Berber sword is razor sharp. If you killed someone with that you'd slice, not bash.'

'Well, if I had a Maxim gun, I'd probably fire it at my victim,' said Sphagnum. 'But if it were empty, I'd drop it on the bastard's head. That won't hold water, Lestrade. Of course, the Berbers hold their women in scant regard, you know.'

'They do?'

'Och, yes. Make the poor wee drabs fetch and carry water, milk the goats. It's barbaric.'

'Isn't that a bit like the Highlanders?' Lestrade asked.

'Ach, "Sticks and stones may break ma bones, but names will never hurt me". Are you saying a Highlander did it?'

'Highlander, Lowlander, tinker, tailor, I don't know, Mr Sphagnum. And I won't commit myself until I've talked to everybody.'

'Of course,' said Sphagnum, 'there is *one* person we've overlooked.'

'Oh?'

'Her Royal Highness, Princess Louise, the Incumbent.'

'Hmm . . . again, not a woman's crime.'

'Oh? You're pretty sure of that.'

'I've been chasing murderers man and boy now for thirty years. Are you seriously suggesting the daughter of Queen Victoria is a maniac?'

'Well, you've met her, Lestrade. What's your conclusion?'

'Point taken,' Lestrade agreed. 'Now,' he topped up their glasses, 'the police report. Your side of the bargain.'

'Right.' Sphagnum pulled out the sheaf of papers. 'Now, it's not exactly Mary Macleod or the Cuchulainn romances . . . By the by, I presume you'd prefer it spoken, not sung?'

'Just the facts,' sighed Lestrade, rather less enchanted by Highland lore since the haggis.

'Man, man.' It was Sphagnum's turn to sigh. 'You've no heart in ye. Well, Amy Macpherson was found at the base of the cellar stairs. Which reminds me, by the by, Lestrade, of Amy Robsart . . .'

'We'll bypass your love life for this evening, Mr Sphagnum. For me, time is running out.'

Sphagnum laughed and went on. 'She was found by Miss Dorothea Anne Pringle, governess, at eight thirty on the morning of November the thirtieth.'

'St Andrew's Day,' Lestrade chimed in.

'We'll make a Scot of you yet,' beamed Sphagnum. 'She'd been dead about three hours. By the time the police were called and a doctor, she'd been dead about seven hours.'

'Any signs of rigor?'

'Er . . . I don't think there's a word for rigour in the Gaelic.' Sphagnum riffled through the papers.

'Is there a word for stiff?'

'Aye, there is, and it's not here.'

'Go on.'

'The doctor thinks she was struck from in front by a blunt instrument, perhaps an iron bar or wooden staff.'

'Didn't he look for bits in the wound?'

'Bits?'

'If it was a wooden staff, there'd be splinters sticking to the blood.'

'Nothing about that here.'

'All right. Anything else?'

'No disarray of clothing. No sign of sexual assault.'

'So that wasn't the motive.' Lestrade was talking to himself. 'Unless . . .'

'Unless our friend was disturbed by Miss Pringle. But it says she found the body at eight thirty and Macpherson died at five thirty. That's a hell of a long time to get doon the stairs, Lestrade.'

'From what I've heard of the forensic information so far, Mr Sphagnum, we can't exactly rely on any of those times. It seems the police north of the border could stand a crash course in professionalism.'

'Ah, but you've not heard the best bit,' Sphagnum smiled. 'It says at the bottom, in English, "Case closed. Probable suicide."'

'Suicide,' Lestrade repeated. 'So Connaught was right.'

'Eh?'

'Never mind. Is it signed?'

'McNab.'

'I thought you told me Gaelic was too difficult for a mere policeman to master?'

'I did,' agreed Sphagnum. 'I smell cover-up, Lestrade.'

'Mr Sphagnum, two minds with but a single nose. How do I get to Glarms Castle from here?'

'By way of a Quadrant Twin Engine and courtesy of yours truly.'

'Now, Sphagnum . . .' Lestrade held up a hand in protest.

'No, Lestrade,' Sphagnum interrupted. '"I am in blood Steep'd in so far, that should I wade no more, Returning were as tedious as go o'er."'

'You and your Scottish poets,' moaned Lestrade. 'Half the words are missing.'

5

The morning of the twenty-second was raw with freezing fog. It swirled around Lestrade's legs as he hauled them into the stirrups of the Quadrant and it crept inexorably up his sleeves as he tried to bury his hands in the tartan rugs Allan Ramsay had lent him. Lestrade was well used to fog; the green moving carpet that crept along the Thames, keeping company with the trailing lighters and the plodding policemen on their nightly beats. What he was totally unprepared for was the cold and even before Sphagnum's machine had roared and coughed its way out of Balmoral's grounds, the superintendent's moustache was a block of ice and his lungs had frozen over.

They stopped in the village of Braemar, whose slate roofs rose like ghosts out of the grey, and Lestrade staggered to the Post Office to send two telegrams. The first told Marshall and Snellgrove where he was bound. The second apologized to Mr Edward Henry, Assistant Commissioner of the Metropolitan Police, for extending the fortnight's compassionate leave. Not only was Lestrade's aged aunt no better, she had had a second fall off her library steps and Lestrade himself had gone down with pneumonia. He timed the whole thing perfectly and jogged the telegrapher's arm as he wrote the name Braemar. Lestrade smiled to himself. The telegram was such a mess, it could have come from anywhere.

Sphagnum wiped the ice off his goggles and with their insides newly thawed by a nip of his flask, he and Lestrade took the high road to the south-east, to the castle of Glamis.

*

It was somewhere on the rocky road to Inverculiarity, where, above the mist, the craggy outcrops of Cat Law stare down, brooding and silent, over Prosen Water. It was here that Sphagnum's Quadrant gave a last cough, a death rattle and stopped.

'Ach.' He thumped the machine with a gauntleted hand. 'The bitch. It'll be that bloody overhead piston arrangement. It's never been anything but trouble.'

He hauled up his goggles and forced his eyes to focus. 'Lestrade, I'd wander around for a bit, if I were you. I'll be a minute or three and if you sit still in this mist, man, you'll likely freeze to death.'

He helped the superintendent out. Lestrade stamped for a while on his good leg and blew on his hands – the obvious thing to do considering the colour they'd gone. He then wandered off a little distance from the road, past the white stones which marked its edge, to risk frostbite and answer the call of nature. Steam rose from the rock against which he stood. It was like standing fully clothed – well, nearly fully clothed – in a Turkish bath. In the distance he could hear the happy sound of tinkering, metal on metal, as Alistair Sphagnum took a crowbar to his Quadrant. The rhythm of man and machine was broken now and then as the metal hit flesh and Sphagnum went walkabout, cursing loudly in Gaelic.

As he adjusted his clothing and turned to trudge back for the road, Lestrade was suddenly aware that he was not alone. Looming out of the mist ahead of him came the great black head of an Aberdeen Angus bull, followed by its shoulders and square, high back. It looked at him, snorting and pawing the frosty heather clumps. It was followed by a second, then a third.

'Shoo!' he said softly, having been a couple of times to Smithfield Market. The beasts didn't move. Lestrade's problem of course was that the cattle he'd seen in Smithfield Market tended to hang upside down, skinned, in half and rather dead. This was a whole new creel of herring.

'Shoo!' he shouted, resolutely standing up to them.

A wild eye rolled and a bellow roared up from the bowels of the nearest beast. As far as the eye could see, hundreds of pounds of beef were outflanking him to east and west – the revenge for all those steak and kidney pies at the Collar. He began to limp backwards, not taking his eyes off the cattle. One or two of them started to crop the stiff grass or browse in the heather, trying to lull Lestrade into a sense of false security. The one that had appeared first, clearly the ring leader, judging by the metal circle in his nostrils, tossed his head and came for Lestrade, snorting and growling.

The superintendent forgot his limp entirely. He threw his bowler at the beast and ran like a madman through the heather, crushing it under his flying feet like so many frozen firecrackers. All the way he heard the bellow of the bull and felt its hot, sweet breath on the back of his neck. He was grateful to feel the road under his feet. Why wasn't there a single bloody tree around when you wanted one? Rather like policemen, really.

'Sphagnum! Sphagnum! Where the hell are you?' he heard himself shouting. The voice was not his own. There was a clatter of hoofs which told him that the minotaur had reached the road. It would outpace him here. In the heather, travelling downhill from the slope to Cat Law, he'd had an even chance, but that evil-coated bastard had four legs to his one and a half and two hundred pounds of muscle to power them. He was just wondering how he could brace himself for an iron head in the small of the back when he collided head on with the Quadrant, throbbing again after Sphagnum's gentle ministrations. The superintendent's knees buckled and he went down.

Sphagnum swung his leg off the machine again and went round to view the sleeping policeman. He was suddenly aware of a giant black bull, alarmed by the twin engines, looking sheepishly at him. The Scotsman walked up to the creature, bent down and kissed it on the matted forehead. 'Awa' wi' ye,' he whispered in its ear, 'or I'll have you for a wee sandwich.'

The beast needed no further bidding. It snorted, showing how little it cared, and wheeled away, rumbling internally to call its wives to it.

Sphagnum stooped and hauled Lestrade upright, steadying him as he lifted an eyelid. 'They're harmless, man,' he told the unconscious superintendent. 'You ran into the Douglas herd, that's all. Yon bull just wanted his ear scratched. Now, if they'd been Highland cattle . . .' and he sucked in his breath sharply, as he tucked Lestrade into the sidecar and wrapped him snugly in Ramsay's blankets. 'You see, your Highland cattle might *look* like bales of hay with a wee welcome mat thrown in, but those horns . . . Man, the smell alone can kill you.'

They rattled through Kirriemuir, pausing only to get a leather bottle full of ice for Lestrade's head. As they passed the manor house at Logie, his vision began to clear and as the Quadrant hissed and jolted its way through the ice of Dean Water, he began to sit up and take nourishment.

Even so, it was a shaky superintendent who was once again lifted out of the sidecar beneath the grey, baronial battlements of Glamis Castle. He seemed to make rather a habit of this.

And it was an even shakier superintendent who somersaulted gracefully over the stone lion on the front doorstep as he was about to enter. And he may have been several miles to the north-west, but the rest was Blackness.

When he awoke, he was in a bed, with a radiant face looking down at him. As his eyes focused in the firelight, he found the nose a little sharp, but the eyes were clear and the hair swept high from a broad, intelligent forehead.

'My dear sergeant, how are you? How's your poor head? It looks rather purple and angry from where I'm sitting.'

'Rather like the rest of me,' moaned Lestrade, 'Mrs . . . er ?'

'Bowes-Lyon. Welcome to Glamis Castle, sergeant.'

'Thank you, ma'am.' Lestrade struggled to sit up in order to bow. 'Superintendent,' he corrected her.

'Oh, he's all right. He's been regaling us at dinner with stories of how you joined the Scottish police in order to improve your experience.'

'I'm sorry . . .'

'Oh, no, please. Don't apologize. There are lots of things the Scots do better than the English.'

'Indeed there are,' Lestrade agreed. 'How long have I been here?'

'In the East Wing? An hour or so. Before that you lay rather still on the hall floor.'

'Is he deaded, Mummy, the man?' a shrill little voice suddenly called from under the counterpane. Lestrade jarred both his head and leg in surprise. A beautiful little girl, not more than three years old, sat on the bed, smiling at him. She had large, bright eyes and her long dark hair was spread over her frothy nightdress. She reminded him of his own Emma, not so long ago.

'No, of course not, dear,' her mother explained. 'You can see for yourself, he's sitting up. Which reminds me, it's time you weren't. Where's that brother of yours?'

Another little head with golden curls popped up beside the first.

'Ah, my two Benjamins,' their mother beamed.

'See,' said the girl to the boy, 'I told you he wasn't deaded. Look. He's sitting up.'

The boy looked Lestrade up and down. He'd probably never seen anything so strange in the whole of his two years on earth. A sallow-looking man with a drooping moustache and a rather nasty, crumpled shirt. There was a clean white bandage around his head above the dark, sad eyes.

'Elizabeth and David,' said their mother, 'I'd like you to meet Sergeant Lestrade, attached to the Leith Police.'

The little girl hopped off Lestrade's bed and did her best with a wobbly curtsey. The ladies looked at David, hoping for some attempt at ceremonial from him. It was not to be. He carried on staring at Lestrade.

'I feel I must explain, Lady Bowes-Lyon,' said Lestrade, 'I am not a sergeant, but a superintendent. And the only thing I am attached to, apart from whatever may be left of my reputation, is Scotland Yard.'

'Oh . . .' Lady Bowes-Lyon blinked first, then frowned afterwards. 'But that means that Superintendent Sphagnum . . .'

'Is a liar,' Lestrade finished the sentence for her.

Lady Bowes-Lyon clapped her hands over her daughter's ears, but it was too late.

'What's a liar, Mummy?' the little girl asked.

'It's . . . um . . . an old stringed instrument, darling,' she explained. 'Now run along to Nanny Moncrieff, both of you. Time for Bedfordshire.'

The little ones scampered away. At the door, little Elizabeth stopped and bobbed again. 'Nice to meet you, man,' she smiled and dashed off in pursuit of her brother.

'You have lovely children, ma'am,' Lestrade told her.

'Thank you, Mr Lestrade.' Lady Bowes-Lyon rose from the bed. 'But from your careless remark just now, I can only assume you have none.'

Lestrade smiled. He thought of golden-haired Emma with the firelight bright on her tresses. 'No,' he said, 'none.'

'I hope you'll be comfortable.' She made to go.

'Lady Bowes-Lyon.' He stopped her, more roughly than he intended. 'I'm sorry, but I am investigating a murder.'

'Good heavens!'

'I take it Mr Sphagnum did not mention that?'

'Why no.' She sat down sharply. 'He merely said that his machine had broken down and begged shelter for the night. With this fog and your collision with old Leo . . .'

'Leo?'

'The stone lion at the door, Mr Lestrade.' She leaned forward. 'I think you'd better tell me everything.'

It was not in Lestrade's make-up to tell *anybody* everything. But he confided in the elegant lady of Glamis as far as he dared. He would upbraid 'Sergeant' Sphagnum for reversing their roles. The man was harmless enough. He just had delusions of grandeur and enjoyed a practical joke, that was all.

In the mean time, as it was not too late, he would like to talk to Mr McAlpine, the builder, if that was not too much trouble. And then to Miss Pringle, Lady Elizabeth's governess.

Robert McAlpine stood square and solid, like one of the many buildings he had erected all over Motherwell. Grey of hair and bright of eye, he suffered no one gladly and fools least of all.

'Well.' He tapped his way along the gloomy corridor past silent suits of steel that stood sentinel. 'I'm a busy man, Mr Lestrade, and time's money, y'ken. Och, will you look at that?'

Lestrade did. Lifting his bandage a little, he peered into the dark of a recess.

'Shocking, isn't it? Bloody Scottish baronial style. I wouldn't give you tuppence for it. It's all turrets and machicolations. You wouldn't think this was the twentieth century, would ye? I tell you, Lestrade, the time's got to come when we have hot and cold running water in all rooms. At the moment we've only got cold and it's running down the bloody walls. Well, come on, man, ye haven't staggered up here to hear ma views on architecture. Out wi' it.'

'It's about Balmoral . . .'

'Aye, well, there y'are. That bloody place is even worse. At least this is essentially medieval. I ask you, what does the bloody Royal Family know about architecture? Man, I practically built the Glasgow sewerage system. There isn't a pipe nor elbow-joint I don't know there personally. Don't talk to me about Balmoral. Plumbingly, it's a bloody joke.'

'It was actually about the girl, Amy Macpherson, I wanted to talk to you.'

'Oh, aye?' McAlpine stopped sniffing the stones and put away his tape measure. 'Battered to death, I understand.'

'Did you know her?'

'Well, *know* is a bit strong, especially in the Biblical sense. I believe she brought ma morning toast once or twice.'

'Did you form an opinion of her?'

'Rather limited, I thought. Not a natural for the Antediluvian Society of Scottish Architects, certainly.'

'What did she say?'

'Er . . . I believe it was "Guid morning, sir." Is that a sort of victimly thing to say? You see, I've never met a murder victim before. I'm a bit out of ma depth as Toulouse Lautrec used to say.'

'Where were you on the Morning in Question?' Lestrade was getting nowhere.

'In ma wee truckle bed, wishing I was *anywhere* but Balmoral. Mind you, I was the first man on the scene.'

'Indeed? Where was your room?'

'At the back, overlooking the stables. Quintessential view, mind. I heard Miss Pringle scream.'

'You knew it was Miss Pringle?'

'Not at the time. But it was loud and female, so I jumped into my breeks and ran to the source of it.'

'What then?'

'When I got to the cellar I saw Miss Pringle standing at the bottom of the stairs, a candle in her hand. She was still screaming, so I slapped her.'

'What happened?'

'She carried on.'

'So what did you do?'

'Slapped her again. This time she went down. I carried her up to the ground floor.'

'And Amy Macpherson?'

'Ah, well, I nearly came a cropper over her. I must have missed her on the way down, what with the poor light and Miss Pringle carrying on. On the way up, I tripped over the wee wretch and nearly fetched ma length.'

'And?'

'I left Miss Pringle with Allan Ramsay and went back. Man, that gel was a mess. Reminds me of a foreman I once had who was a little hard of hearing. His mate shouted, "Einer liner" – to which, of course, the stock reply is "Burr" – and he got no response.'

'So?'

'So the mate dropped three hundredweight of bricks on him. The merest chance, mind you. The foreman should have been three feet to the left.'

'Is this relevant, Mr McAlpine?'

'Probably not, but the result was the same.'

'You think Miss Macpherson was hit by falling bricks?'

'You're the police,' McAlpine said. 'You tell me.'

'When I know, I will. Do you know which is Miss Pringle's room?'

'Certainly not.' McAlpine straightened. 'I'm a married man.'

'Ah.'

'Och, very well. Up the stairs, third on the left, past that particularly nasty stone lintel.'

Lestrade found the nasty stone lintel, albeit with his head, but there was no reply from Miss Pringle's room. He hobbled back to the library, meeting Alistair Sphagnum on the way. Two guests stood warming their hands before the roaring log fire. They turned at the arrival of the pair.

'Sholto!' they chorused.

'Harry! Letitia!' Lestrade had crossed to them in one bound. 'I don't believe it.'

'What are you doing here?'

'I was about to ask the same of you.'

The radiant Letitia hugged him to her, kissing his cheek and whispering in his ear, 'It's so good to see you again.' She pulled back. 'Sholto, you're hurt.'

'Actually, it's my head,' he said. 'Nothing to worry about.'

'Missed his brain by several feet,' beamed Sphagnum.

'Oh.' Lestrade's face fell. 'May I present? Letitia and Harry Bandicoot, this is Alistair Sphagnum.'

'Bandicoot.' Sphagnum extended a hand. 'I know that name. Where are you from Mr Bandicoot?'

'Huish Episcopi, in Somerset,' Bandicoot told him.

'Oh, aye,' Sphagnum nodded. 'There's a place with a guid broa' Scots ring to it. But I've never been there. It's your face I know. And yours, madam . . .' He took Letitia's hand and kissed it. 'Yours I will get to know.'

'How are the boys?' asked Lestrade. 'And Emma?'

Letitia broke away, a trifle too reluctantly for Harry's liking. 'They've all gone down with mumps, Sholto,' she said, holding both Lestrade's hands in hers. 'They're right as rain, of course. I hated to leave them in quarantine but I couldn't risk Harry. It does strange things to men, I understand. The Bowes-Lyons suddenly asked us – out of the blue. We met them in Town and decided on the spur of the moment to spend Christmas up . . . here. We hadn't seen them for years. A pity we had to leave the children. Little Elizabeth is such a darling. And David. They'd all have had a marvellous time. Emma talks of you constantly, Sholto. After Christmas, you *must* spend a few days with us.'

'We'd have been here sooner,' said Bandicoot, 'but the points were frozen on the Tay Bridge. What a disaster!'

'Were you at Cambridge, Mr Bandicoot?' Sphagnum asked.

'No,' said Harry.

'Come and sit down, Sholto.' Letitia patted the sofa beside her. 'Tell me, how long have you known the Master of Glamis?'

'Well, actually, I've yet to meet him . . .'

'Eton!' Sphagnum suddenly roared. 'You boxed for Eton.'

'That's right,' said Bandicoot.

'And I boxed for Fettes. Let me see, was it '86 or '87?'

''87. I had dysentery in '86.'

'School mince?'

Bandicoot nodded.

'Same at Fettes. You knocked me out in the eighth round.'

A strange light of realization dawned in the limited brain of Harry Bandicoot. 'Slaughterer Sphagnum!' He clicked his fingers. 'You were bally good.'

'Aye, laddie, but you were better. I'd like a return match some day, Basher.'

Harry glanced at Letitia. 'Some day,' he said and watched the Scotsman sit beside his wife, on the other flank from Lestrade.

'Your husband has a powerful right hook, Mrs Bandicoot,' he said.

'I know.' Letitia smiled at Harry. 'Now, Sholto . . .'

Suddenly, there was an ear-piercing shriek. A flunkey by the wall dropped a silver salver which rolled and clattered on the polished floor. Everyone was on their feet. 'What was that?' Bandicoot found his voice first.

'It's the *Bean-Nighe*,' Sphagnum whispered. 'The Wailing Woman. There's a death in this hoose tonight.'

And the three men made for the door.

'It came from over here,' Sphagnum shouted.

'No, up the staircase, surely.' Bandicoot peered upward.

'I hate to be an old stick-in-the-mud, gentlemen,' said Lestrade, 'but it actually ruminated from the cellar.'

He tried the door. It was locked.

'Is there a key?' He turned to the flunkey.

'I say, steady on,' a voice called from the stairs, and turning to his lady behind him, 'One of the guests, my dear, shoulder-barging the furniture. Is that strictly on?'

'Strictly, no, dear, but I don't have a key and he is a police superintendent. Mr Lestrade, this is my husband, the Master of Glamis.'

Lestrade bowed to Bowes-Lyon whose military moustache swept magnificently in return.

'We heard a scream. Was it you, Mr Lestrade?'

'No, Lady Bowes-Lyon, it was not,' the superintendent assured her.

'Letitia! Harry!' The gracious lady glided gracefully down the staircase. 'I'd no idea you'd arrived.'

'We've just this minute come.' Letitia kissed her old friend. 'We wanted to thaw a little first.'

'Harry.' She held the big man to her. 'It's been too long.' She smiled. 'Claudie, you remember Harry and Letitia.'

'Do I? Oh, yes, yes, of course. Merry Christmas, everyone.'

'A little premature, dear,' Lady Bowes-Lyon reminded him. 'That's tomorrow.'

'Ahem!' Lestrade coughed. 'We may have a damsel in distress here somewhere, gentlemen. Perhaps you youngsters could have a go at that cellar door? With your permission, of course, Lord Glamis?'

'Oh, don't mind me.'

'I think we're the youngsters he's referring to, Bandicoot,' said Sphagnum. '*Floreat Etona*, eh?'

'Absolutely,' said Bandicoot, 'or even *Floreat Fettesia*,' and shoulder to shoulder, they rushed the door. It crashed back under their collective weight and a second scream was heard.

'Sphagnum?' Bandicoot asked. 'Was that you?'

'Sorry,' said the Scot, waving a throbbing finger. 'Splinter.'

'My lord,' said Lestrade, 'do you have a light down there?' He pointed to where the cellar steps fell away into total darkness.

'Here, sir.' The flunkey had reappeared before anyone had noticed he had gone and was carrying a candle.

'Well done,' said Lestrade and, taking the brass handle, he gingerly descended the steps. They felt worn and uneven under his feet. His head still ached and his foot still throbbed, but a job was a job and he was easily the most experienced scream-investigator there. True, Harry Bandicoot had once served as a constable of the Metropolitan Police, but that was for less than a year and anyway, it had all been a case of mistaken identity – a rash career move best forgotten.

In the flickering light he made out two bodies, one sprawled across the base of the steps, the other propped up against the far wall. Lestrade crouched as well as he could in a confined space with a gammy leg and checked each one. The first was thirty to thirty-five with a deathly pale countenance. Judging by the cut of her bodice, she was a woman. The other one was a man, but a man no longer. What was left of his head lolled against the whitewashed brick and great sweeps of blood

87

daubed and spattered the wall. His left eye was lost in a pulverized mass of blood and bruising. His right, still partly open, eyed Lestrade quizzically. It taunted him in its dull, dead way – ' Well, here I am,' it seemed to say, 'what are you going to do about it?'

'This one's still alive,' he said and Sphagnum and Bandicoot joined him on the steps to haul the woman's body across their shoulders and up the passageway above.

'Good God, it's Miss Pringle,' Lestrade heard Lord Glamis say. 'Has she been . . . interfered with?'

Lestrade heard the silence in which he knew all eyes, except Miss Pringle's, had turned to face the master of the castle. But it was a proper question and Lestrade wanted the answer to it too.

'She's all right,' he heard Lady Glamis say. 'Letitia, help me get her to her room, would you?'

'There's somebody else.' Sphagnum had come back down the stairs, peering through the gloom.

'I'm afraid so,' Lestrade told him. 'Harry, get me more light, there's a good fellow.'

To get past the flunkey on the steps, Bandicoot did a little pas de deux, as befitted a father of twins, and returned with a second candle.

'Anybody know him?' Lestrade asked. As both Sphagnum and Bandicoot were relative strangers to Glamis, the question was a little optimistic.

'I do.' Lord Glamis perched above Bandicoot half-way up the stairs. 'It's Alexander Hastie, one of my grooms.'

He edged his way past the crouching figures and knelt beside the dead man, on the other side from Lestrade. 'My God, what's happened to him?' he whispered, afraid his usual voice would betray him.

'His skull has been smashed,' Lestrade told him, clinically viewing the ghastly wound by the flickering light. 'With a heavy, blunt object. I'd say he's been dead about an hour.'

'That would make it . . .' Sphagnum conjectured.

'Five o'clockish,' Lestrade said.

'The murderer can't have got far, Lestrade.' Sphagnum stood up. 'I'll assemble the guests.'

'No, you won't, young man.' The Lord of Glamis was on his

feet too. 'It's Christmas in a few hours. I won't have that spoiled, murder or no murder. Besides, apart from yourselves and the Bandicoots, there's no one else here. Mr Lauder hasn't arrived yet.'

Sphagnum groaned.

'Who?' Lestrade asked.

'Harry Lauder,' Glamis told him. 'He's our Turn.'

'Which is precisely what he gives me,' muttered Sphagnum.

'You've forgotten Mr McAlpine, my lord,' Lestrade reminded him.

'No, I haven't. Man's a tradesman. Can't number him among the guests.'

'Of course,' said Sphagnum. 'It's this English fascination with the nobs – begging your pardon, my lord, of course – this conviction that only they can be guilty of so dastardly a crime. Why can't it be one of the servants?'

'Not *my* servants, Sphagnum,' Lord Glamis assured him. 'Lady Bowes-Lyon has hand-picked them herself. We're most particular about references. Not one of them said anything about murder.'

'Oh, good,' beamed Lestrade, enormously reassured. 'My lord, would you be so kind as to assemble the domestics? I'd like a word with them before I start work.'

'Very well,' said Glamis. 'But I warn you, Superintendent, I will not have Christmas spoiled. Nothing comes between me and my plum duff of a Yuletide. I don't want the children upset.'

'Quite right, my lord,' and Lestrade bowed as the Master went in search of his servants. 'Well, Sphagnum . . .' He knelt again with some difficulty. 'Since you seem to have appointed yourself honorary policeman, let's have your views.'

'Er . . .' The Scotsman nodded in Bandicoot's direction.

'Harry Bandicoot is the salt of the earth,' Lestrade informed him. 'I'd go through fire with that man. In fact, I probably have. Your theories?'

'Oh, Sholto.' Bandicoot knelt there too, grinning rather sheepishly.

'It's the same method of attack,' Sphagnum said, 'as poor Amy Macpherson. Head all but disintegrated.'

'Just what I was thinking,' Lestrade nodded.

'Was it?' Bandicoot was lagging a little behind the others. Why, he wondered to himself, and not for the first time, did bodies start appearing when Lestrade was around?

'So all we have to do,' Sphagnum was in his element, 'is to find a link between them and hey, presto! We have our man.'

'Or woman!' chirped up Bandicoot.

'No, no, Harry,' Lestrade explained, 'we've been through all that. Not a woman's crime.'

'Although,' Sphagnum mused in the eerie half-light, 'curious is it not, that yon Miss Pringle should have found *both* bodies?'

'"When a body meets a body", eh?' Bandicoot smiled.

Sphagnum turned to his old sparring partner. 'You're not just a pretty right hook, Mr Bandicoot,' he said. 'I think you and Mr Lauder will get on famously.'

'What did you mean?' Lestrade asked him. 'When we heard Miss Pringle scream?'

'Eh?' Sphagnum was lost for a moment.

'You said it's the Been She or something.'

'Och, the *Bean-Nighe*,' Sphagnum chuckled. 'Aye, the Wailing Woman. I told you this place was haunted, Lestrade. Well, old Alexander Hastie's just added another ghost to it. Legend has it that she is small and green and has red webbed feet.'

'Well, that rules out Miss Pringle.' Bandicoot prided himself on his observation. 'Miss Pringle's feet are perfectly normal. I know because at one point on the stairs, they were up my nostril.'

'Thank you, Harry,' said Lestrade.

'Ask among the ghillies,' said Sphagnum. 'One of them will have seen her at the local burn, washing the smalls of wee Hastie here. The Irish call her banshee.'

'Ah yes, she wails.' Lestrade had heard that one.

Bandicoot looked at him. His old chum must be getting a little hard of hearing in his fiftieth year. Sphagnum had distinctly said the Irish, not the Welsh.

'That's funny,' said Lestrade. 'I didn't hear anything in the British Hotel.'

'The British Hotel?' Sphagnum echoed.

'It's in Edinburgh,' Lestrade told him.

'Capital!' said Bandicoot.

'I ken fine it's in Edinburgh,' said Sphagnum. 'I was there with ye, man, when . . . Mr . . .'

'. . . Acheson died,' Lestrade finished the sentence, nodding.

'Och, how stupid.' Sphagnum slapped his forehead. 'He's another in the series. *His* head had been caved in too.'

Lestrade nodded.

'But that's a hell of a coincidence, Lestrade,' frowned Sphagnum. 'That . . . wait a minute. You changed rooms with him, didn't you?'

Lestrade nodded again.

'So, in other words,' Sphagnum's brain was racing, 'whoever killed Mr Acheson thought he had killed . . . you.'

They looked at the weathered face in the candlelight.

'Scots wa' hae,' Lestrade whispered.

And Bandicoot whispered too, 'I'm sure they do.'

'Well?' asked Snellgrove. 'Shall we or shan't we?'

Marshall checked his hunter. 'It's not midnight yet,' he frowned.

'Oh, go on, Tass. Be a devil.'

'Oh, all right. Merry Christmas, Wim,' and he handed him an elaborately wrapped package.

'And to you, Tass,' grinned Snellgrove, returning the compliment. 'Oh, you shouldn't have! Dates. My favourite.'

'Ah, but look at the fork.' Marshall winked.

Snellgrove did. 'Gold!' he gasped. 'Pure bloody gold.'

'Oh, Wim.' Marshall had finished his unwrapping. '*The Lustful Turk. And* it's bound in calf-skin with silver clasps. Well, I think this calls for a toast,' and he reached across for the Jeroboam in the ice bucket. 'Here's to the Duke of Connaught.' He raised his glass.

'And to Mr Lestrade?'

'Oh, yes,' chuckled Marshall, 'and to Mr Lestrade.'

6

Dorothea Pringle lay sprawled as elegantly as her hysteria
would allow on the *chaise-longue*. Her eyes flickered open and
saw the blur of a moustachioed man in a rather nasty check
suit. She screamed.

Outside in the ante-room, Letitia Bandicoot caught the arm of
Lady Bowes-Lyon. 'It's all right, Nina,' she said. 'Sholto said
she'd do that. He's interviewed hundreds of women, not a few
of them governesses. He'll be gentle with her.'

'You *will* be gentle with me?' Miss Pringle gasped, clutching
the locket at her throat. Her wild eyes flickered to the left.
'Wait. I must turn mother's portrait to the wall.'

'That won't be necessary,' Lestrade assured her. 'I only want
to ask you some questions.'

'I know,' said Miss Pringle, vaguely appalled that Lestrade
should have thought she meant anything else.

'I realize you have had rather a shock, Miss Pringle.' The
superintendent clasped his hands around his knee. The governess fell back, a little faint. He unclasped immediately, realizing
he was showing rather too much sock. 'Can you tell me how
long you have been in service here?'

'Nearly three years,' she said. 'I was governess to the boys
and will, after the New Year, begin my tutoring of Miss
Elizabeth.'

'And you were recently at Balmoral, I understand?'

'Yes,' she said. 'A short vacation before my term began.'

'Will you tell me about events that occurred there?' he asked.

She snorted smelling salts with a fierce inhalation. 'I was
looking for a candle. Balmoral is a dark old house, Mr Lestrade,

and I could not see clearly in the upper rooms. Mr Ramsay told me the candles were in the cellar.'

'He didn't send a servant for one?'

'He offered,' she said, 'but I didn't want to bother anyone. I could manage by myself.'

'This was early morning?'

'When I went in search of the wretched things, yes. I had asked Mr Ramsay the previous evening. I found myself unable to sleep and became aware that my one remaining candle would not last much longer.'

'And when you went to the cellar, what did you find?'

She shuddered so that her imitation pearls rattled. 'I couldn't see the bottom stair,' she whispered. 'I could make out what I thought was a bundle of rags. I thought it was a draught excluder. The late Duke of Edinburgh was always making them.'

'Was he?' Lestrade raised the eyebrow of surprise. The Duke of Edinburgh was a funny old bleeder.

'I stepped . . . over it, found the candles on a shelf . . . and then turned. Oh!' She clapped a hand over her mouth.

'Take your time, Miss Pringle.' Lestrade tried to reassure her without moving. A wrong move now might prove fatal.

'I could see it was a girl . . . and that she was dead.' She closed her eyes. 'I don't remember any more.'

'Did you know the dead girl?'

'Only by sight. She made up my fires daily. Frankly, she wasn't very efficient. Trail of coal along the carpet, you know the sort of thing. Not inefficient enough to be bludgeoned to death, of course.'

'Of course not,' agreed Lestrade, though he knew several men back at the Yard who fitted that bill. 'Tell me . . .' He ventured a slight forward movement of the head, a tilt of the torso. Instantly, Miss Pringle's nether limbs shot upward and she curled herself up on the *chaise-longue* like a disturbed spider. 'Tell me, afterwards, was there any talk of what might have happened to Miss Macpherson?'

'The police talked to me,' she said. 'A nasty, inferior sort of person named McNab. He and a disgusting sergeant whose name I have avulsed from my memory.'

'Quite,' Lestrade nodded. He knew sergeants who could turn milk.

'I told them essentially what I have just told you. They told me it sounded like suicide.'

'And does that sound likely to you?' Lestrade asked.

'I really don't know. All I know is that Mr McAlpine left startlingly soon afterwards. Now, I'm not one to gossip, Mr Lestrade, but that other fellow – Sir Harry Thingamajig. The one who dresses like a Kaffir.'

'Yes?'

'Well, that can't be normal, can it? The man's a Moslem. Imagine, a Moslem at Balmoral. It defies belief.'

'I thought the late Queen-Empress had several Indian servants,' Lestrade reminded her. 'Surely some of those were rather less than Anglican?'

'I suppose you're right, Mr Lestrade,' she said. 'I'm only a governess. What do I know?'

At last Lestrade had found one who admitted it. 'Now,' he said, 'earlier today. Here at Glarms.'

'It was silly of me, I know.' She sniffed into an embroidered handkerchief. 'But I had to go down into a cellar again. To prove that I could. That everything would be all right . . .'

'And?'

'And it wasn't.' She wailed like Sphagnum's *Bean-Nighe* until Lestrade raised a hand, the very threat of which quieted her. 'I thought I was dreaming,' she sobbed. 'Having some ghastly nightmare – I saw another bundle of rags at the foot of the stairs.'

'Another draught excluder?'

'No, no. This one wore a kilt and had . . . lower limbs protruding from it. When I realized what it was, I simply . . .' and she trailed away, forcing the smelling salts up her nose anew.

'Did you know Alexander Hastie?' Lestrade asked after a moment.

'Of course. He often saddled the children's ponies when they went riding.'

'A friendly man?'

'Not to me,' Miss Pringle was quick to assure him.

'I mean, the sort of man who makes enemies?'

'I really don't know,' she told him. 'He didn't live here on the estate, but over at Kirk Douglas. His family were crofters, I understand.'

Lestrade nodded. 'And you saw no one else in the cellar?'

She shook her head. He risked a charge of rape by reaching out and patting her hand. 'You're a very brave lady, Miss Pringle,' he said, 'but please, do us both a favour? Stay out of the cellar from now on?'

She nodded silently, flushing crimson from the touch of a man's hand on her own. And though Lestrade was never to know it, for the rest of her rather solitary life, she never washed that hand again.

Early the next morning, while Lestrade wrestled with the problems of *another* body in a cellar, the Bowes-Lyon family threw reality to the winds and welcomed Christmas. The Lord of Glamis himself wore a ludicrous white wig and beard and rushed about the castle bellowing, 'Ho, ho, ho,' while children of various sizes scampered after him, shrieking with laughter. The cooks bustled in the kitchen and there was the merry cracking of nuts alternating with the festive popping of champagne corks. Ribbons and wrapping paper flew in all directions, and there was laughter and games and the joy of Christmas. Exactly as Lord Glamis insisted it should be. As *every* Christmas was to be for the Bowes-Lyons.

Lestrade felt an unwelcome guest and although Sphagnum had the brass neck to take breakfast with the family and the Bandicoots, the superintendent left early and, following the servant's instructions in almost comprehensible English, wandered through the raw mist of the morning to Kirk Douglas, 'just over the hill'.

In fact, Lestrade seemed to have crossed several hills before he came full circle in the Lowland heather and knocked on the door of a thatched hovel with whitewashed stone walls. A little old crone opened it and stood there, puffing resolutely on her pipe. 'Yes?' she trilled.

'Merry Christmas, Mrs Hastie.' Lestrade tipped his headgear.

'So it is, laddie.' She peered up at him through pince-nez that appeared to have more cracks than Harry Lauder. 'But we make little o' it up here. I'll be stepping gaily, row on row, heel to heel and toe to toe come Hogmanay.'

'Oh, good,' said Lestrade, astonished that the woman was even standing.

'I never buy from pedlars on Christmas Day,' she told him and began to close the door.

'I'm not selling anything, madam,' he said. 'I'm afraid I have some bad news for you.'

'Och, if it's about that shiftless son o' mine, I know all about it. They came from the castle to tell me last night.'

'I see. Well, you have my condolences then,' said Lestrade.

'That he's dead or that he was ma son at a'?'

'Well, I . . .'

'You'd best come in.' She held the door open again. 'It's raw enough to freeze the bollocks off the Bruce.'

'Indeed it is,' Lestrade found himself agreeing.

He was offered a hideously uncomfortable monks' bench which the monks had long ago vacated and only hit his head twice on the beams of the ceiling before he sat down. The peat fire smouldering in the grate was some compensation, however, even if his left arm was jammed up against a large frame in the corner of the room.

'Did your son have any enemies, Mrs Hastie?' Lestrade asked.

'Hundreds.' The old girl rekindled her flagging pipe. 'He got right up my nose the day he was born. Some say you canna blame the bairn for the afterbirth, but I've never held wi' that.'

'Quite.' Lestrade felt strangely out of his depth.

'You'll have to excuse me,' she said. 'I have this gum disorder. My eldest, Angus, had me some false teeth made a wee while ago, but I canna bear the things. I havena had 'em in ma head since 1883. So I have tae have regular treatment.'

She reached into a little cupboard by the fire and produced a bottle. 'Will you join me?' she asked.

'Er . . . no, thank you,' Lestrade said, 'I have my own teeth.'

'Suit yoursel',' and she swigged from the bottle, screwing up her brown, wrinkled face and shuddering from head to foot. 'Man, but that's a guid brew.'

'Yes, indeed. Now, about your late son.'

'Aye, he was late. Rude. Stupid. Smelly.'

'But he was at least a good groom?' Lestrade thought *someone* had to speak up for the dead man.

'So he may have been.' The old girl took another swig. 'But his place was here. Wi' all the other Hasties. Man and boy, ma family and ma husband's have been crofters. In the summer we croft and in the winter we weave. What d'ya think of yon loom?'

Since yon loom filled almost the entire room, Lestrade could see that it would be a conversation piece.

'Very nice,' he said.

'It's been in ma husband's family for generations.' She puffed again on the yellowed stem of her pipe. 'When the late Bonnie Prince was wandering the Heelands wi' dysentery and had to change his kilts so often, it was broadcloth from that very loom that kept him decent.'

'Fascinating,' nodded Lestrade. 'Can you think of anyone who hated him enough to kill him?'

'Charlie? Well, that old German bastard King George for a start . . .'

'No, no, I meant your son.'

'He had a wee drink problem.' Old Mrs Hastie winced as the drink hit her gullet again. 'I've no idea where he got that from.'

'And drink got him into trouble?'

'Och, aye. If you looked at him funny, he'd lay one on ye. He may have been the fruit of ma loins, but he was a noxious bastard. Take ma word for it. Will you stop and have a bite of skillie?'

'Er . . . thank you, no,' said Lestrade. If the old girl didn't need teeth for it, he wasn't sure it could be bitten into. 'I'll leave you to your Christmas.'

'Och, aye, it's a barrel of laughs here,' she said. 'Come back at Hogmanay, boy, and I'll put ma stays on for ye.'

'Marvellous.' Lestrade rose, his grin frozen, and crunched his head on a beam. He peered out of the tiny, cobwebbed panes to the grey nothingness outside. 'Lovely vista,' he said. 'A sort of loom with a view.'

They sat that night in the little drawing-room overlooking the front lawns. The lights and trinkets of Christmas shone back at them from the leaded windows.

97

'I must confess . . .' sighed Lady Glamis. Lestrade edged forward on his seat. 'I'd be happier for the children's sake if Allah was with us.'

Lestrade raised an eyebrow. First, Sir Harry Maclean. Now the Bowes-Lyons. Islam seemed to be spreading. 'I'm sure he is, ma'am,' the superintendent comforted her.

All eyes looked a little oddly at Lestrade. It was not the first time such a thing had happened.

'No, no,' Lady Glamis laughed. 'I should explain that Allah is the children's nurse – Clara Knight. When the children were little, "Allah" was as close as they came to Clara. She's one hundred per cent Anglican, I assure you. Only, she's in Hertfordshire. It's her Christmas off.'

'My lord,' Lestrade addressed the Master of Glamis warming his backside by the fire, 'I have tried not to intrude on your Christmas, but a man, I fear, is dead. I have to ask some questions.'

'Yes, of course, Superintendent. Rather a busman's holiday for you, what? Well, fire away. Or should the ladies leave us?'

'Tosh, Claudie,' said his wife, 'if you think that Letitia and I are going to bustle off and talk about needlepoint at a time like this . . .'

'Nina's quite right Claudie.' Letitia Bandicoot seconded her hostess. 'Besides, we've been cross-examined by the superintendent before.'

The superintendent smiled.

'Have you now?' Alistair Sphagnum crossed the Persian carpet in one bound and perched himself on the arm of the settee next to Letitia. 'That must have been an exhilarating experience.'

Harry sat in the far corner, next to the hideous Jacobean sideboard, and continued to sip his brandy.

'My lord.' Lestrade turned to Glamis. 'The late Mr Hastie was one of your grooms, I understand.'

'Indeed he was.'

'A good servant?'

'Quite good with horses.' Lord Glamis took up his pipe. 'There were those who said he drank, of course.'

'Really?'

'Oh, yes. Apparently he kept a still of sorts over at Kirk

Douglas. Well, I didn't object to that. Illicit drinking and Scotland go hand in hand, Mr Lestrade. I love this country. I'm part of it. I wouldn't object as long as the man remained sober on duty. I believe he did.'

'I think the members of the Distillers Company would see it a little differently, my lord,' said Sphagnum.

'Who?' Lestrade asked.

Sphagnum shifted a little. 'Those wee gentlemen in Edinburgh who produce the Scotch you're drinking now.'

'Ah, well, no, not exactly,' said Lord Glamis. 'That particular drink is a little simple blend they haven't got their evil clutches on yet. It's a recipe known only to a few!'

'Indeed?' Sphagnum smiled. 'I'll stick to my brandy – and very good it is, eh, Letitia?'

She smiled disarmingly at him.

'How long had Hastie worked for you, sir?' Lestrade asked.

'Since he was a boy, I believe. When one is only here for half one's year, one doesn't get to know the staff as well as one would like. One confuses faces and names. Isn't that so, George?' he turned to Bandicoot.

'Er . . . yes,' said Bandicoot, never one to give offence.

'His mother didn't seem particularly sorry to see him go,' Lestrade observed.

'Oh, how dreadful,' said Lady Glamis. 'Still, grief strikes people in peculiar ways sometimes.'

'Sholto,' Letitia leaned forward, 'what are your theories?'

Again, all eyes came to rest on the superintendent.

'Yes.' Lady Glamis leaned forward too. 'How do the Leith Police operate on horrible matters like this?'

'I didn't know you were an authority on the Leith police, Sholto,' Bandicoot chirped. 'Or any other Australian constabulary.'

'It's your theories on the Hastie murder we are anxious to hear, sir,' Sphagnum butted in.

Lestrade felt the ground shift beneath him. 'All right,' he said suddenly. 'The whole thing hinges on how easy it is to lure a groom into the cellar of a castle, bludgeon him to death and walk away scot-free.'

'So you're assuming it's a Scotsman?' Sphagnum was quick to see the implication.

'A figure of speech . . . um . . . sergeant. I hope you're taking notes, by the way.'

Sphagnum's sneer turned into a smile. 'Och, I've forgotten my pad, Superintendent.'

Lestrade's eyes rolled heavenward.

'Why couldn't the murderer have simply walked away, Sholto?' Letitia asked.

Lestrade paused. 'He'd be covered in blood.'

'Well.' Lady Glamis leaned back after a moment. 'It could of course be one of our ghosts.'

'Nina!' The quietly spoken Lord of Glamis roared so that the pretty blue and white Delft on the hideous Jacobean dresser jumped and rattled. His lordship was emptying his pipe into the grate and bending an elbow for his wife's arm. 'We've a long day tomorrow, gentlemen. The Boxing Day shoot. We've a few hinds in the covers thanks to Angus Laidlaw.'

'Laidlaw?' Lestrade repeated.

'The head ghillie on the Royal Estate,' Glamis told him. 'There's not a man in Scotland knows more about deer. He's a little cranky, but a broa' Scot for all that. You'll join us Mr Lestrade? Mr Sphagnum?'

'Thank you.' Sphagnum accepted for them both.

'Good-night and God bless.' Lady Glamis kissed the Bandicoots, nodded gracefully to the policeman and the other one and swept with her husband from the room.

'Would you have called the ghillie cranky?' Sphagnum asked Lestrade.

'I'd have called him Mr Laidlaw,' said Lestrade. 'We do that in the Leith Police, you know.'

'What is all this about the Leith Police, Sholto?' Bandicoot was confused. 'I'm confused,' he said.

'Well, sergeant?' Lestrade lolled back in the armchair, arms folded.

'Ah,' Sphagnum grinned. 'A wee subterfuge. A slight smoke-screen. When you're a student of politics like me, you have to be a little devious.'

'That's funny,' commented Lestrade. 'I thought you were a student of law.'

'And politics,' said Sphagnum. 'It's a new course at the University. Combined honours.'

'Odd how Claudie reacted then,' mused Letitia, 'when Nina mentioned ghosts.'

'Letitia,' Lestrade smiled, 'though I never thought I'd hear myself say it, you'd have made a damn fine detective. I expect Mr Sphagnum here has some intelligence on these ghosts of Glarms.'

'Intelligence, yes.' Sphagnum helped himself to a little more of Bowes-Lyon's brandy. 'Rather a lot of it, actually. All these old castles have ghosts, Lestrade, but I assume you don't think one of them cracked Alexander Hastie's skull?'

'Well,' Lestrade ever kept an open mind, 'in my experience the flesh is weak.'

'So the spirits may be willing?' Letitia added.

'What are these ghosts then, Sphagnum?' Bandicoot asked. 'It *is* Christmas, after all.'

Sphagnum smiled. 'Well, I don't want to upset your charming wife here . . .'

'Oh, you won't, Mr Sphagnum,' she assured him. 'We've a Grey Lady at Bandicoot Hall.'

'Ah, but the Things that walk these passages would put your Grey Lady in the shade, Letitia,' the Scotsman said. 'First, there's Shakespeare . . .'

'Don't tell me he died here.' Bandicoot was sceptical.

'No, no,' said Sphagnum. 'I mean the play. "Thane of Cawdor and of Glamis . . ." Of course, Sassenach propaganda. Macbeth was a nice old boy. Loved dogs and children, that sort of thing. But nevertheless, *somebody* is said to have murdered Malcolm II here. I'm sure if you ask Lady Glamis nicely, she'll show you the bloodstained room.'

' "Who would have thought the old man had so much blood in him?" ' Letitia quoted.

'Quite,' agreed Sphagnum. 'Then of course there's the tongueless woman . . .'

'That's unusual,' beamed Bandicoot, but the flash of a frown from Letitia wiped the smile from his face.

'Not to mention the little Black Boy who, if the servants' gossip is to be believed, sits on the wee stone seat outside this very room.'

They all turned to the door.

'Of course, there is something alive in these tragic halls.

101

Something that walks the night. That's why the Lord of Glamis reacted as he did. The master of the castle alone knows the secret and he passes it to his eldest son when that son comes of age.'

'That's Pat. It *is* his twenty-first soon, I believe,' Letitia said.

The air had become strangely chill. The logs in the fireplace settled and threw grey ash out over the firedogs. Bandicoot sat impassive, but he had not touched his glass.

'What thing?' Lestrade found his voice first.

'Take your pick,' said Sphagnum. 'Is it the Vampire-Servant caught sucking blood years ago and walled up alive? A hunted refugee of the Ogilvy clan, fleeing from the Lindsays after a particularly atrocious Highland clearance? Is it Earl Beardie who is doomed to endless games of dice with the Devil? They do say', he leaned nearer to Letitia whose eyes were wider in the firelight, 'that there is a room at Glamis that has a window and no door. Something is walled up for ever here. A living tomb.'

The clock struck eleven as Sphagnum finished and the whole room jumped.

'Time to retire, I think, my dear,' said Bandicoot. Lestrade nodded his agreement. He should have retired years ago. One by one they took their candles and walked up the stairs in a huddle, back to back.

As chalk is to cheese, the weather changed. The swirling grey mist had gone. The Feast of Stephen opened with a watery sun gilding a sparkling field of frost. After a sumptuous breakfast of kedgeree, bacon, eggs and pressed-meats, during which little Elizabeth crawled under the tablecloth busily tying everybody's shoelaces together, the shooting party set out.

Now, Lestrade had to admit he was never at home with guns. Some years before, on just such a Boxing Day shoot, his own superior at the Yard, no less, had stumbled in a bolt hole and peppered Lestrade's shoulder. This time he trailed a little behind everybody else. Just in case. And this time at least he had Harry Bandicoot with him. Whether he was ordering champagne, cantering in the Row or brutally murdering inno-cent animals, Harry Bandicoot behaved impeccably, as befitted an old Etonian with a pedigree as long as your skean-dhu.

Lord Glamis had lent Lestrade a huge fur duster coat to wear in place of his totally inadequate Donegal. Away had gone the bowler earlier, hurled at the Aberdeen Angus, to be replaced by a tweedy deerstalker of the type the late Sherlock Holmes was reputed to have worn: the check peak offset his bandage beautifully. Around his forehead, the swelling still rose dim and purple, rather like the snow-capped Grampians to the north-west.

Their feet crunched on the frozen tufts of coarse grass and ahead of the slowly advancing line, the beaters of the Glamis estate leaped and roared like some Forlorn Hope of the tartan army, screaming defiance at Culloden or hurtling through the heather so as not to be late for the massacre at Glencoe. They banged kettles with sticks and leather bucklers with blunted swords. All they lacked was a handsome man on a white horse, a prey to dysentery.

In this bewildering world, not a word was spoken along the line of gentlemen. Lestrade scanned them from his wary position on the right flank. In the centre, Lord Glamis and his sons, guns unbroken now in the morning, eyes hard and jaws set firm. Beyond that, the figure of Robert McAlpine, as square and craggy as one of his own buildings, and beyond him again, various neighbours, the gentry of Angus and the pride of the clans, nattily tweeded against the weather. Beside Lestrade himself, swinging with jaunty strides, two ex-public school-boys, Bandicoot and Sphagnum, their barrels still broken in the crooks of their arms.

Suddenly, the line stopped dead, apart from Lestrade, who collided with the motionless Bandicoot. The Bowes-Lyons were blasting away in the centre, McAlpine cocking his gun. Lestrade heard the roar, saw the smoke die away on the frosty air. What they were shooting at, he couldn't see at all.

'This way,' shouted Sphagnum and he and Bandicoot sprinted forward, hurtling down the hillside before them over the tumbling frills of frost. Gammily, as was his custom, Lestrade followed suit. In no time, the line of shooters had gone. Even the Highland beaters seemed to have vanished and Lestrade found himself descending in a valley of fir trees where the bracken was waist high and razor sharp in the winter air. He could see Bandicoot trotting ahead, head cocked like a spaniel. Any minute now, he'd cock his leg. Sphagnum had cut away to the right, leaping over the glazed outcrops of icy rocks where the stream had frozen on them. A curious silence descended. Lestrade stood still. He looked to his right. Nothing. To his left. Only the silent firs on which the sun dappled. Behind him the tracks of three trackers in the silver. Ahead, nothing now. Not even Bandicoot. He felt vaguely like the little crippled boy in that bloke's poem – the one who couldn't follow the piper. But what piper had drawn on Bandicoot and Sphagnum and lured them away? And where was the cave in the mountainside through which they vanished? Lestrade did in this situation what he had been trained to do. What one would expect of a professional suddenly alone and exposed to an eerie, silent, hostile environment. He panicked.

He ran forward, stumbling, trying desperately to keep his balance. He didn't see the sign which said 'No Trespassing. Keep Out.' He didn't see the barbed wire stretched taut over the broken wall and hanging on it the dead weasels, stiff and strangled in the sunlight. Omens like that just passed him by.

In the end, the gravity of the situation got him and he tumbled headlong, his empty twelve-bore bouncing into the bracken somewhere to his right, and he rolled like some giant hedgehog to crunch against the rough bark of a Douglas fir.

It wasn't a rough bark that brought him to his senses, however, but a sharp whine. And it went straight to his head. He sat bolt upright, the deerstalker at a ludicrous angle. He blinked several times, but other than that was motionless. He was staring into the little yellow eyes of a full-grown wolf, its pink tongue hanging stupidly out of its mouth, its breath smoking away on the crisp air. It cocked its head once, twice, as puzzled by Lestrade as he was by it.

'Shoo,' he whispered, proving yet again man's sovereignty over the beasts of the earth.

The beast looked back at him, sniffed his left boot and turned, cocking its leg and spraying Lestrade's trousers liberally before wandering away. The superintendent did not know it, but he had become part of the animal's territory. As soon as he saw the sinewy grey haunches vanish through the undergrowth, Lestrade rolled sharply to his right, snatching up the gun and holding it level, forgetting in his panic that it was empty. As his eyes focused along the barrel and he lined up the sight, he was aware of two fingers inserting themselves in the business end.

'Fire now and we'll both be blown to oblivion,' a quiet voice said.

Lestrade peered out from behind the weapon. 'Right,' he said. 'If you take your fingers out, I'll take my thumb away. That way we should both be all right.'

'Who are you?' the man enquired politely, kneeling beside the sprawled superintendent.

'Sholto Lestrade,' he said. 'I'm with the shooting party of the Master of Glamis.'

'Tut, blood sports.' The man shook his head. 'I'm Ned Chapman.'

'I didn't see you at breakfast.' Lestrade took the man's hand and allowed himself to be hauled upright.

'No, no, my dear fellow. I share this part of the Tayside with the Bowes-Lyons. Our estates adjoin. I realized my fences were in need of repair and that's when I saw your little tumble. You seem to have a blow to your head.'

'It's nothing,' said Lestrade, 'unless of course, it's worse than I thought and I'm seeing things. I could have sworn I was just looking at a wolf. Aaghh!' He flung himself backwards against a tree, his finger pointing harmlessly beyond Chapman's shoulder. 'I *did*. I *did* see a wolf.'

'My dear Mr Lestrade, do be comforted. That's just old Romulus.'

'Just old Romulus? Oh good,' gulped Lestrade. 'I thought for a moment it was a vicious carnivore with a killer instinct.'

'Well, really. Romulus! Here, boy.'

The animal stood in the bracken, looking at him.

'One word from me and he does exactly as he likes. Here, Romulus!' Chapman slapped his jodhpured thigh and the wolf padded over to him, licking his fingers and rubbing his head against the man's knee. 'Actually, he doesn't have a tooth in his head. I have to marinade his beef for hours in claret before he'll touch it. Of course, it doesn't help that he's a dipsomaniac.'

Lestrade was beginning to realize that the wolf wasn't the only maniac in these forests. 'But aren't they dangerous?' he asked, uncoiling from the tree trunk.

'Only when cornered,' he said. 'They are orderly, fastidious

105

creatures with a great sense of clan, just like the Scots. I've three others somewhere. I'm thinking of reintroducing them to the wild.'

'The wild?' Lestrade was horrified.

'Oh, it would take a while, of course. They're all rather fond of dog biscuits and Dundee cake at the moment, but they'll soon revert to sheep slaughtering.'

'Won't that rather upset the farmers hereabouts?' Lestrade kept Chapman between himself and the great, grey beast.

'Yes, well, that is one problem. The other one's disembowelling. Contrary to popular belief it doesn't come naturally. I'm particularly inept at it and so how can I expect my beasties to cotton on?'

'How indeed?' Lestrade's face bore a frozen look of horror.

'Actually, perhaps you can help me.'

'No, no,' Lestrade was quick to assure him. 'I really must be getting back. It's been years since I did any disembowelling.'

'Well, have you seen in your perambulations a tall man with blond hair and a hunch?'

'A hunch?'

'Yes. He'd be incredibly tall without it. As it is, he's no slouch. About six foot one.'

'I've seen no one,' said Lestrade, 'apart from the men of the Bowes-Lyon shooting party. He wasn't among them, I don't think.'

'No, indeed. His name is Dick MacKinnon. He's a guest of mine, from the Isles. He went off as usual for his constitutional before breakfast. I haven't seen him since.'

'You don't think . . .' Lestrade nodded to the wolf without letting the wolf see him do it.

'Lord, no,' said Chapman. 'It's not merely a flight of fancy you know, that book by Mr Kipling. There are many examples in India of feral children – humans brought up by wolves in the wild. They'd have taken to Dick like a duck to water.'

'They wouldn't have practised their disembowelling?' Lestrade wanted to be sure.

Suddenly there was a long, low howl that seemed to fill the firs and still the spruces. Lestrade had never heard anything like it. The hairs on his neck stood on end. So did those on the neck of Romulus.

'It's Remus,' said Chapman. 'I think he's spotted Dick. Come on!'

Lestrade stumbled in the wake of the running Chapman, holding back to let the running wolf pass them both. Clearly this man was mad. Even if Romulus had no teeth to speak of, could that also be true of the other one? Besides, Lestrade had read that book by his old friend Mr Kipling. He knew the sly, grey bastards hunted in packs. They couldn't *all* be gummy, surely?

'Over here!'

At first, all Lestrade saw was the outline of a wolf against the darker firs, leaner, more muscular than the first. It sniffed and pawed at something in the bracken. Then he saw an arm against the tree, stiff with rigor or the morning frost. And a twisted figure, hunched against the cold, the straw-coloured hair matted with blood. It was the sight below the waist that made Lestrade catch his breath. The kilt was thrown back to reveal not what a Scotsman wears under it, but what is under his skin. The bracken was dappled with crimson. The man had been disembowelled. Lestrade shook himself free of the sight. He'd seen it all before. But not since those dark nights in Whitechapel had he seen anything quite like this. It could have been Long Liz lying there, or Annie Chapman . . . He looked up at Chapman, whose face was as grey as the hoar frost.

'Dick MacKinnon?' he asked softly. The other Englishman nodded, his eyes wide with shock and disbelief. Then he turned and vomited into the bracken.

'Your wolves?' Lestrade asked, at a loss to explain the ripped corpse in any other way.

'No.' Chapman was as insistent as his own bowels would allow him to be. 'I told you. They're tame. You might as well say your hamster did it. My God, Lestrade, what's going on?'

The superintendent fought down the revulsion in his stomach and crouched over what was left of Richard MacKinnon. He turned the drawn, pale face towards him and saw for the first time the dozen or so blows that had shattered the skull. He drew back his lips so that his breath smoked out on the morning air. He nodded to himself. 'No, Mr Chapman, you're right. Your wolves didn't do this. A man did. Your friend MacKinnon was bludgeoned to death first. The disembowelling was an afterthought.'

'An afterthought?' Chapman was trying to rationalize all this, and he could not. 'In the name of God, Lestrade, why?'

'To point the finger at those animals of yours,' Lestrade told him. 'And that means one thing.' He stood and looked to the higher ground where Bandicoot and Sphagnum were hacking their way through the bracken, looking for deer or superintendents, he couldn't be sure which. 'It means our man's beginning to panic. I'm getting close.'

7

When Lestrade had marked out his ground with a length of hemp provided by the ever-helpful Alistair Sphagnum, they rigged a makeshift bier and carried the mortal remains of Richard MacKinnon down into the glen where Chapman the Laird lived in a fortified manor house of grey granite, an unlovely bastion which may have given the late Sir Walter Scott his idea for Castle Dangerous.

The three newcomers had never seen so many different animals under one roof in their lives. As they staggered past a row of cages a half-grown panther, as black as Lestrade's usual hat, turned behind its bars with lashing tail and spat at the superintendent.

'Ignore that cat,' Chapman told him. 'It's barking mad. As soon as I can, I'll release the poor creature. They're territorial, you see. Need to make their boundaries by cocking their legs and so on.'

Lestrade had known a mastiff like that. Unfortunately, Lestrade's left trouser leg seemed to be the only boundary it knew and soggy serge was inevitably the result. The wolf Romulus had behaved the same way. They laid the bier and its mangled load in an outhouse, while Chapman went off to send his man for the local constabulary and the wolves slunk off into their kennels.

'Well, Lestrade?' Alistair Sphagnum perused, as closely as he dared, the remains under the tartan blanket.

The superintendent looked at the others. 'Victim number four, gentlemen,' he said. 'Harry, I don't think for a moment there's any cause for alarm, but when did you and Letitia plan to leave?'

'Nothing's been settled yet, Sholto,' Bandicoot told him. 'Should I take her away?'

'It's probably best,' Lestrade said. 'There must be *some* method in our man's madness, but mad he is, nonetheless.'

'What do we know about this one, Lestrade?' Sphagnum asked.

'At the moment, very little. His name is Richard MacKinnon and he's not local. Apart from Mr Acheson, who I suspect is rather a different kettle of fish, MacKinnon breaks the pattern.'

'Can you make sense of it, Sholto?' Bandicoot asked, watching in horrified fascination as Lestrade washed the blood from the pulped head.

'He's been dead about two hours. Chapman said he went out for a walk just after dawn.'

'That's a risk in itself,' murmured Sphagnum.

'What? With Chapman's menagerie, you mean?' Lestrade asked.

'Not just that. The cold. It's Boxing Day, man. The temperature fell way below freezing last night. This man's not even wearing a top coat – just a jacket and kilt.'

'Which tells us what?' asked Lestrade.

'Och, awa' wi' ye.' Sphagnum lapsed into a broader Scots than was strictly necessary. 'You don't want to hear ma wee theories.'

Lestrade began to probe the tip of his switchblade into the gashes along MacKinnon's skull. Bandicoot and Sphagnum turned away. 'About now, Mr Sphagnum,' the superintendent said, 'I'd settle for any wee theories anyone's got.'

'This man's from the Isles,' Sphagnum said. 'A true Highlander. Only a true Highlander would have the hardiness for such dress in this weather.'

'Does that tell us why he was murdered?' Bandicoot asked.

Lestrade was unused to such perceptive questioning from his old friend, but he wasn't going to say so.

'It might,' nodded Sphagnum cryptically.

The Englishman looked at the Scot for an explanation. None was forthcoming. The latch on the outhouse door clicked up and Ned Chapman had returned. 'There's a hot toddie inside the house,' he said. 'I think we could all do with a dram. I've sent for the police.'

110

'McNab?' Sphagnum raised an eyebrow. 'He's got a bloody big patch. First Balmoral, now Glamis.'

'I believe the inspector is the chappie they turn to in moments of violent dispatch, yes.'

'I'd better make myself scarce,' said Sphagnum. 'He may have the odd constable with him who'll recognize me from my visit to the station at Abergeldie.'

'This McNab,' said Lestrade, 'is he any good?'

'Perfect beast,' Chapman told him. 'Threatened to shoot my wolves if their noses so much as poked through the fence. He's the sort who'd worry sheep and pin it on my beauties.'

Lestrade had met policemen like that before. 'Where did MacKinnon come from?' he asked.

'The Isle of Skye,' Chapman told him. Lestrade saw Sphagnum beam smugly. 'That's why I invited him down here. Better all round, I thought, if I could release my babies on an island like Skye. Once they'd proved themselves, I could introduce them on to the mainland later.'

'And what did Mr MacKinnon think of that?'

'All for it. As a principal landowner on the island, he gave it his blessing. Of course, he'd have had to discuss it with the others.'

'Tell me,' Lestrade said, 'did Mr MacKinnon seem in any way worried? Preoccupied?'

'It's funny you should say that.' Chapman stood frowning at the corpse. 'He said something to me only last night.'

'Oh?' Lestrade and Sphagnum chorused.

'Yes, he said, "I hate all these secrets, Ned." I asked him what secrets and he said, "That's just it. I can't tell even you." Odd, wasn't it?'

'Did Mr MacKinnon *do* anything,' Lestrade asked, 'apart from landowning, I mean?'

Chapman and Bandicoot chuckled. Lestrade looked nonplussed.

'That's a pretty full-time job you know, Sholto,' Bandicoot grinned, 'landowning.'

Lestrade shrugged. He came from the wrong class to appreciate the assertion. He just took the gentlemen's word for it. 'May I see his room?' he asked.

'Of course,' said Chapman and led the way.

'What killed him?' Sphagnum asked.

Lestrade turned back for a moment to the corpse. 'The nearest I can come to a weapon is an axe,' he said. 'As to the motive, I can't help thinking that the answer lies somewhere with Mr MacKinnon's secrets. The real question is how many secrets lie hidden here?'

While Sphagnum and Bandicoot retired to the main hall to stiffen their sinews against the grisly shock of the morning, Chapman led Lestrade to the North Tower, where the late Richard MacKinnon had slept the night before. As he slid back the bolts and raised the heavy Jacobean latch, Chapman stood rooted to the spot.

Lestrade peered around the door, lifting his nose over his host's hand. The place was in chaos, cushions ripped, leather wallets and suitcases torn apart at the hinges.

'A trifle untidy, was he, Mr MacKinnon?' Lestrade asked.

'I've been burgled.' Chapman threw the door back.

'Not you, Mr Chapman.' Lestrade stepped over a fallen stag's head. 'Mr MacKinnon.'

'Why?' Chapman was nearly speechless for the second time that morning. 'Who would do such a thing?'

'I can tell you approximately when,' said Lestrade. 'While you were out walking your wolves. And I can tell you why – almost. Because Mr MacKinnon carried whatever secrets he was talking about in his belongings, not merely in his head. Or at any rate, that's what his visitor assumed. What I can't tell you, at the moment anyway, is the answer to your question, who? Would you be so kind as to assemble your servants?'

Thankfully, Ned 'The Laird' Chapman had far fewer servants than either Glamis or Balmoral. Rumour had it that the eccentric actually combed his own hair. Apart from his manservant, Gloag, an unprepossessing, monosyllabic character who had once been a dumb waiter, the only other occupant in the house was a Mrs Dalziel who 'did' for them both in different ways. All the others – four ghillies of indifferent intellect who never crossed Chapman's threshold – served entirely in the capacity of looking after the laird's extensive menagerie. They spoke warmly enough of their charges, to which they had become

112

quite attached, but none of them could shed any light on the comings and goings of the late MacKinnon. Mrs Dalziel had made his bed just before breakfast that morning and had noticed nothing amiss about the guest bedroom. Even to a lady who had a faint whiff of inebriation about her, Lestrade noticed, the signs of disturbance would surely have been evident.

In short, his investigations had got nowhere. And they were still getting nowhere when Gloag, towards evening, announced the arrival of Inspector McNab of the Forfar Constabulary and Sergeant Pond. Bandicoot and Sphagnum had returned to Glamis, where they were sworn to secrecy by Lestrade to say nothing of the latest outrage. How they explained Lestrade's absence was up to them, but they were to let Sphagnum do the talking. Harry Bandicoot was straight as a die. He couldn't invent a lie, let alone stick to it. To Alistair Sphagnum however, Lestrade suspected, such things came rather more easily.

'Rum business, eh, Lestrade?' William McNab was a shriv- elled little man with a shapeless tweed hat and an extremely long muffler. He appeared to be about forty years too old for any police force Lestrade had encountered, but his grey eyes had a twinkle all their own and his wrinkles belied the speed of his brain. Alongside him, Sergeant Pond was a vegetable.

'You know who I am?' Lestrade asked, rising from the rather uncomfortable library chair.

'Mr Chapman has been filling me in, so to speak. I canna help wondering what a superintendent from the Yard is doing this far north?'

'Spending Christmas with friends,' Lestrade told him.

'Oh? Who might they be?'

'The Bandicoots,' Lestrade told him, 'of Bandicoot Hall, Huish Episcopi. They're staying at Glarms.'

'Och aye? The Lord Lieutenant's place. Hideous. You won't mind if I ask you some questions, seeing as how you don't exactly have jurisdiction here an' a'?'

Lestrade sat down again as Sergeant Pond positioned himself by the fire with pencil and notepad at the ready.

'I'll help if I can,' Lestrade told him.

'We're sure you can,' Pond snarled with a sneer that Lestrade did not care for. 'You found the body, I understand?'

'Not exactly,' said Lestrade, frankly unused to being on the receiving end of a police enquiry. 'A wolf did.'

McNab produced a churchwarden pipe from the bowels of his Harris jacket and proceeded to light it. 'Aye, well, I've waited for a chance to shoot those bloody animals for quite a while. This might be it. Cause of death, would you say?'

'A blunt object to the head,' Lestrade said. 'Several blows, possibly an axe.'

'And the disembowelling?'

'You've seen the body?'

McNab nodded.

'Well, I'm no expert,' Lestrade lied, 'but I'd say that was an afterthought. To throw suspicion on to the wolf.'

'Tsk, tsk,' McNab said. 'How despicable can some people get?'

'Well, sir, in my experience . . .'

'Thank you, sergeant,' McNab interrupted his man, 'it was what we with intelligence call a rhetorical question.'

'I'd need a medical opinion,' Lestrade said.

'Aye, well, it's old Dr Finlay in this parish, so you won't get that. Has anyone sent for him?'

Lestrade shrugged.

'He'll have to do a wee bit of mugging up on murder,' McNab said, 'and that'll take a while. I happen to know there isn't one book on medical jurisprudence on Dr Finlay's bookcase. Sergeant, get Mr Chapman to send a man over to Finlay's, will ye? Tell him we've a murder on our hands and I'd like his views. This week would be nice.'

'Very good, sir.' Pond put away his pad and pencil. 'Don't think we've finished with you, Sassenach. Not for a moment,' and he stumped out.

'Pleasant chap, your sergeant,' Lestrade commented.

'Gorbals,' said McNab.

'Just an observation,' Lestrade assured him.

'No, I mean he was born and raised in the Gorbals, the worst slums in Glasgow. It's astonishing that he became a policeman, let alone a human being. But his heart's in the right place. I'm just not so sure about his brain. However,' McNab's smile had vanished as quickly as it had appeared, 'he does have a point, Mr Lestrade.'

'Does he?' Lestrade could be as bland as McNab and, as the superintendent lit his cigar, both men looked inscrutable behind their respective smokescreens.

'You see, I have this wee problem,' McNab murmured. 'First, I'm called in to investigate the suspicious death of a serving girl over at Balmoral.'

'Really?' Lestrade played dumb – something at which he was very adept.

'Well, that was plain, old-fashioned suicide. Unhappy childhood, history of lunacy, odd behaviour dependent on the tides – you know the sort of thing.'

Lestrade nodded.

'Then, lo and behold, there's *another* body, not a capercaillie's fart away, at Glamis, which is, if my memory serves me correctly, the place you're staying at, Mr Lestrade. And then, here we are – yet *another* body, at Mr Chapman's wee zoo. Now, what's the common denominator, laddie? Do you remember your mathematics?'

Lestrade clicked his tongue. 'Damned if I can,' he said.

'And damned if you can't,' McNab said coldly. 'The common denominator, laddie, is you.'

The door of the library crashed back and Sergeant Pond stood there, square, menacing, huge, his knuckles whitening around a telegram.

'Beggin' yer pardon, Mr McNab, sir,' he said, 'Constable John has just arrived wi' this. It came soon after we left the station.'

McNab crossed the room to take it. He read the contents briefly, then looked at Lestrade. Pond was looking at him too. 'It's from ma old friend and comrade in arms, Thaddeus McFarlane of the Leith Police,' he said. 'He's looking for a man posing as a detective from Scotland Yard. A man who he believes has something to do with the mysterious demise of a Mr Acheson in Edinburgh. A man called Lestrade. Noo, that makes three murders you're involved with. The fragile threads of coincidence are getting more fragile a' the time, are they not?'

'Actually, that's four murders,' said Lestrade. 'You see, I too was called in to investigate the death of Amy Macpherson – and if that was suicide, I'll eat my hat.'

'I wonder how bowler tastes in this season?' McNab smiled. 'I assume you *do* wear a bowler.'

'Only when I'm not stalking murderers,' said Lestrade.

'Can I break his jaw, sir?' Pond asked.

'No, no.' McNab patted the sergeant's biceps. 'Think of Mr Chapman's Axminster. I don't think Mr Lestrade is going to give us any bother, are you, Mr Lestrade?'

The superintendent rose to his feet. 'Am I under arrest?' he asked.

'Och, aye,' said McNab, 'and I don't recommend resisting it. Young "Goldfish" here has a marked personality disorder and a massive fist.'

Looking at Pond, Lestrade didn't doubt it. 'What's the charge?' he asked.

'Murder, Mr Lestrade,' McNab smiled. 'You don't have to say anything, ye ken, but anything ye do say will be taken down and used in evidence.'

'I believe I'm allowed one telegram,' Lestrade said.

'South of the border, maybe y'are.' McNab clenched on the stem of his pipe. 'Up here it'll probably be Hogmanay before we give you breakfast. Shall we go?'

Pond snapped the handcuffs on to Lestrade's right wrist and the other loop on his own. Briskly, McNab ran his fingers over the superintendent's person, causing him to adjust his clothing.

'Och, I'm sorry,' he said, 'I don't recall goosing a superintendent before.'

'It's been a long time for me,' Lestrade told him. 'May I take laughing boy here to get my Donegal?'

'Why not? From now on, whither thou goest, he goest. And I hope neither of you has to take a leak before you part company. Sergeant Pond's left-handed.'

Harry Lauder was well into the thirty-fourth verse of 'I Love A Lassie', having roamed for quite a while in the gloaming, when Harry Bandicoot leaned across to Alistair Sphagnum. 'What can be keeping Sholto?' he whispered.

Only Letitia noticed. The entire Bowes-Lyon family, including the little Benjamins, who had been allowed to stay up specially, were lost in Caledonian admiration as the Scottish favourite of kings leapt and cavorted in front of them, complete with false beard and huge tam-o'-shanter.

116

Sphagnum checked his hunter. 'I was wondering that myself,' he said. 'What say we skip the next two hundred stanzas and wander over to Mr Chapman's? Alternatively, I've a yen to watch the Tay Bridge girders rust.'

As unobstrusively as possible, the six-foot Old Etonian kissed his wife on the cheek and sidled out of the door. After a suitable interval, during which Lauder showed everybody a tantalizing glimpse of his wee sleekit, Alistair Sphagnum yawned ostentatiously and followed suit. Out into the freezing night they went, the Old Etonian and the Old Fettesian, wrapped in furs against the cold, crunching on the frosty tussocks under a fitful moon.

Ned Chapman had already retired for the night by the time they reached his portals, but his man Gloag peered out from under a ludicrous night cap to tell the latecomers that Mr Lestrade had left earlier in the presence of the police officers. To Sphagnum that didn't bode well.

'He has no jurisdiction up here,' he told Bandicoot on their way back across the heather to Glamis. 'He's as defenceless as a wee bairn.'

Now Bandicoot had no idea how defenceless bairns were, wee or otherwise, but he shared Sphagnum's concern. It wasn't like Lestrade to talk to strange policemen, let alone wander off with them. 'What shall we do?'

'Well, when I was reading classics at the University,' Sphagnum said, 'I read a few chapters of Caesar's *Gallic War*. You'll remember that from Eton.'

Bandicoot looked blank. He knew that the country was divided into three parts, but he hadn't dreamt Caesar was referring to Scotland.

'Well,' Sphagnum's rapier mind was racing. 'That in turn led me on to the tactics of Vercingetorix. The wily old barbarian was pretty adept at dividing and conquering – before the Romans got to him, of course.'

'What was he adept at then?'

'Nothing much. Dangling in chains. Being exhibited in Rome, that sort of thing. However, you miss ma point, Bandicoot. I know this McNab, at least by reputation. He doesn't suffer fools gladly, so Lestrade's in for it. He'll probably have arrested him for interfering with the course of justice.'

'Can he do that?'

'Can Rabbie Burns write a jingle?'

'Er . . .'

'Never mind. The point is, that McNab or at least one of his muscle brains at Forfar might recognize me as I appropriated some confidential information from the Abergeldie station safe recently. So, we do a Vercingetorix. They don't know you – you go in the front door and find out where Lestrade is. If he's there sippin' a wee cup of tea, no harm done and we'll all go home together. If he's not, I'll be nippin' in the back door. Done?'

'Very well,' agreed Bandicoot, vaguely aware that he had been.

'Right. When we reach Glamis, I must pop up to ma room for a few items. Can you get ma Quadrant out of the stables?'

'Does it work like a deDion?' Bandicoot was a child of the new technology.

'Man, it works like a dream. As long as it's dry and not too cold. Oh, and remember to crank it into the wind. On the south side of the castle.'

Once all this was accomplished and Harry Lauder had finally put the entire household to sleep – not for nothing did Sphagnum call him Harry Laudanum – the Quadrant rattled to a halt outside the black, austere walls of the police station in Forfar.

It was a groggy desk sergeant who snapped to something approximating to attention at the arrival of a youngish man in immaculate furs.

'I am looking for Superintendent Lestrade,' he said.

'Eh, who?' the desk man asked.

'Superintendent Sholto Lestrade,' Bandicoot repeated. 'I understand he is here.'

'Was, sir,' a thin voice called from a back room. Inspector McNab walked into the light. 'I've told you before aboot this bloody lamp, sergeant,' he hissed. 'It'll have somebody's eye out before the night's out. Who might you be?' He expended one of his sinister smiles on the Englishman.

'My name is Bandicoot,' said Bandicoot. 'I am a friend of Mr Lestrade and I was told he was here.'

'Yes, Mr Bandicoot. Yes, indeed, the superintendent was here, but he left, oh, when was it, sergeant?'

'Half-past eleven, sir. I remember it specifically because his watch had stopped and he stood just where you are, sir, and he said, "Do you have the time?" and I said, "Do you mind, I'm a married man. None of your Lunnon ways here." And he said . . .'

'Yes.' McNab held up his hand. 'Sorry, Mr Bandicoot. I expect your friend is back at the Bowes-Lyons's by now.'

'But I . . .'

A constable swathed in a cape burst through a side door.

'Now then, Pascoe,' the desk sergeant growled, 'who's chasing ye?'

'Harry Lauder's outside,' said the constable. 'Said he was passing and would the nicht shift like a wee bit of cheering up?'

'If it's Harry Lauder, that's a contradiction in terms,' said McNab.

'Och, it's him a'right, sir,' the constable assured him. 'He give me his card.' He flicked it out to the inspector.

'Hallo, hallo, hallo.' A figure wrapped in an outsize kilt and tam-o'-shanter suddenly swept in through the same side door. 'Did ye hear the one aboot the inspector and the Highland cow?'

'No,' said Pascoe.

'Damn,' said Lauder, clicking his fingers. 'I'd love to add that one to ma repertoire. Well, who's in charge?'

Everybody looked around them, then they all pointed to McNab.

'Harry Lauder, at your service.' The entertainer bowed low and swept his tam across the floor. 'Tsk, tsk,' he said, 'the muck in 'ere. Well, where can I perform?'

'First things first,' said McNab. 'What do you charge?'

'Och, it's Christmas,' said Lauder. 'I'm feeling generous. This is a charity event for the Police Benevolent Society. If you can call the police benevolent, that is?'

'But it's two o'clock in the morning, man,' the sergeant said.

'Aye, and in half an hour it will be time for the Chinaman to go to the dentist.' Lauder stamped his foot and held out his hand for applause. There was none.

'Well,' said McNab, 'I'll be awa' hame. Sorry, Mr Bandicoot, that your journey was wasted, but I think you'll find Lestrade tucked up in his little bed by now. Good-night, gentlemen,' and he left with a knowing glance at the sergeant.

119

'So,' said Lauder, adjusting the huge black beard looped over his ears, 'where would you like me?'

'Out in the street,' muttered the sergeant, but he'd read that this man was the Idol Of The Halls north of Carlisle so he humbly asked him for his autograph and showed him into the operations room, an elongated broom-cupboard with a privy at one end. Two or three policemen dozed in corners.

'Hallo, hallo, hallo.' Lauder shook his gnarled stick at them. 'What did Adam say to his wife on the twenty-fourth of December?'

One of the constables looked up disconsolately from an abandoned game of dominoes. 'It's Christmas, Eve,' he said.

Lauder's grin froze. 'Aye, quite right.' He took up another pose. 'What were Anne Boleyn's last words?'

Another constable yawned himself awake. 'I think I'll go for a walk around the block.'

'Right.' Lauder's grin remained frozen. 'What's the difference between a married man and a bachelor?'

'I don't know.' Harry Bandicoot, lolling on the door frame, was convulsed at all this, guffawing loudly. 'What's the diff . . .?'

'One kisses his missus; the other misses his kisses,' said the sergeant, stony-faced.

'Aye, well, that was just for openers,' said Lauder. 'Now, by popular request, I'd like to give you ma own, ma very own "I Love a Lassie".'

Bandicoot clapped vigorously until he realized everyone was looking at him; then he stopped. Lauder cleared his throat. 'Sadly, I've left my accordion behind,' he said, 'so I'll have to sing unaccompanied.'

'You mean we can't join in?' one of the constables asked.

Lauder glowered at him. 'Who writes your material?' he scowled. '*Oh, I love a lassie, a bonnie Heeland lassie, she's as bright as a fire down in hell; I love a lassie, a bonnie Heeland lassie, I bet you do as well.*'

These were obviously the more Rabelaisian lyrics, intended for a rough male audience. Harry Bandicoot didn't recognize the words he'd heard all evening. Even the tune seemed different. Then, as Lauder pranced past him, his kilt swinging around his ankles, he pulled down the woolly beard to reveal

120

the rather desperate face of Alistair Sphagnum. Bandicoot gasped, then resumed his casual loll on the door frame. Sphagnum dropped to one knee and slid across the floor, pounding the furniture as he laed his way through the song that had made Lauder famous.

'I love a lassie,' he went on, 'a bonnie Heeland lassie.' He twirled with the speed of light and pressed a ring of keys silently into Bandicoot's inside pocket, and, nodding to the corridor, under his breath sang, 'Third door leads to the cell.'

'Oh . . .' He broke away, snatching the hands of the desk sergeant, and proceeded to whisk the bemused man around the room in some mad Highland fling. 'I love a sergeant, a bonnie Forfar sergeant, he is just ma cup o' tea . . .'

Bandicoot couldn't stand to hear the outcome of the rhyme and while the policemen's attention was held by the extraordinary confession of the Idol Of The Halls, he slipped away down the gaslit passage and found the relevant door. Because it was dark, because he was in a hurry, because he had sixteen keys to choose from and because he was Harry Bandicoot, it took him a while to get in. Once he had, he found himself descending a stone staircase at speed, praying there wasn't a guard on duty. He was in luck. He peered into the first cell, sliding back the little iron grille.

'Father!' the occupant cried and Bandicoot slammed the thing shut fast.

The second cell elicited nothing but snoring. The third elicited a double-take from Bandicoot. 'My nanny used to tell me that would send you blind,' he whispered through the grille.

The view through the fourth opening made him spring back. It was a yellow face with a once-waxed moustache. 'Yes?' Lestrade hissed. 'If you're singing carols, you're a day or so too late.'

'Sholto,' Bandicoot whispered, 'Sphagnum thought we'd find you here.'

'Did he?' Lestrade asked. 'That man's too clever by half. Where is he?'

'Upstairs, impersonating an entertainer. And he's not, between you and me, doing very well. What are you doing in here?'

'I'm advising the Forfar Constabulary on the latest ulterior decoration in prison accommodation,' said Lestrade. 'Either that or I've been McNabbed on four counts of murder. Or is it three? I missed the lecture on mental arithmetic for policemen.'

'Murder?' repeated Bandicoot.

'It's a rather quaint old-fashioned Scottish custom,' Lestrade told him. 'And the way this case is shaping up, I'm beginning to think McNab might be right. Perhaps I did do it.'

Bandicoot frowned. 'Sholto. You've got jail fever. They haven't hit you, have they? Over the head, I mean?'

'Just get me out, Harry,' Lestrade said. 'The rats in here could pass for Shetland ponies.'

'Right,' and the Old Etonian began fumbling with his keys.,

'No, no,' said Lestrade. 'If I break out of here, I'll be on the run from *two* constabularies. Now you've found me, get back to Lord Glamis. As Lord Lieutenant of the County, he can get me out. Of course, there may be a matter of bail . . .'

'Don't worry about that, Sholto. Letitia and I will be happy to provide any amount.'

'Harry Bandicoot,' said Lestrade, 'if these bars weren't in the way, I'd kiss you.'

'Oh, Sholto.' Bandicoot shifted uneasily from foot to foot, vaguely glad that the bars were in the way. 'See you first thing in the morning.' And he tiptoed back up the passageway, pausing at the first cell again, where the same paralytic voice now hailed him as 'Mother!'

In those days, nothing stopped the Royal Mail, especially the Telegraph Department. As Scotsmen were too mean to acknowledge Bank Holidays, it was bright and early next morning that an errand boy knocked on the door of the cottage rented by Detective Constables Marshall and Snellgrove in the frozen little village of Coldstream. Eyebrows had been raised at the two young men living in a cottage anyway. The arrival of an errand boy with a jaunty cap and buttocks like jelly on springs merely confirmed the suspicions of the locals.

'It's from Lestrade,' said Marshall. 'He's under arrest for murder.'

'Get away.' Snellgrove sat upright in the smoking jacket

newly arrived from the Army and Navy Stores, courtesy of the Duke of Connaught's chit.

'It's a fact. Though what he expects us to do about it, I can't imagine.'

'It's a cry for help, Tass,' Snellgrove assured him.

'Do you think so? What's today?'

'Thursday.'

'The twenty-seventh. Well, I expect everything's closed now in Scotland until after the New Year.'

'Where's it from?'

'Er . . .' Marshall perused the telegram head. 'Some place called Forfar.'

'Where's that?'

'Buggered if I know. More to the point, where's that hamper from Fortnum's? It should have been here two days ago. Oh, give that boy a tip, will you?'

Snellgrove padded down the passageway to where the lad stood shivering in several degrees of frost. 'Never stand under a tree during a thunderstorm,' he said, patting the lad on the head, and he closed the door.

Dawn came up like thunder back at Forfar in the persons of a recently changed Alistair Sphagnum, a determined Harry Bandicoot and a totally bewildered Lord Glamis.

'I've no one by that name, sir.' The desk sergeant was a different man from six hours earlier. The night man had had to go home to lie down. It wasn't many hard-bitten sergeants of the Forfar Police who could claim to have danced the night away with Harry Lauder.

'Look again,' Sphagnum insisted.

'Haven't we seen you somewhere before?' The sergeant scrutinized the student.

'The name.' Sphagnum tapped the register with a rapidly tensing finger.

'May I remind you', said Glamis, 'that I am Lord Lieutenant of this County.'

That had not indeed dawned on the sergeant, who suddenly stood to attention. 'Cell Four, sir. I'll get him now.'

And before Sphagnum could sing a single refrain, Sholto Lestrade stood before them. There were broad grins all round.

'Come on, Sholto, I expect Lady Glamis has some delicious kedgeree for you.' Bandicoot led the way.

'Er . . . oh, yes, indeed,' said Glamis. 'I'm sure she has. Er . . . what's going on, Lestrade?'

'Look,' the desk sergeant said, 'I canna just let him go.'

Sphagnum turned to the man. 'At the moment,' he said, 'I'm only leaning on your counter. In a wee flash, I'll be leaning on you . . . constable.'

'Sergeant,' the sergeant reminded him, pointing to his stripes.

'Och, aye,' grinned Sphagnum. 'How remiss of me. You can send any necessary paperwork to Glamis Castle.'

The five of them stood on the rocky outcrop, where the Douglas firs stood dark and brooding in the grey morning light. The huge Highlander knelt in the bracken, sniffed the air, straightened, stepped to his left, then to his right.

'Looks like the Gay Gordons,' whispered Sphagnum.

'What's he doing?' asked Bandicoot.

'Ssh,' Lestrade ended the conversation. 'He's doing my job for me, with a bit of luck. Well, Mr Laidlaw?'

Mr Laidlaw stood like a Douglas fir in a kilt. 'Well, it's only ma opinion,' he doured, 'but I've been trackin' noo this past thirty years, man and boy.'

'And?'

'Your man was killed up there,' he said, 'by that fallen tree. Then whatever did for him dragged him doon here, to lie amongst the bracken.'

'And what did "do" for him, Mr Laidlaw?'

'Aye, well, that's the five-sheelin' question, Mr Lestrade. I'm not familiar wi' the disembowellin' techniques of wolves, mind . . .'

'Mr Chapman is,' said Lestrade. 'He says wolves wouldn't have done it.'

'Aye, well, he would, wouldn't he?' Laidlaw grunted. 'On the other hand, if a man did it, it's a pretty bosh shot. The sort of thing a Lowlander might do.' He grimaced at Sphagnum. 'Or a Sassenach,' and he grimaced at the other two. 'The question, if you'll forgive the bluntness of a simple ghillie, is why should anyone want to?'

Lestrade nodded. 'That's the same question a simple policeman is asking too, Mr Laidlaw,' he said. 'But I'm grateful to you. You and your boy have earned yourselves a drink.'

Lestrade and Bandicoot began passing round the toddies kindly provided by Lady Glamis.

'To the little gentleman in velvet.' Wee Fingal raised his glass.

'Whisht!' the older Highlander suddenly snapped, glaring at the disappointment that had sprung some twenty summers ago from his loins. A great hairy hand snaked out and fetched the lad a sharp one around the ear. Laidlaw senior grinned sheepishly at the others. 'An ould Heeland custom,' he explained.

They had only just got back to the turreted splendour of Glamis when a telegram arrived for Lestrade. It was not from his constables on the border offering help. It was not from the Commissioner of the Metropolitan Police demanding his resignation. It was from Balmoral. Someone had tried to kill Allan Ramsay.

8

Dusk was falling on that short winter day with the promise of snow. They had to winch Lestrade out of Sphagnum's sidecar again and carry him in a body under the clock entrance to Balmoral. There was no dourly pompous Allan Ramsay to meet him. That gentleman was lying quietly in his darkened room, a wet hanky across his forehead. His eyes were closed and a small rosary leapt between the fidgeting fingers of his right hand.

'Mr Ramsay.' Lestrade forced his blue jaw to work.

The Steward of the Household sat bolt upright, a look of terror on his face. 'Who's there?' The cry was strangled.

'Lestrade,' said Lestrade. 'You're among friends,' and he pointedly closed the door on Alistair Sphagnum, who was content to creep out and risk pneumonia, hovering by the wisteria at the back. Just as the draught of Angus swept in through the leaded windows, so snippets at least of conversation swept out.

'Lestrade,' Ramsay sank back. 'Thank God you're here. Some maniac has tried to kill me.'

'So your good lady wife told us in the hall.' Lestrade began to unwrap his numerous layers and suffered agonies as the heat of the log fire got to work on his fingers. 'What happened?'

'Och, it was terrible. Terrible.'

'Calmly, now, Mr Ramsay. I need all the details. Everything you can remember. Slowly and carefully.'

'It was yesterday evening.'

'The twenty-seventh?'

'Aye. Sir Harry Maclean had left that afternoon. I went to see to his room.'

126

'Isn't that usually maid's work?'

'Not here, Lestrade. Sensitivity, you see. Some of the most powerful and famous people in the world have crossed these portals. What if they left something behind? Something, shall we say, delicate? It wouldn't do to have a tweenie discovering that now, would it?'

'Er . . . no, I suppose not. Go on.'

'The door appeared jammed. I put my shoulder to it and fell into the room . . .'

His voice trailed away. 'And?' Lestrade sat on the bedside chair.

'The force I exerted threw me forward. There was an almighty twang and a steel blade hovered an inch from my nose. An inch, Lestrade. I tell ye, if I hadn't checked myself, it would have gone right through my skull.'

'The camel castrator,' murmured Lestrade.

'What?'

'Tell me, Mr Ramsay, this blade. Was it attached to a leather or hemp thong, designed like a catapult to operate when the door opened?'

'The very same,' gasped Ramsay. 'How did you know about it?'

'Well, I could say they're all the rage as murder weapons in London,' said Lestrade, 'but in fact I doubt you'd see it used outside Morocco.'

'It was used on *me*,' Ramsay shouted, 'here in Angus. Only yesterday.'

'Indeed,' mused Lestrade. 'Who else knows about this?'

'The entire household, I expect. I'm sorry, Mr Lestrade, but discretion tends to go by the board when your life's on the line.'

'Quite understandable, Mr Ramsay,' Lestrade assured him.

'You don't think . . . it wasn't Sir Harry, was it?' Ramsay was sitting bolt upright, astonished that the thought hadn't struck him before.

'Well, things certainly look stacked against him,' said Lestrade. 'Did he know you were in the habit of checking departing guests' rooms?'

'I don't know,' said Ramsay, 'but I'll tell you this. That's one little piece of royal protocol that's changing around here. Next time, I'll send in a tweenie, sensitive or not.'

'Good for you,' smiled Lestrade.

'Will he have got far, Lestrade?' Ramsay propped himself up on one elbow. 'Can you stop him?'

'The answer to the second depends entirely on the answer to the first,' Lestrade said, for the moment at one with Confucius. 'Did he say where he was going?'

'Out of the country if my eavesdropping over dinner last night was anything to go by. Maclean was up-wind of Her Royal Highness, so he was able to break the old hoose rule about silence at mealtimes.'

'Right.' Lestrade remembered. 'He had some business in Morocco, I understand. That means Southampton.'

'Or London,' said Ramsay.

'Which means he'd have to travel south, crossing the border at Coldstream.'

'Or Gretna Green.'

'No matter,' said Lestrade. 'I'll have my men spread out along Hadrian's Wall.'

'Or the Antonine,' moaned Ramsay, realizing the hopelessness of the situation.

'Will you get a ghillie to send a telegram for me?' Lestrade asked.

'Consider it done. But why should Sir Harry Maclean want to kill me?'

'I'm not sure he did,' said Lestrade, 'any more than he wanted to kill Amy Macpherson. You've had a shock, Mr Ramsay, but the perpetrator to whom the evidence points has gone. How can I get to the Isle of Skye?'

'Skye?' Ramsay frowned. 'Man, are you mad? You're talking about going as far north-west as Hudson in the thick of a Scottish winter. You'll not find a train. It'll kill you.'

Lestrade smiled. 'Perhaps I'll be luckier than Hudson,' he said. 'I'll find a back passage.'

The wind whipped and roared through the abandoned hill forts, grey stones with the moss of centuries where the legions slept in the heather.

'No wonder the Romans left this bloody place.' Detective

Constable Snellgrove jumped up and down and tried to bury his hands in his armpits.

'Well, we'll give it another half an hour,' mumbled Marshall, behind his muffler. 'But let's face it, we're not likely to spot him, are we? How long do you think this bloody wall is?'

Snellgrove shrugged. 'Fifty, sixty miles,' he suggested.

'Well, there you are. We can't really form much of a human chain, can we? There again, it should be quite easy to spot a chap dressed like a nigger. Especially with these new Zeiss binoculars.' He scanned the dull, purple lowlands ahead of him.

'You don't think the Duke of Connaught will mind all this expenditure, do you?' Snellgrove asked.

'Day-to-day running costs, son,' Marshall grinned. 'I mean, we've pared things down to the bone really.'

Snellgrove wrapped his Savile Row scarf tighter around his ears. 'I suppose you're right. I just can't help thinking Sir Harry Maclean would take a train south. Shouldn't we be watching a railway station or something?'

Marshall concentrated for a moment. 'Chance in a million,' he said. 'If he's as steeped in Moroccan culture as Lestrade says in his telegram, he'll either thunder out of the dust on a pure Arab charger or he'll lope.'

'Lope, do they, Moroccans?' Snellgrove asked. It had to be said he didn't have Marshall's experience.

'All Islam does, son,' Marshall told him. 'That's why they're always complaining about foreign interlopers. Well, that's it; half an hour's up.'

'Is it?'

Marshall whipped out his silver-chased hunter, the new one that had just arrived. 'Indubitably. Anyway, they're open. Duke of Connaught's shout, I think.'

Everywhere, the story had been the same. At Ballater, at Braemar, at Blair Atholl. Snow to the north. Points failure at Fort William. In a siding on the Tunnel Bridge stood the only working locomotive with a sign tied to it in Gaelic saying 'Froze'. Besides, Hogmanay was only two days away now, and the whole of Scotland was preparing for the New Year. Vast quantities of coal which ought to have been used to fuel the Scottish railway system were being spirited away by mysterious alcoholics calling themselves First Footers.

It was all beyond Lestrade, but snow or no snow, Hogmanay or no Hogmanay, he had to get to the Isle of Skye. There, he knew, lay unanswered questions. His time allotted by the Yard had long since run out. But that didn't matter now. There were evil forces at work in Caledonia and he had to move fast before they claimed another victim. Allan Ramsay had been lucky. Lestrade was right. The bungle with the camel castrator, the disembowelling designed to put the wolf in the frame – it all bore the signs of panic. So speed was of the essence. Now his man was rattled. Unpredictable. Now was the time to strike. For Richard MacKinnon was different. In the whole series of head batterings, he was the only stranger. Amy Macpherson, Alexander Hastie, Allan Ramsay, they had all been local, and all, after their own fashion, servants. MacKinnon was neither of these things.

And so Lestrade was forced once again to undergo Sphagnum's transport of delight. He bade farewell to the Bandicoots and the Bowes-Lyons by telegram, urging Harry and Letitia again to go south for the winter; and he explained to Her Royal Highness that he was merely passing through, but that an arrest was imminent. Then he and Sphagnum loaded up the Quadrant with extra furs and thick tweeds and shovels and motored away to the north-west.

In their wake, Inspector McNab of the Forfar Constabulary rubbed his hands together, and not merely with cold. The Lord Lieutenant's posting of bail had got Lestrade out of Forfar jail, but by leaving first Glamis and now Balmoral, he had jumped bail, not once, but twice. McNab got the necessary release from his superiors and, with Sergeant Pond happily cracking his knuckles in anticipation, set out through the Grampians by pony and trap.

The road was closed beyond Dalwhinnie with snow drifts as high as a very tall man, or two dwarfs standing on each other's shoulders. Alistair Sphagnum, who knew the Highlands like the back of his hand, decided instead to head across country. Unfortunately, here the drifts were even bigger and progress was painfully slow. Lestrade battled against the vast, white wilderness with his little shovel, while Sphagnum nursed and cajoled the Quadrant's engines, now in serious danger of seizing altogether.

They were to have spent their first night at the Loch Laggan Hotel, but as Sphagnum pointed out, although they were now deep in Macpherson territory, the place was owned by a member of the clan Macdonald. And Sphagnum would rather die than eat at Macdonald's. In the event, the roaring fire and bannocks of Mrs Benbecula were as acceptable as anyone else's to the two frozen travellers, who dripped ice all over her sheepskins. It had to be said that Sphagnum wasn't Lestrade's ideal companion in the double bed, but he comforted himself that it could have been worse. It could have been Mrs Benbecula.

Fresh snow overnight blocked their road to Fort William, so that the Quadrant coughed and spluttered its way north through Lochaber, deaf to the soft padding of pony and trap only fifty or so miles behind them. Again, the way was arduous and Sphagnum caught Lestrade's drift several times in the course of the morning. It was evening, strangely bright in the snow's light, when they reached Fort Augustus. It gave them time to wander the banks of Loch Ness under a threatening sky and ponder the case as it stood. Lestrade sheltered his cigar in the lee of his Donegal as they strolled.

'Will we reach the coast tomorrow?' he asked.

'Well, we've a choice,' Sphagnum told him. 'We can go south to Invergarry and even if the roads are blocked, take a boat to Loch Linnhe and the Firth of Lorn. That'll mean a day at sea past Muck and Rum to reach Skye.'

'I'll mull that over,' said Lestrade. 'What's the alternative?'

'The road – or the moors – to the Kyle of Lochalsh. But the going will be rough.'

'Is that it?'

'Well, we can split the difference. As the crow flies, we should reach Mallaig by this time tomorrow. Mind you, I canna answer for the wee machine much longer. It wasn't designed for this climate. High time they made a Scottish motor cycle. Good God, what's that?'

Lestrade followed Sphagnum's pointing finger, a skill he had recently acquired, and saw a dark shape break the surface of the loch, ripples thrown out in its wake.

'Looks like a sheep,' said Lestrade, 'with a very long neck.'

'Och aye.' Sphagnum turned back towards the hotel. 'That'll be Scottish Blackface. There's said to be a whole flock in the loch.'

'Isn't that rather odd?' Lestrade asked. 'Waterborne sheep? I had no idea they were aquatic.'

'This is Scotland, laddie,' Sphagnum reminded him. That, in effect, said it all.

They spent most of the night bouncing ideas off each other. Sphagnum was all elbows in bed and Lestrade snored, although he swore he didn't, so sleep was an impossibility anyway. A mass murderer was at work. They knew that much. Someone with a penchant for cracking skulls like eggshells. He tended to go for servants mostly, hitting them in cellars in the dark. But there was always the exception of Richard MacKinnon, killed in the open. And he was nobody's servant. There again, there was Acheson, who had died by mistake, in lieu of Lestrade. Whoever their man was, he was well informed as to the superintendent's movements. And now he was ragged, frightened, making mistakes: the feeble attempt to involve the wolf; the complete change of tack in rigging up Maclean's castrator to kill Ramsay.

And the more they talked about it, the more nightmarish it became.

By morning, having made no progress, they took a light breakfast of poached salmon.

'What's it been poached in?' a suspicious superintendent had asked his hostess.

The hostess hovered near the plate with his nose. 'Kirkudbrightshire,' she said.

Then they split the difference. Nearer the coast, the weather improved and the road to Mallaig was open, if wet and rutted with brown snow. The next day was the first of the New Year and Lestrade and Sphagnum had to do some pretty hefty haggling to find a boatman to take them across to Skye.

'Who pays the ferryman?' Sphagnum asked, true to the doctrines of his race.

'Both of ye,' the salty old seadog at the tiller assured them. The waves butted and slapped as the little boat, neat in red and white, nosed outward for the island wreathed in mist.

'Can you not feel it?' shouted Sphagnum above the wind. 'This is the way Bonnie Prince Charlie went a hundred and fifty years ago.'

'It's not the best way to go,' Lestrade agreed, trying to keep down what he could of breakfast. He was glad now he hadn't accepted Mrs Benbecula's offer of Atholl Brose. One for the road now would have had him vomiting over the side. And besides, his own Havanas were infinitely superior to her Arbroath smokies.

'*Speed, bonnie boat, like a bird on the wing.*' Sphagnum was doing his Harry Lauder again. '*"How much?" the sailors cry. Carry the lad that's born to be a superintendent, over the sea tae Skye.*'

Loud the wind howled, loud the waves roared. At least there were no thunderclaps rending the air.

'Aye, but I love the Sound of Sleat,' Sphagnum said.

Lestrade had never thought about it, but on balance he preferred good old English rain.

Lestrade was never so glad to see the steps of a quay in his life and his knees had turned to jelly by the time he reached the top.

'Now what?' he asked Sphagnum.

'This is Ardvasser,' the Scotsman said. 'Macdonald country. We'll find the MacKinnons to the north. But it's nearly dark. And without the Quadrant, we'll not get far.'

Lestrade looked to the little cluster of whitewashed houses and beyond to the black of the hills. 'Are there *any* roads here?' he asked.

'Och, awa' wi' ye,' laughed Sphagnum. 'I told you, man; this is Scotland.'

Now Lestrade had felt some hard beds before, but even he wasn't prepared for the steely qualities of the half-tester he slept in that night. At least, unlike the Skye boat, the thing kept relatively still. Once again however, he was elbow to elbow with Alistair Sphagnum. He repeatedly told his host they were not even good friends, but it fell on deaf ears. Times were hard.

Beds were scarce. No one had quite recovered from the Highland Clearances of a few years back, nor the great woodworm
plague of '83. Why, even the kings of Scotland were crowned
on a stone and wasn't it time the bastard English gave it back?

Dawn of the Year of Our Lord Nineteen Hundred and Four
passed off quietly enough, considering this was Scotland and
Hogmanay. Lestrade and Sphagnum made the most of the
smouldering peat fire at the inn and Lestrade experienced his
first and last porridge.

'It's not the best of times to be talking to the MacKinnon,'
their host had warned them, but he was less than specific and
time was of the essence. They grabbed a passing crofter's cart
and padded through the fresh, crisp snow along the vague road
to Strathaird. Here, the world was one mass of grey and white
and the Cuillin mountains rose craggy and ominous into the
winter mist. Even the fast-flowing streams were finding difficulty in gurgling and rushing their way to the sea and the ice
gripped them in a chill silence.

They paid the crofter for his trouble and stood up to their
shins in the snow.

'Are you sure this is right, Mr Sphagnum?' Lestrade looked
around him. All he saw was desolation.

'Well, at the inn, they said . . .' and Sphagnum's voice trailed
away. His finger rose in disbelief.

Lestrade tracked it again, expecting to see another long-
necked, aquatic sheep. Instead, he saw nothing. At first. Then,
through the mist he heard the most appalling sound in the
world – the skirl of the pipes.

'What is it?' he whispered.

'The skirl of the pipes,' Sphagnum told him.

'Yes, yes, I know that,' said Lestrade, having difficulty
making his lips move in the cold. 'But what does it mean?'

'It's the MacKinnon war chant. Rather similar to your
"Soldiers of the Queen".'

'War chant?' Lestrade frowned. 'We aren't at war with
anyone, are we? Unless, of course, this is Tibet.' From the mist
a ragged line emerged; infantry, hungry, wild, plodding stead-
ily over the craggy outcrops.

'Lamas?' Lestrade asked.

Sphagnum shielded his eyes from the glare of the snow.

134

'Dress MacKinnon,' he said. 'That tartan. Their kilts and plaids. Spectacular sight, isn't it?'

Lestrade noticed the lack of conviction in Sphagnum's voice. 'Any minute now,' Sphagnum said, holding up his hand. 'Aye, there it is.'

Above the pipes, Lestrade heard a guttural, imcomprehensible shout. 'What are they saying?' he asked.

'*Cuimhnich bàs Ailpein*,' Sphagnum repeated.

'Trespassers will be prosecuted?' Lestrade attempted a rough translation.

'Remember the death of Alpin,' Sphagnum corrected him.

'Something I ought to investigate?' Lestrade proffered.

Sphagnum whirled round. 'There,' he said.

'What?' Lestrade spun too to see nothing but the hills and the mist.

'The Macdonalds of Sleat.'

Through the mist before him another line of clansmen was forming, wilder and hairier than the first, their tartan redder, their tread more daunting. Their piping was better, though, and Lestrade found himself humming along.

'Whisht, man,' Sphagnum said, 'do you know what this is?' Lestrade had not seen the Scotsman without his composure before.

'Celtic versus Queen of the South?' Lestrade suggested.

Sphagnum turned again, this time to his right, nodding slowly. 'I thought as much,' he said.

A third line of Highlanders was tramping over the frozen water courses from the hills, their banners lifting on the wind, whipping snow now into the faces of all present, their tartan a dark and deadly green.

'What's going on?' Lestrade asked Sphagnum.

'Yonder,' Sphagnum pointed to the latest arrivals, 'the clan of Macleod of Macleod, the sons of Rory Mor. They've come doon from Dunvegan.'

'What for?'

'For them.' Sphagnum jerked his head to the left, towards the line of Macdonalds who halted and formed ranks.

'And what about them?' Lestrade pointed up the hill to his right, where an ancient man with a wild, white beard was being lowered into an ancient chair.

'Och, they'll watch for a while, see how the battle's going and then join in on the stronger side.'

'Battle?' Lestrade repeated.

'The Battle of the Bloody Bay,' said Sphagnum. 'They re-enact it every five years.'

'Er . . . for real?' Lestrade heard his own voice crack.

'Och, no,' said Sphagnum, 'it's all a game these days. There's hardly any actual maiming. And the widows are all looked after by the Scottish Widows Pensions Fund.'

'Oh, good.' Lestrade tried to smile. 'Are we in the way, do you think?'

'Completely,' Sphagnum assured him. 'If I remember my Scottish military formations from when I was a history student at the University, they'll strike from the centre, then bring the wings round to hit them in the flank.'

'They don't . . . er . . .' Lestrade squinted at the three armies. 'They don't use firearms, do they?'

'Whisht,' said Sphagnum, 'these men are Highlanders. They'll rely on their broadswords and claymores.'

'Good.' Lestrade was relieved, then a thought struck him. 'What's the range of a claymore?'

'You'll know when you feel one,' Sphagnum assured him.

An alien shout rose from the Macleods. The piping had stopped and the lines stood silent.

'What did he say?' Lestrade asked. 'Is it a battle cry?'

'No,' said Sphagnum. 'He said "If you want to watch the battle, that'll be three and six".'

'Three and six?' snapped Lestrade. 'That's outrageous. Are they MacKinnons over there?' He pointed to his left.

'No, they're the MacKinnons over there.' Sphagnum pointed to his right.

'Right.' Lestrade marched forward in as sprightly a fashion as he could in a soaking wet Donegal, wading through drifts two feet deep, and by the time he'd reached the MacKinnon line was totally out of breath.

One of the Scotsmen said something incomprehensible to him.

'I'm sorry,' said Lestrade. 'Does anyone here speak English?'

'We all do,' said the man behind the throne. 'Only we're too bloody-minded to do it. Who the bloody hell are you?'

136

'Superintendent Lestrade, Scotland Yard,' he told them.

'Where?' said the old man in the chair.

'London, father,' said the younger man. 'It's the Sassenach capital.'

'I ken reet enough what it is.' The old man glared at his son.

'Are you on holiday, mister?' the younger MacKinnon asked him.

'No, sir,' said Lestrade. 'Tell me, are any of you related to Mr Richard MacKinnon?'

'Aye,' the entire clan chorused, 'we all are.'

'What's it to ye?' the old laird asked. 'Why isn't Dickie here? He's never missed a muster in his life.'

'It's my painful duty', said Lestrade, 'to tell you all that Richard MacKinnon is dead.'

Even the wind dropped at that moment and the old man's red eyes grew wide. 'What was it?' he piped. 'Amoebic dysentery? Beri-beri? Intermittent claudication?'

Lestrade's mouth hung slack. It must have been the cold.

'You'll have to excuse The MacKinnon,' said his son. 'He used to have a flourishing medical practice in Edinburgh before he inherited the Lordship of the Isles.'

'*I'm* the bloody Lord of the Isles,' a voice wafted from the lines of the Macdonalds.

'Och, dear,' said the younger MacKinnon. 'That's Angus "The Bat" Macdonald. Got the best set of jugs north of the Firth.'

'Jugs?' said Lestrade. 'That's a curious phrase for a Highlander.'

'Dinna let these theatricals confuse you, Mr Lestrade,' the younger MacKinnon told him. 'Next week, I'll be back in Lincoln's Inn wi' ma bum on a bundle of briefs.'

'You're a barrister?' Lestrade blinked.

'Scottish or English law. Take your pick. Now, what happened to my brother?'

'He was murdered,' Lestrade told him.

The whole clan gasped.

'Who was?' The Bat shouted across the field of battle.

'By whom?' The old laird rose trembling to his knees.

'I don't know, yet,' said Lestrade, 'but rest assured, I'll find out.'

137

'How?' said MacKinnon KC. 'You have no jurisdiction here.'

'Is there no police force on the island?' Lestrade asked.

'Hallo, hallo, hallo,' a voice called from the ranks, and a huge Highlander burst forward, his chest and socks bristling with skean-dhus. 'Constable MacKinnon, at your service.'

'How many men do you have?' Lestrade asked.

'Men?' The constable blinked. 'Man, I *am* the Isle of Skye Constabulary.'

'You've as many men as you need, Jock.' The MacKinnon growled. 'It was a Macdonald killed my son.'

'Ptarmigan shit!' roared The Bat. 'You're a senile old bugger, Ewart MacKinnon. And by the way, you owe me ten shillings from last Thursday.'

'That's the Macdonalds for you,' sighed the KC. 'Murderous *and* mean.'

'No, no.' Lestrade sensed the MacKinnon line tensing. 'You misunderstand me. I don't know who killed your brother.'

'Look, Mr Lestrade.' The KC took the man aside, and placed a leather-strapped arm around his shoulder. 'When I go home tonight, I shall listen to Mozart on my gramophone. My maid will be cleaning with her François Billet vacuum machine and when this bloody snow clears, I'll be driving to the ferry in my deDion. Contrary to what the world thinks of us, Mr Lestrade, we are a civilized people. But to that man there . . .' He jerked his head back towards his father. 'It's not that Dada has gone gaga. It's just that he is The MacKinnon, you see. He has a sworn duty. The Macdonalds and the Macleods have been our enemies for centuries. And when something like this happens, well . . .'

'But something like this hasn't happened,' Lestrade persisted. 'Your brother could have been murdered by the Akond of Swat for all I know.'

'Ah, you suspect an oriental connection?' The KC nodded shrewdly. 'Tell me, how did he die?'

'Blunt instrument,' said Lestrade.

'Quite,' thundered the old man. 'It was a Macdonald claymore.' He turned to his clan and roared something incomprehensible in Gaelic which filled his flowing beard with spittle.

'Just a minute . . .' Lestrade said, but the drone of the pipes drowned his words. There was a rush of steel on all sides of him and the MacKinnons began whooping and yelling, tumbling down the snowy hillside, bashing their leather shields with their swords.

'Not now, Mr Lestrade,' said the KC. 'Look after the old man, will you? I'll be back in aboot half an hour,' and clawing free his tasselled broadsword, screamed like a *Bean-Nighe* and plunged after his clansmen.

Beyond the charging line of the MacKinnons, Lestrade saw Alistair Sphagnum running to his right, away from the converging armies. On the right, the dark-clad Macleods, without the benefit of the aural skills of The Bat in the Macdonald ranks, dithered in confusion. The MacKinnons had never led the charge before. It was traditional. Everybody had forgotten, centuries before, what caused the MacKinnons to delay in the first place. Now the Macleods took umbrage anew. If anybody was going to get to the centre of that field first, it was going to be a Macleod, so they whipped out their weapons and ran for it, helter-skelter, the pipers struggling to play in their wake.

The Macdonalds threw forward their red tartan line, hurling insults in English and Gaelic at MacKinnon and Macleod alike. Alistair Sphagnum just had time to throw himself into a ravine when the three armies collided like a tidal wave and steel rang on steel in the Scotch mist. Muscle and sinew flexed and jarred, teeth flew from skulls, fingers jabbed into eyeballs, knees rammed into groins.

'You can stop this,' said Lestrade to The MacKinnon, who sat quivering with bloodlust on his throne.

'Never,' hissed the old man.

'You,' Lestrade turned to the solitary piper by the chair, 'sound the recall or something. This instant.'

'The MacKinnons don't have instant recall,' the piper assured him. 'A MacKinnon only goes forward.'

Lestrade frowned. 'Someone's going to get killed,' he said.

'It's the way of it,' said The MacKinnon firmly. 'It has always been so.'

'Balderdash,' said Lestrade, the nearest to Gaelic he could get. 'You're a doctor, for God's sake. You took an oath to save life, not to take it.'

'I took an oulder oath, laddie,' snarled the laird, 'as my father did and his father before him. Whenever a MacKinnon dies, it's the fault of the Macdonalds. It has always been so.'

Faced with such blind inversion, Lestrade resorted to unreasonable tactics of his own. He whipped the brass knuckles from the pocket of his Donegal and clicked out the four-inch blade. He jerked back the bonnet of The MacKinnon and held the blade at the old man's throat.

'Sound the recall!' he bellowed to the piper. 'Or you'll be swearing in a new laird come morning.'

'Whisht!' gurgled the old man. 'He's bluffing, wee Jimmy. Don't you play a single note.'

'But grandfather . . .' The piper was wavering.

'But nothing.' The old man clawed ineffectually at Lestrade's sleeves, the arm locked around his windpipe.

'I'll count to three,' said Lestrade. 'One, two . . .'

The pipe grated into action at his elbow, the wee lad going purple in the face as the notes wailed out. Lestrade held the blade rigid until he saw MacKinnons of all shapes and sizes emerge from the carnage on the lower slopes. They began to regroup and march stolidly away, carrying their shields over their backs, while the Macdonalds and the Macleods backed away too, cheering and jeering like young muleteers.

When they'd gone, the litter of weapons and fallen bodies and the blood on the snow made it look like a battlefield.

'Well played,' said Lestrade to the piper, and he released his grip and let the old man go.

The MacKinnon staggered to his feet and fetched the confused boy a nasty one around the side of the head. 'Dimwit!' the laird roared. 'Remind me to cut you oot of ma will entirely. Oh, by the way, I just doubled your rent. As for you . . .' He turned on the superintendent.

'Da?' A panting KC in ripped plaid, bleeding profusely from a head wound, came slogging up the hill. 'We'd only just started. I hadna' begun to fight.'

'Dinna blame me,' the laird snapped. 'Ask this Sassenach here. He's to blame.'

'Mr Lestrade,' said the KC, 'play the white man. We only do this once every five years. Have a heart.'

'Mr MacKinnon,' said Lestrade, 'I'm sorry to break up your

little game, but I'm pursuing a murder enquiry. And, whatever your father thinks, my quarry is not down there.'

'Are you suggesting he's bloody well up here?' Constable MacKinnon bellowed in Lestrade's ear.

'Excuse him,' said the KC. 'Cousin Jock *is* a policeman.'

'I understand,' said Lestrade. 'Can we talk in private?'

'Aye,' said the KC, 'but first, I must bathe ma wounds in yon burn.' He caught Lestrade's glance. 'Och, I know, but it's tradition.'

'All right. In the mean time, I'll try to find my friend. If I remember rightly, the last I saw of him, he was lying face down in just such a burn.'

'You handle our quaint little Scottishisms very well,' beamed the KC, flashing a gap where a tooth used to be, 'for a Sassenach an' a'.'

'When in Rome,' shrugged Lestrade as they walked the battlefield to the stream. He had never shone at geography while in Mr Poulson's Academy.

'Aahhggh!' The KC stifled the scream as best he could as the icy water dripping over the ledge hit the cut above his swollen eye.

'You can get up now, Mr Sphagnum,' said Lestrade, crouching beside them both.

'Is it over?' Sphagnum peered through a clump of frozen reeds. The tartan armies were scattering to their clan lands, muttering imcomprehensibly as they went. 'You know, Lestrade, there are times when discretion is the better part of valour.'

'Who's this?' the KC asked.

'Alistair Sphagnum,' said Sphagnum, extending a hand, 'Leith Police.'

Lestrade's eyes rolled upward to the Cuillin Hills.

'You're a bit off your beat, Mr Sphagnum,' the KC observed. 'Not as much as Mr Lestrade here, of course.'

'Mr MacKinnon is a barrister,' said Lestrade, 'with a practice in London.'

'Is that right?' Sphagnum brushed the snow off his coat. 'I was a student of the law before I joined the police, you know.'

'That's extremely rare,' the KC commented. 'If either of you is easily embarrassed, by the way, turn your backs. I think I took a dirk in my testicles,' and with that he whisked up his kilt to examine the extent of the problem.

'Flashing again, MacKinnon?' A distant figure disappearing in the mist stopped to wave a claymore at him.

'See you in five years, Bat Macdonald,' the KC called. 'No, missed my fishing tackle by a whisker.'

'Tell me, Mr MacKinnon,' said Sphagnum, 'in the case of Regina versus Stott, what are your views?'

'Ah, well, it depends of course on one's ability to bugger a duck . . .'

'Gentlemen, I'd love to discuss British bestiality with you,' said Lestrade, 'but there are more pressing matters.'

'Not for the duck, I fear,' said the KC.

'This may seem a rather redundant question, Mr MacKinnon, in view of the little display I just stopped, but did your brother have any enemies?'

'Och, this little display was just a friendly.'

'I thought your father was ordering mass murder,' Lestrade told the younger MacKinnon.

'Och, he'll calm down by nightfall. In answer to your question, Mr Lestrade, Dick was rather an odd cove. Some English idiot, begging your presence of course, kept pestering him to let him unleash wolves and such on the Isle of Skye.'

'Mr Chapman.'

'Yes, that's right.'

'It was on his estate that your brother met his untimely end.'

'I see. Do you suspect this Chapman, then?'

'No, I think he's clean,' Lestrade told him.

'You never told me why a Yard man is this far north, Mr Lestrade.'

'It's a long story, Mr MacKinnon. I believe your brother was but one victim in a series of five. And yet . . .'

'And yet?' Mackinnon made his way from the stream, the detectives, real and imaginary, in his wake.

'And yet . . .' Lestrade was still loath to be too open with friend Sphagnum. 'There is something different about your brother's death. I can't put my finger on it, but he stands out, like a sore thumb.'

'Oh, here.' MacKinnon ferreted in his badger-head sporran

and produced a hip flask, which had obviously slipped a little. 'It'll warm your cockles on this raw morning.'

'What is it?' Lestrade asked, wary of anything taken by mouth north of Macclesfield.

'*An dram buidheach*, we call it – The Drink That Satisfies, to you English. And to you Lowlanders, Mr Sphagnum.'

'I get by,' Sphagnum assured the KC. 'I studied the Gaelic under Professor Auchtermuchty himself.'

The KC seemed impressed.

'Tell me, Mr MacKinnon,' Lestrade said. 'Oh . . .' His eyes watered anew as he swigged the flask's contents. 'I've drunk this before, somewhere.'

'No, you haven't laddie,' Mackinnon assured him. 'No one has outside this clan. Mr Sphagnum, will you have a dram?'

The mock Leith policeman accepted gratefully and he felt his ears tingle.

'You were about to ask me something, Mr Lestrade.' The KC picked up a fallen sword and slid it home in his scabbard.

'Was I? Ah, yes. Was your brother in the habit of carrying anything valuable with him when he visited?'

'Valuable?' repeated the KC. 'Such as?'

'Well, gold, jewels, money.'

'Och, no. He was a Heelander through and through. Tight as a gnat's arse. Unless . . .'

'Unless?' Lestrade halted the little trio at the foot of the Cuillin Hills, the mist as grey and grim as it had been at first light.

'Unless you're talking aboot the secret,' the KC said.

Lestrade looked at Sphagnum. Sphagnum looked at Lestrade.

'What secret?' Lestrade said.

'Man, you've just drunk it.' MacKinnon stooped to pick up a length of tartan and swing it over his shoulder. '*An dram buidheach*. The Drink That Satisfies. It's a secret recipe, known only to the MacKinnon of MacKinnon and his eldest son. Oh, bugger, that's me now.'

'Why is it secret?' Lestrade asked.

'Ralph Holinshed – who was an Englishman, but a man for a' that – once said of Scotch that it sloweth age, helpeth digestion, abandoneth melancholie.'

'Did he have a speech impediment?' Lestrade wondered.

'Och, no, he just lived in Tudor times, that's all, before the Stuarts. Anyway, that's not the point. Although in a way it is. Are you familiar with the Pretender, Mr Lestrade?'

'The Duke of Buccleuch's filly at Epsom last year?'

'Nay, laddie. Charles Edward Stuart, the Young Chevalier. His grandfather was the rightful king of Scotland and England – in that order, mind you – and that boring old fart Dutch William took it away from him.'

'Aye,' Sphagnum nodded. 'Never trust a man from a flat country, Lestrade.'

'I'll try not to,' said the superintendent. 'What's the link?'

'Well, there you have it,' said MacKinnon. 'A link with the '45. Charles Edward – Bonnie Prince Charlie to his scores of female followers – tried to get his grandaddy's throne back and was routed at Culloden Muir by a German bastard whose name we do not use here in the Highlands. The Prince, exhausted by dysentery, abandoned by his friends, out of French money, and almost totally devoid of hair powder, wandered the heather until Flora Macdonald brought him in a frock over here to Skye.'

'I told you all this, Lestrade,' Sphagnum said. 'I knew you weren't listening.

'But what has all this to do with . . .?'

'Whisht,' said the KC, 'I'm coming to that. Charlie took refuge with my ancestor, MacKinnon of Strathaird, and got a ship to France.'

'The Ould Alliance,' Sphagnum chipped in.

Strange name for a ship, Lestrade thought, but it was hardly his business to say so.

'In exchange for saving the Prince's life, Charlie gave The Then MacKinnon a recipe. A recipe for what you've just drunk. The laird and his eldest son have kept the ingredients all these years.'

'So why is it secret?' Lestrade asked.

MacKinnon visibly rocked. 'I may practise law in London,' he said, 'I may be appallingly civilized, I may even deign to talk to you, but this drink is my birthright, laddie. I'm not about to share its ingredients with you.'

'Apart from which,' said Sphagnum, 'it's worth a mint.'

'There's mint in it?' Lestrade frowned.

'Most of the ingredients are no secret at all,' said MacKinnon.

'It's made from a blend of sixty whiskies, mostly malts, aged between eight and twenty years . . .'

'That's what I have in the last three weeks,' Lestrade muttered.

'What gives it its rich, yet dry and light texture with that subtle blend of herbs and honey is the secret essence that we add in a ratio of one gallon to five thousand gallons of whisky.'

'You have five thousand gallons of the stuff?' Sphagnum was astonished.

'Man, this is Skye. Apart from the odd woman and the odd sheep, what else is there to do?'

'So,' said Sphagnum, 'if I offered you . . . say . . . one thousand pounds for the secret ingredient, would you give it to me?'

MacKinnon thought for a moment. 'Not for a hundred thousand, no. But in any case, it's not within my power. Until Da tells me, I don't know what's in it any more than you do.'

'It doesn't matter now,' said Lestrade.

'What doesn't?' asked the KC.

'Bonnie Prince Charlie's secret's out, Mr MacKinnon,' he said. 'That's why your brother's room was ransacked. That's why he died. He didn't have gold or jewels in his belongings. He had something far more valuable. And now his murderer has it.'

'Good God,' murmured MacKinnon. 'What will I tell the old man?'

'Whatever you tell him,' said Sphagnum, 'I'd get him to give you the ingredients first.'

9

The weather relented sufficiently for the Quadrant to take them safely back to Balmoral. Safely that is except for the little incident in the Sound of Sleat. The small boat taking Lestrade and Sphagnum back to the mainland passed within hailing distance of the small boat taking McNab and Pond across to Skye. In accordance with Scottish Police Regulations 1893, published by McEyre and McSpottiswoode. McNab did just that – he hailed. It had to be said that Lestrade and Sphagnum *had* heard such language before and merely raised their hats in silent acknowledgement. The staunchly Presbyterian ferryman in McNab's boat however had not and he not only refused to turn round, but threatened to tip the policemen over the side unless they refrained.

It was then that McNab forgot all about Regulations and started lobbing anything that came to hand at the other boat. It was to no avail however. The tide and the ever seeping mist soon swallowed up his quarry.

That little incident gave Lestrade and Sphagnum a day's advantage, for there was at that time only one ferry crossing a day. Just in case however, as Lestrade sauntered past the Forfar Constabulary's trap, parked illegally on the quay at Mallaig, he casually kicked out enough spokes to make the thing unusable.

They were back at gloomy Balmoral by the next day, the wind being with them, and Lestrade was carried in again by various lackeys now used to the situation. A telegram awaited him from the border signed 'Anthony and Cleopatra' to throw any miscreants off the scent. Neither the General nor his Ribaudred Nag had had any luck in sighting 'a certain Moroccan gentleman' and what did Lestrade suggest they did now?

Lestrade toyed with asking them to stop anyone who looked

as though he was about to make a fortune out of a stolen recipe, but even he realized the impracticalities of that. In the event his return telegram told Marshall and Snellgrove to sit tight and asked them again if they had come across the Duke of Connaught's chit as his money had all but run out. And Lestrade was too preoccupied to notice that he received no reply.

Meanwhile a telegram had also arrived for Alistair Sphagnum. He didn't tell Lestrade about it, but quietly packed his things and tweaked and cajoled both engines of the Quadrant.

'Ready for the road?' Lestrade asked him, standing in the driveway, blocking Sphagnum's exit.

'Er . . . just going for a spin, Lestrade,' the Scotsman grinned. 'You know, get some air.'

Lestrade looked at the luggage piled high on the sidecar. 'It looks to me as if you're changing hotels,' he said.

'Well . . .' Sphagnum's chuckle was brittle. 'It's actually the start of the University term in a day or two. I have to get back to Edinburgh.'

'Really?' Lestrade was unimpressed. He calmly removed two of Sphagnum's suitcases and lashed his Gladstone to the sidecar. 'We'd better hurry then,' he said. 'Can't have you missing any lectures. Oh, go the pretty way, will you, via Glarms? If the Bandicoots are still there, I want a word with Harry.'

Lestrade had his word. Everything seemed calm after the death of Richard MacKinnon, and the Bandicoots had stayed into the New Year to keep an eye on Nina and Claudie. After all, it wasn't every day that a body was found in one's cellar and the entire Bowes-Lyon family were at pains to be as cheerful and normal as possible under the circumstances. Letitia missed the children and longed to be back with them, but little Elizabeth and David cuddled against her of an evening until they fell asleep. She was content with that.

Lestrade had been careful not to be seen by any of the Bowes-Lyons. While Sphagnum waited with his engines purring, the superintendent tiptoed down the drive, past the avenue of limes, and did his talking to Harry in hushed tones. Bandicoot was to keep his eyes and ears open and to report anything amiss on Lestrade's return. He knew Inspector McNab was on his tail. He also knew that if the Lord Lieutenant hadn't seen Lestrade, then he wouldn't be placed in an invidious position when McNab asked him if he had.

The Quadrant rattled south-east.

They crossed the Tay together, but somewhere around Coaltown of Balgowrie, the infernal machine suddenly cut out. Sphagnum pounded the handlebars and got off.

'Lestrade,' he called to the half-frozen man in the sidecar, 'can you lend a hand? I've got my piston stuck.'

Lestrade could not stand by when a fellow human being was in this predicament, so he somehow clambered off his perch and knelt down beside Sphagnum. 'What's the problem?' he asked.

'Och, nothing,' Sphagnum answered, 'except perhaps you.'

Lestrade felt his new bowler crunch and his head cave in. For a second, the Quadrant's pistons swam in his vision, then he toppled forward and lay in the muddy slush. Sphagnum checked to see that his spanner hadn't done too much damage. Just a wee concussion, he guessed from his medical training. Then he dragged the prone policeman to the side of the road and wrapped him securely in all the blankets he had to spare, sprinkling a little Scotch over him, so that to any passing Samaritan, he'd resemble just another Scotsman getting over Hogmanay. The countryside was littered with them. Then he kicked his perfectly healthy machine into action and purred away.

Sheep. A little tar perhaps. A hint of the heather. But mostly and especially sheep. That was what hit Lestrade's nostrils as he woke up. He found his eyeball staring into the eyeball of a Scottish Blackface. He hoped it wasn't one of those who lived in Loch Ness. There was no telling what *they* smelt of. He craned his neck as best he could and his vision blurred. He'd never seen a sheep with four eyes before, nor eight legs, yet here they were all around him. He clawed upwards, his hands reaching fresh air above the woolly backs. With difficulty he sat upright. The Blackfaces moved grumpily to accommodate him. One of them bleated.

'Och, you're awake, are ye?' He heard a voice. He was aware of movement, a jolting sensation and of wind ruffling his hair. He was on a wagon, bound for market.

'Where am I?' He thought it best to be predictable in these circumstances.

'Just coming into Cowdenbeath,' the carter said, then cracked his whip and said something fairly appalling to his horse. 'How's the heed?'

'Painful,' said Lestrade, gingerly running his fingers over the lump on the back of his cranium. 'Where did you find me?'

'By the side o' the road,' the carter told him. 'Man, you've got to take more water with it.'

'With what?' asked Lestrade.

'Scotch, laddie. What else? You're a foreigner, aren't you?'

'If you say so,' muttered Lestrade, trying to free his legs from the fleecy flock around them.

'Aye, well, there y'are. A Sassenach should never take whisky neat. They canna cope.'

Lestrade sniffed the lapels of his Donegal. The carter was right. He stank not only of sheep, but of Scotch.

'I'm a police officer,' he said.

'Och, aye?' The carter continued to cart, utterly unperturbed.

'How far is it to Edinburgh?'

'Edinburgh? Ooh, let's see. As the crow flies, aboot ten mile. 'Course, that means swimming across the Firth of Forth. I wouldna recommend it, it bein' January an' a'.'

'How much for you to take me?' Lestrade asked.

'Whoa!' The carter hauled on the reins. 'Well, now. We'd have to go via the Queen's Ferry, which means I'll be late for market wi' ma sheep. Then there's the wear and tear on ma wheels and ma horse. Noo.' He shook his head. 'It wouldna be worth ma while.'

'Half a crown?'

'Done,' and they rattled south.

The carter filled Lestrade in on the current affairs he had been without for the past three weeks: the price of mutton per pound

149

at Cowdenbeath; the total lack of skill of Paul McGascoine who played inside out for Partick Thistle; and Glasgow's chances of winning this year's Beautiful City Award. By the time he'd finished, Lestrade realized he'd have had a better conversation with the sheep.

It was drizzling in Edinburgh when he found the opulent square of the University. Sphagnum? The clerk didn't think he'd heard the name. Student of law? Not in that faculty. Medicine? No. Politics? No. Perhaps history? Ancient or medieval? There was no such thing as Modern History; that was really current affairs and there was no faculty of current affairs. That was not quite how Lestrade saw it. He had been brushing currants off his Donegal all day. But everywhere he went, the answer was the same. There was no student named Sphagnum in the entire University. Come to think of it, was there anyone named Sphagnum in all of Caledonia? Lestrade thanked the clerk and pointed out that the clerk had missed the point. It was Scotland Lestrade was talking about.

The superintendent wandered the alleyways and courts off the Netherbow. He had no luggage, no hat, no bed for the night and precious little money. He had four unsolved murders and one attempted murder on his plate, and the constabularies of two counties were looking for him. So much so, that every time he saw the silver finial of a bobby's helmet, he ducked the other way or pressed what was left of his nose against a shop window selling ladies fol-de-rols. By evening, he was beginning to get some very funny looks from passers-by.

It was then, just before he limped westward in search of a slightly salubrious doss-house, that he tried a longshot. The death of Richard MacKinnon, heir apparent to the Lordship of the Isles, hinged on the theft of the secret ingredient in The Drink That Satisfies. Perhaps some light could be shed on all this by the Distillers Company, whose premises he found in an imposing building in George Street. Lights burned dimly in the upper windows. Late for the premises to be occupied, he thought, but gratifying nonetheless. Perhaps he could see somebody who could help before he resigned himself to a night's scratching on the ticking.

An extremely large man answered the pull of the bell.

'Aye?' he asked.

150

'Inspector Thomas McFarlane,' Lestrade lied, 'Leith Police.'

The large man squinted at him. 'Aye?' he repeated.

'I'd like to see your employer.'

'Which one?' The large man was less stupid than he appeared.

'The top man.' Lestrade struck a match on the gargoyle by his shoulder and proceeded to light his last cigar.

'There's no one here,' and the man proceeded to close the door.

Lestrade wedged his foot in the way, but against superior weight, quickly withdrew it. It was his good foot too. He rang the bell again. Again the large man opened the door but this time he was accompanied by another large man. They looked like Gog and Magog. The two of them standing shoulder to shoulder could have blocked Princes Street.

'I told ye,' the first man said, 'there's no one here but us porters. Come back tomorrow.'

'What time?' Lestrade asked.

'Well, now. It's a Wednesday. Better say eleven.'

Lestrade obliged. 'Eleven,' he repeated and sauntered away. As soon as he heard the heavy door slide and grate behind him, he doubled back. There was an alleyway to his left, narrow and dark, and he hobbled into it. It was not the best of times to go mountaineering. He was forty-nine years old with a painful leg and a painful head, the same one that wasn't really for heights. The alley was pitch dark and he had no ropes. His only chance to get into that building was to use the rather awful Gothic stonework as hand and foot holds to lever his way up. There had been something in the manner of the porters he didn't like. Something that told him the very man he sought – the Chief Distiller himself – was in one of those gaslit rooms on the first floor. And why had the porter specifically said 'Eleven'? Was it that the Chief Distiller would have been long gone by then and another clue would be blown like haggis-wrapping along the windy gutters of Edinburgh?

He climbed. By the time he was ten feet or so off the ground, he sensed the drainpipe swaying above him. It was like the last yard of the 4,300 feet of Ben McDhui. Lestrade's boots were planted each side of the pipe and the wind rushed up it making weird howling noises. His fingers gripped desperately at the wet sills of a small window. His heart was in his mouth, which made breathing difficult, and his ear was pressed against rough, cold metal, listening to the skirl of the pipes. Suddenly, there was a jarring, gurgling sound that made him slip. His right foot swung wide, his sole scraping frantically on the grey-faced stone. Someone had just flushed a lavatory and the light in the window above his head went out.

His feet found a ledge in the darkness. It was now or never, and he forced himself upwards until he was battering his forehead on the frosted glass of the window. Grunting and sweating, he forced his body up on to his arms and, closing his eyes, performed a feat he hadn't tried since the D. D. Hume Levitation Case, when he was a sergeant back in the Stone Age. He rammed his head, since both arms supported his body, against the right-hand side of the window frame and it swung outwards. Haven't lost the touch, he thought to himself. It was all about knowing where to knock. His touch may still have been there, but his timing was off and the window caught him a nasty one on the jaw. He reeled back, the pink clouds of the Edinburgh sky and the black bulk of the building reeling in his vision. For a second, his left arm gave way, his life flashed before him. But it made such unpleasant viewing, he shook himself free of the clammy hand of terror and squeezed himself in through the open window.

It came as no surprise, with his intimate knowledge of civic plumbing, when his foot plunged heavily into a particularly unattractive lavatory pan in white and blue. He wasn't even perturbed when the brass thing on the end of the chain hit him in the eye as it swung wildly. Clearly, these Distillers had all mod. cons. at their disposal. He wasn't prepared, however, for the height of a very odd-looking chair, designed by Mr Mackintosh, which caught him in the ribs as he stumbled forward wetly in the dark.

Still, he was made of sterner stuff and gingerly turned the knob. A stubby nose and jaundiced eye peered round the door. He was now standing in a corridor, lit by gas and plushly carpeted. A creak on the stair to his left made him dash down the corridor and embed himself into a doorway, his back to the veneer.

The creak had been caused by one of the huge porters,

Magog, doing his evening rounds and the canny great oaf stopped at the glass-fronted door marked 'Private. Distillers Only.' He saw in the crimson carpet the spoor of a wet foot snaking off down the passageway. He crouched, dabbled his fingers in the indent. Then he sniffed his fingers. Household bleach. He jerked open the door of the Usual Office, noted in the darkness the open window, the swinging chain, the wrecked chair. In a trice, his porter's mind had it sorted. The place had been burgled by a one-footed man with an obsession with cleanliness.

Magog hauled from his trouser pocket something which would have amazed the girls of the Netherbow. Well, you didn't see an ebony life-preserver every day. He wrapped the leather round his fist and tiptoed forward, his finger tracing the raised wallpaper with its motifs of barleycorn and rye.

Lestrade's fingers nestled tighter on the brass knuckles in his pocket. The big ape would take some felling. And it all seemed so unnecessary. All he wanted to do was to ask the Head Distiller a question. He'd met some obstinate doormen in his time, but this one and his gargantuan Number Two were above and beyond.

Without ceremony, Lestrade's dilemma – fight or flight – was resolved. The weight of his body on the door caused it to crash back and he rolled haphazardly into a large, gaslit room. Before he could scramble to his feet, Magog had leapt on to him, forcing his right arm behind his back and his head on to the floor.

'Clarice,' Lestrade heard a voice say, 'who is this gentleman?'

'Inspector McFarlane of the Leith Police, your lordship,' Magog grated, struggling to hold him.

'Well, let him up, man. You can't go around assaulting police officers.'

'Very guid, sir,' and Lestrade felt the iron grips leave his wrist and neck.

He stood wavering on a plush carpet, staring at a startled body of men sitting on three sides of a large table. Another man stood before this table with his back resolutely to Lestrade.

'Thank you, Clarice,' said the spokesman, a benign, silver-haired gentleman in the centre. 'We'll ring if we need you. I expect Eustace will have your cocoa ready by now.'

'Aye,' muttered Magog, and bowed before exiting.

'Now . . .' The silver-haired man stood up. 'Inspector McFarlane. This is rather an unorthodox way of effecting an entry.'

'I'm sorry, sir.' Lestrade moved forward, vaguely uneasy at the sixteen hostile eyes that stared at him. 'It was urgent that I talk to the managing director of the Distillers Company.'

'You're in the wrong building,' said the man with his back to Lestrade. 'This is a faculty meeting of the University.'

Lestrade stiffened and looked to his right. He was staring at the arguably handsome profile of Alistair Sphagnum.

'Er . . . that's right,' said the silver-haired man. 'I am Professor McReady. These gentlemen are my fellows.'

Lestrade noticed for the first time that McReady wore a silk apron over his suit and all the men present, apart from Sphagnum, wore sashes and orders around their necks. 'Oddfellows?' Lestrade asked.

'McFarlane . . .' McReady began.

'Lestrade.' The superintendent squelched forward. 'Superintendent of Scotland Yard.'

A murmur ran like indigestion around the table.

'I think it's time this subterfuge came to an end,' Lestrade said. 'I know enough about Scotland to know that Mr McReady is a famous actor. I also know, having spent an hour or so with a clerk at Edinburgh University this morning, that there is no professor of that name.' He turned to the man at his elbow. 'Neither is there a law, medicine, politics or history student called Alistair Sphagnum.'

Sphagnum looked at Lestrade. Then at the silver-haired man. 'He's a fair cop, my lord,' he said. 'I don't feel we have any choice.'

'One moment,' the silver-haired man said. 'First, I'd like to know why an officer of Scotland Yard feels he has to impersonate a police officer and break into a private building.'

'One explanation at a time,' said Lestrade. 'You first. You see, gentlemen, Mr Sphagnum here is wanted for the theft of a Gladstone bag, assault on a police officer with a deadly weapon and conspiring to pervert the course of justice, viz. and to wit by dousing me liberally with Scotch having knocked me out.'

There was a gasp of horror throughout the room. One of the gathering stood up. 'Man,' he growled in an octogenarian sort of way. 'Pouring whisky over someone is blasphemy.'

There were cries of 'Hear! Hear!'

'Sphagnum,' said the silver-haired man, 'perhaps you'd better explain yourself.'

Sphagnum hesitated, then whipped something small and white out of his jacket. 'My card,' he said.

Lestrade read it. 'Alistair Sphagnum, Consulting Detective. You mean you're a sort of Scottish Sherlock Holmes?'

'Who?' asked Sphagnum.

'Nobody,' said Lestrade. 'I just made the name up. So you aren't attached to Edinburgh University?'

'Not any more,' said Sphagnum. 'Ten years ago, I was, briefly. I needed a cover when I met you at the North British Hotel. What better way to explain the fact that I was loafing about in Edinburgh doing nothing? That's what students always do – especially, I understand – at *this* University.'

'Of course.' Pieces of the puzzle were beginning to fit in Lestrade's tired old brain. 'I should have smelt a rat when Harry Bandicoot said he knew you. If you'd boxed with him, you had to be approximately the same age. Rather long in the tooth for a student.'

'Quite. I counted on you not knowing much about universities, but having made that stupid mistake with Bandicoot, I had to cover my tracks – hence the lines about different faculties. That way, I could have stayed at the University indefinitely.'

'But why the subterfuge?' Lestrade asked.

'That brings me to these gentlemen here,' said Sphagnum. 'Superintendent Lestrade, may I present the Most Honourable the Marquess of Tullibardine, MVO, DSO, MP.'

The little silver-haired man nodded. Lestrade did likewise.

'These other gentlemen are, from left to right, Mr John Haig, Mr John Walker, Mr John Dewar, Mr James Mackie – he of the White Horse, Mr James Buchanan, Mr T. R. Sandeman and Mr William Sanderson; the cream of Lowland grain distillers.'

Lestrade nodded to them all. Thank God, he thought, not a Teacher in sight.

'You'd better sit down, gentlemen.' Tullibardine returned to his elaborate chair and waited until Lestrade and Sphagnum had their backsides on twin Mackintoshes. 'Mr Sphagnum has not told you the whole story, but before I do, I want to know

155

what you are doing here, rather poorly disguised as a Scottish policeman?'

'There you have it, my lord,' said Lestrade. 'As you must know, an English policeman has no jurisdiction north of the border. Neither does he cut much ice with the likes of Clarice on the door. I had hoped Inspector McFarlane could open doors Superintendent Lestrade could not.'

'I see,' nodded Tullibardine. 'And why did you need to see us so urgently?'

Lestrade looked at the sober, dignified men before him. Between them, they must have represented millions.

'I am engaged on a murder enquiry,' he said, 'unofficially, of course. And I have reason to believe that at least one of the deaths I am investigating has to do with the production of a whisky-like beverage.'

'The Drink That Satisfies,' said Tullibardine.

'You know about that?'

'We do,' the silver-haired Scot said. 'And now, to my explanation. I am not actually a distiller at all. More a stone cutter, you might say. I am the Grand Master of the Grand Lodge of Scotland.'

'Mason?' Lestrade blinked.

Tullibardine nodded.

Lestrade blinked again. He had tangled with the Masons before and he didn't care for them. For a start, they were so free. And so rich. And so powerful. And they all had names likes James and Perry.

'Who is the Grand Z?' Tullibardine asked him.

'I beg your pardon?'

'The Grand Master of the United Grand Lodge and Supreme Grand Chapter of the Royal Arch?'

'Er . . . ah,' Lestrade confessed, 'that's a difficult one.'

'The Duke of Connaught.' Tullibardine simplified it for him. 'Since his brother became King, the Apron has fallen upon him. He appointed you, did he not, to enquire into the death of this wretched Macpherson girl?'

'He did,' said Lestrade, now that all the cats appeared to have long ago left their bags.

'Arthur of course is merely concerned about a royal scandal. I had other doubts when he confided in me.'

'Oh?'

'You see, the girl Macpherson was done to death on November the thirtieth of last year.'

'She was,' Lestrade agreed.

'Does that date have any significance for you?'

'I believe it is St Andrew's Day,' said Lestrade.

'Well done,' said Tullibardine, impressed that a mere Sassenach should care. 'It is also the night of our Grand Festival.'

'Which means?'

'Which means, by the time you've cut through the quaint ceremony, we all get pissed as a crofter's sporran. Tell me,' Tullibardine leaned forward, as confidential as he could be in a room the size of Hampton Court, 'as a London policeman, are you familiar with the Whitechapel murders?'

'Jack the Ripper?' said Lestrade. 'I worked on that case, yes.'

'There was an ugly rumour at the time, I seem to remember, oh, baseless of course . . .'

'Of course,' nodded Lestrade.

'. . . that there was some Masonic connection with the killings.'

'Indeed,' said Lestrade, remembering the old ritual. 'Jubela, Jubelo, Jubelum.'

'Yes,' chuckled Tullibardine, as well as a nervous man with ill-fitting dentures can. 'What nonsense.'

And the whole table of distillers broke into a paroxysm of sniggering.

'It occurred to us as Masons that some maniac was trying to discredit us once again by tying in the untimely death of the girl Macpherson to a Masonic ceremony.'

'And further,' chimed in Haig, 'it occurred to us as distillers that there was something brewing in the Heelands.'

'There's always something brewing in the Heelands,' Sphagnum explained to Lestrade.

'Now, we're not opposed to honest competition,' Dewar assured him. 'We know about the dram of the MacKinnons; that old MacKinnon is thinking of marketing it commercially. All perfectly above board and fair, I assure you. But man, its worth. What if that secret ingredient were to fall into the hands of someone less scrupulous? The MacKinnons, for all they're Heelanders, are gentlemen through and through. There'd be no

157

sharp practice, merely the usual cut-throat competition. It's always been that way since the days of the Picts.'

'We'd heard rumours,' said Haig, 'that someone was about to steal the formula, handed doon by the Bonnie Prince himself. That's where friend Sphagnum came in.'

'He did?' Lestrade glanced at him.

'For royal, Masonic and commercial reasons,' said Tullibardine, 'we didn't want great policemen's feet – begging your pardon, Lestrade – thundering all over the place.'

'On the other hand,' said Haig, 'we couldn't *not* inform the local constabulary if a corpse should turn up unaccountably. How would it look?'

'Odd,' nodded Lestrade.

'Quite,' nodded Tullibardine. 'Mr Sphagnum's credentials were excellent – Fettes, Edinburgh, descended from Sphagnum Of That Ilk (or so he tells us), got a right cross like a steam hammer . . .'

'Hung like a donkey,' Sphagnum whispered out of the corner of his mouth.

'. . . and a brain to boot.'

Yes, reflected Lestrade; that was probably where Sphagnum *did* keep his brain – in his boot. 'I'll vouch for his right cross,' and he ruefully rubbed his head.

'We knew from the Duke of Connaught that you were on your way,' Sphagnum said. 'I must have met every down train into Waverley Station for three days. Then I followed you to the North British Hotel.'

'And then there were complications,' Lestrade said.

'The fire. And the death of poor Acheson. Burns night, you might say.'

'A bump on the head and a fire that were intended for me.'

'Quite. I worked that out over a few days. And then had to pretend surprise when you told me about it. It was bloody hard being an amateur sleuth. But that meant that someone else knew you were on your way up. The question is who?'

Sphagnum leaned back, as well as he could on one of Mr Mackintosh's early efforts.

Lestrade did likewise. 'Anyone in this room,' he said.

A ripple ran round the table.

'Now, just a minute, Lestrade . . .' Dewar began.

Tullibardine held up his hand. 'No, John, Lestrade's right. Not one of us is above suspicion. But having said that, who else knew?'

'That depends on who else Prince Arthur spoke to,' said Lestrade. 'And I suspect most if not all of the staff at Balmoral were aware of my arrival.'

'These aren't the sort of murders which servants commit, Lestrade.' Tullibardine had had servants all his life. He knew a deranged domestic when he saw one.

A lull fell in the conversation.

'Well,' said the Grand Master, 'all our cards appear to be on the table. Where does this leave us?'

'Up the loch without a paddle, I'm afraid, my lord,' said Sphagnum, 'unless, Lestrade, you know something I don't?'

Lestrade looked at his man. 'I suspect there are a lot of things I know that you don't,' he said. 'The point is, the answers to things neither of us knows lie north of here – somewhere between Glarms and Balmoral.'

'Well then, gentlemen,' said Tullibardine, 'let us not keep you. Thank you, Sphagnum, for your report. And Mr Lestrade, for yours. Keep in touch.'

'Of course,' said Lestrade, to whom a thought had just occurred. 'We could catch our monkey by doing one thing.'

'What's that?' asked the Grand Master.

'Waiting,' said Lestrade. 'If we are right about the motive for the death of Richard MacKinnon, whoever killed him will tip his hand sooner or later by manufacturing The Drink That Satisfies. When he does that, we've got him.'

'Och, man,' said Haig, 'he can hide behind a corporate identity for ever. He only has to assume a different name, create a Swiss bank account, employ an army of solicitors. You'd never find him.'

'We have our methods,' Lestrade told him.

'And what if anyone else is battered to death in the mean time?' asked Tullibardine.

Lestrade stood up. 'We are on our way, gentlemen,' he said. He and Sphagnum bowed to the Marquess of Tullibardine and left.

*

159

It was a scowling Gog and Magog, with cocoa skin all over their sneering lips, who watched them go, this time via the front door.

'Sorry about the tap on the head, Lestrade,' said Sphagnum. Lestrade shook his wet foot. He was well acquainted with Scottish plumbing by now.

'Was your violence really necessary?' Lestrade asked.

'I must admit I almost panicked there,' the Scotsman confessed. 'Not like me of the sure hand, the firm jaw; but there it is. We all have our weak moments. I was summoned by that wee witches' coven up there to report my findings. Unfortunately, you were behaving like a plaster cast. I couldn't shake you off. So, how can I make amends?'

They turned into the Edinburgh night.

'A bed. A fire. A plate of food – something edible preferably. My Gladstone bag, which I *think* still has one clean pair of socks left. Another new bowler. And the truth from now on.'

'Cross ma heart, hen,' said Sphagnum. 'By the way, what did Tullibardine mean when he said about somebody else being battered to death? Surely, our murderer's finished, hasn't he? He cut down a few hapless individuals at random to disguise the real victim – Richard MacKinnon. He thought that would throw us off the scent.'

'I wish it was that simple,' said Lestrade.

10

'I see they've beatified Joan of Arc.' Letitia Bandicoot read from the January issue of *Horse and Hoond*.

'Is that possible?' Harry looked up. 'She's been dead for years, surely?'

There was a commotion at the door and Sholto Lestrade was helped in by a begoggled and gauntleted Alistair Sphagnum.

'Sholto, you're back!' said Bandicoot, rising to help him into a chair.

'That's the least of my worries,' said Lestrade and proceeded to moan and whimper as he held his feet and hands out to the crackling fire.

'Scotch, Sholto?' Letitia asked. 'I'm sure Claudie won't mind.'

'Three fingers, please,' said Lestrade, 'and a small one for Mr Sphagnum here.'

The Scotsman pulled off a fur mitt and touched Letitia's fingers just a *little* longer than was strictly necessary. 'Thank you,' he said.

'Well, Harry, all quiet?' Lestrade asked, as soon as his mouth was working again.

'As the grave,' said Bandicoot. 'Oh, perhaps I shouldn't have said that.'

'Did you and Mr Sphagnum find what you were looking for in Edinburgh?' Letitia asked.

'Yes and no,' Lestrade told her.

'You know I once met him, don't you?' Harry suddenly said.

Everybody looked at each other.

'Who, heart?' Letitia asked.

Bandicoot lolled at the fireplace, his elbow on the Adam. 'John Brown.'

All eyes followed the nod of his head in the direction of a rather ghastly painting above him. The late Queen-Empress, God Bless Her, sat on a dumpy pony, as short in the leg as she. The nag's head was held by a dour-looking Scot in glengarry and kilt.

'Really?' Lestrade yawned.

'You never told me that, Harry.' Letitia took up her sampler again.

'Well, it's a bit embarrassing really.' Bandicoot quietly wished he hadn't embarked on this.

There was a silence. 'Well, come on, Bandicoot,' said Sphagnum, 'you can't just leave it at that now. Around here, admitting to knowing John Brown is a bit like saying you're on intimate terms with God.'

'Well, it was all rather silly.' Bandicoot shifted. 'It was while I was at school. Her Majesty was due to arrive at Windsor Station. A group of us had a half-holiday to wave to the old girl. I was with old Priapus Parsons of the Remove, when a maniac ran forward and fired at the Queen.'

'Good Lord!' gasped Letitia. 'That's astonishing.'

'Yes, isn't it? I believe it was the seventh attempt on the old girl's life, so I expect she was quite hardened to it.'

'What has this to do with Brown?' Lestrade asked.

'Well, he was normally on hand, it was said, to cope with such things. But he was a bit slow that morning.'

'Of course, he died the following year,' Sphagnum said. 'Hardening of the arteries.'

'Really?' Letitia asked.

'Och, that was well-known,' said Sphagnum. 'Cut John Brown and he'd bleed pure malt.'

'What happened, Harry?' Lestrade continued to toast his feet.

'Well, we were in training for the annual Eton v. Harrow fencing tournament, Parsons and I, and our minds, I suppose, were on that. We burst through the crowd and both lunged with our umbrellas simultaneously.' Bandicoot sidestepped and placed his large hands over his wife's ears. 'I got him in the left testicle, Priapus in the right.'

'That must have made his eyes water.' Letitia pulled a face, demurely taking Harry's hands away.

'It was highly embarrassing,' Bandicoot chuckled. 'Her Majesty came to Eton three days later and addressed us all in the Quad. Then she thanked Priapus and me personally. She was a sweet old trout, in an odd sort of way. Funnily enough, though, it was Brown who struck us both.'

'His appearance, you mean?' Letitia asked.

'No, I mean, he hit us. We had this maniac lying at our feet, having saved our dear Sovereign's life, and this hairy ghillie swiped us both around the head and said, 'That's my job. Do you mind?" It *was* a bit hurtful.'

Lestrade looked at the biceps in the painting. 'I should think it was,' he said.

'Ungrateful old bastard – oh, begging your pardon, Letitia,' smiled Bandicoot.

'I remember that one vaguely,' said Lestrade. 'I was a sergeant at the time. What was the name of the would-be assassin?'

'Er . . . now you've asked me,' said Bandicoot. He had a mind like a rapier. 'Maclean, I think. Yes, that's it. Roderick Maclean.'

Lestrade looked at Sphagnum. Sphagnum looked at Lestrade.

'You don't think . . .?' the Scotsman began.

Just then, Lestrade didn't have a chance to think at all, because the door crashed back and the Lord of Glamis Castle stood there, white as a winding sheet.

'Lestrade,' he blurted. 'Thank God you're back.'

'Claudie.' Letitia joined the men on their feet. 'You look as though you've seen a ghost.'

'Oh no,' said Bowes-Lyon, his moustache bristling stiffly. 'This one's real enough.'

Letitia joined Nina in the Great Hall and the men told them to stay where they were. Led by Lord Glamis, the intrepid little group climbed stair after stair until they reached the Red Room, off the Clock Landing. No one spoke. The electricity had not ascended to this height. Neither had the gas. On the landing, Bowes-Lyon snatched a candle from the table and led them to the nearest door.

Here another candle spluttered and burned, throwing huge,

163

eerie shadows on to the walls. It was Lestrade who crossed to the body first. It lay face down beside the bed, a dark daub of blood already drying on the quilt.

'Dougal McAskill,' said Glamis, 'second under-butler.'

Bandicoot knelt to turn the body over, but Lestrade held his arm. 'No, Harry. Best not,' he said. 'I'm not sure the Forfar Police have heard of fingerprints, but we ought to give them the benefit of the doubt.'

'That'll mean McNab again,' said Sphagnum. 'He'll have you this time, Lestrade.'

'Who found the body, sir?' Lestrade checked McAskill's bloodied neck for a pulse. He estimated he was about three hours too late.

'Morag, the upstairs maid. She's very upset, poor thing. Would you like to talk to her?' Glamis asked.

Lestrade nodded. 'Sphagnum, will you extinguish that candle? I want this room locked. There's not much we can do here until morning. I'll have the key myself. Oh, and I don't think we need bother the local constabulary until about lunchtime.'

'What's going on, Lestrade?' Glamis asked. 'There are bodies in the cellar, bodies in the Red Room. People will begin to talk.'

'Rest assured, sir,' said Lestrade, 'as soon as I have any answers, so will you.'

Morag, the upstairs maid, was a slip of a thing, the slip probably being her father's. When Lestrade saw her later that night, she had a purple nose and two red eyes, the latter caused by crying, the former by a stiff gin, the cure-all of Mrs Comfrey, the castle cook.

'What time did you go to the Red Room?' the superintendent asked her.

'About half-past eight, sir.'

'Why?'

'In search of Mr McAskill, sir.'

'Why?' Lestrade was as tenacious as a mastiff with lockjaw.

'He was needed to help serve the brandies, sir.'

Lestrade had been a guest in this house before. He knew the

164

custom was to serve drinks to those who wanted them at nine o'clock.

'What was he doing in the Red Room?'

'Her Royal Highness complained of mice, sir.'

'Her Royal Highness?' Lestrade was confused. Or perhaps Morag was. 'Do you mean Lady Glarms?'

Morag looked at him oddly. With a nose like hers, there was really no other way. 'No, sir. I mean Her Royal Highness. The Duchess of Argyll.'

'Argyll?' Lestrade repeated. 'What's she doing here? I thought she was at Balmoral?'

'I believe she's spending a few days prior to going abroad, sir.'

'Abroad? Where?'

'A place called Sandringham.'

'Ah. So Her Royal Highness had mice?'

'Aye, so she claimed. Well, what can ye expect? This is an awful old hoose.'

'And Mr McAskill was looking for them?'

'Aye.'

'Which would explain his position.' Lestrade remembered the body, half crouched, half sprawled beside the bed.

'Aye. He was second under-butler,' Morag confirmed.

'Indeed. Tell me . . . er . . . Morag, did you see anybody else in the Red Room? Or near it?'

Morag let out an ear-piercing scream which brought two men running in. Lestrade looked at them again. On more careful examination, one of them was a woman – Mrs Comfrey.

'Morag, my pet.' She swept the hapless girl to her feet and proceeded to crush the life out of her in her huge biceps, fiercely patting her white-bonneted head as she did so. 'What did the horrid, nasty man suggest? What unnatural act did he ask you to commit?'

Lestrade thought it best to ignore her in the circumstances. 'Mr Ramsay,' he said. 'I hadn't expected to see you here.'

'Nor I you,' said Ramsay. 'Her Royal Highness insisted I accompany her, at least as far as the Border. She's formed an unnatural attachment to my finnan haddies.'

'Butlers cooking!' snorted Mrs Comfrey, allowing Morag the odd gulp of air between her balloon-like bosoms.

165

'Steward, madam,' Ramsay hissed archly. 'I am a steward, not a butler.'

'Hair-splitting,' she bellowed. 'Whether ye buttle or whether ye stew, it's a' one to me. Come away, Morag.'

'Madam,' said Lestrade, 'I have not yet finished with this girl.'

'Beast!' the cook thundered. 'This wee bairn has been through quite enough for one night. You may talk to her again in the morning, but this time in my presence,' and she whisked the trembling girl out.

'I like the way I handled that,' Lestrade mused to himself.

'Is it true, Mr Lestrade?' Ramsay lowered himself carefully into Morag's chair. 'There's been another murder?'

'It's true,' Lestrade nodded. He jerked his head in the direction of Ramsay's lap. 'Are you . . . er . . . all right, after your little problem?'

'Well, you notice how carefully I lowered myself into Morag's chair,' Ramsay said. 'Polishing the silver isn't as easy as it once was. Tell me, Mr Lestrade, as the Duke of Connaught's representative, as it were, are you any nearer to solving this mess?'

Lestrade sat down too. 'I believe so,' he said.

'Is it Maclean? Have you found him?'

'Perhaps yes and perhaps no,' said Lestrade. 'I've got men out combing the border, of course, but I fear he may have slipped through the net.'

'Why?' said Ramsay. 'What could be his motive?'

'He's mad, Mr Ramsay,' the superintendent said. 'Oh, there's probably method in his madness, as Macbeth said, but who can fathom the deranged mind?'

'He's a lunatic, you mean?'

'How many other Scotsmen do you know who wear Arab dress *and* eat haggis?'

'Aye,' Ramsay nodded. He had to admit it was a rare combination.

'The point is,' Lestrade said, 'if Maclean is our man, he didn't intend to kill Dougal McAskill.'

'Not? How do you know?'

'Because Richard MacKinnon was the real target in all this.'

'MacKinnon? Why?'

'This is strictly between ourselves, Mr Ramsay,' Lestrade warned.

'Sir,' Ramsay reminded him, 'I am Steward to the Royal Household at Balmoral. Secrecy is my middle name.'

It was a strange monica, but Lestrade had come across odder in his time. 'Very well,' he said. 'The MacKinnons of Skye have a secret brew – a drink they call The Drink That Satisfies.'

'Have they?'

'They have. Maclean, if he's our man, wanted the magic ingredients.'

'Why?'

'It could make him a fortune on today's market.'

'I see.'

'But what can he do? If he merely killed MacKinnon and stole his formula, that would point the finger straight away.'

'So?'

'So, he disguises his target. He multiplies the victims. Instead of one victim, there are five.'

'Five?'

'The first was Amy Macpherson, the second need not concern you. That one was altogether different yet somehow similar. The third was Alexander Hastie, the fourth Richard MacKinnon. I think Dougal McAskill was in loo of you.'

'Me?'

'He bungled things with you and I think I know why.'

'You do?'

'Our man's having a hard time of it recently. He's panicking. Probably, although it's hardly my place to say so, because of my presence. He's rattled and he's making mistakes.'

'That's why he bungled things with me?'

'Not entirely. I fear I cannot say more. Suffice it that you and McAskill were mistakes. And those mistakes leave me more confused than ever.'

Ramsay scratched what was left of his hair. 'Well, that makes two of us,' he said.

'We've met, surely?' Her Royal Highness the Duchess of Argyll focused her encrusted lorgnette on Lestrade.

'Indeed, ma'am,' he said. 'Some three weeks ago at Balmoral.'

'Yes,' she nodded, narrowing her gaze. 'You tried to sell me a brush.'

Clearly Her Royal Highness was a daft as one, but Lestrade demurred. 'No, ma'am. I am a superintendent of Scotland Yard. Investigating the strange death of Amy Macpherson.'

'What person?' The Duchess swung her head to bring her good ear in line with Lestrade.

'May I ask,' Lestrade had no time to humour her, 'why you are here at Glarms?'

'You may,' she said.

Lestrade paused before complying. 'Why are you at Glarms, Your Royal Highness?'

'Nina invited me,' she told him. 'Such a sweet thing. She was a Bentinck-Cavendish, you know.'

Lestrade did not know, and it would have been of no advantage to him if he had. 'And when did you arrive?'

'Yesterday,' she said, then rose and turned to the window. 'Ah, love was such an easy game to play. Now, Glamis is a nice place to hide away. Ah, how I long for yesterday.'

'Quite,' said Lestrade, perhaps a little too curtly. He was in no mood to be lyrical. The body count was rising and he was flat broke. 'I understand you had mice.'

'Rice? Can't stand the stuff. What has this to do with the death of the butler?'

'Under-butler, ma'am.' Lestrade was a stickler for accuracy.

'Don't say another word.' The Duchess snapped shut her lorgnette. 'If there was anyone under the butler, I certainly don't want to know about it.'

Lestrade cleared his throat. 'I belive you saw vermin in your bedroom?'

'The Red Room, yes. That's where they put me. Mind you, I shan't sleep there tonight. It had mice, you know.'

'Really?' sighed Lestrade, feeling his moustache wilt with the sheer effort of being alive.

'Still, now that this new chappie has been found dead, I doubt if I'll ever sleep again. After all, I haven't slept with the Duke of Argyll for years. Don't print that in your wretched paper, by the way.'

'I am a policeman, ma'am, not a journalist,' Lestrade reminded her. 'May I ask what time you retire?'

168

The Duchess of Argyll raised herself to her full five foot or so and shook her jowls at Lestrade. 'Royalty never retires,' she told him. 'We rule until we drop.'

'Indeed. What time do you go to bed, Your Royal Highness?'

'Seven o'clock.'

'Isn't that a little early?'

'Burly?'

'Early.'

'Curly?'

'Early.' Lestrade knew enough about Royalty never to shout in their presence. His enunciation became crisper with each attempt, until it was as clear as the Virgin Mary's.

'I always retire at that time. It is my habit. The only one I have,' and she sucked her thumb, just for a second.

'But you did not go to bed at that time tonight?'

'Of course not. I told you, that wretched little man was looking for mice. I could hardly retire with a man in my room, especially a butler.'

'Indeed not. May I ask . . . er . . . that is . . . where were you in the early part of the evening?'

'I was in the library, resting.' She suddenly straightened again. 'Do I understand you think *I* killed the horrid little fellow?' she asked, lips frozen in silent outrage.

'No, ma'am, most assuredly not,' Lestrade smiled. 'Who did you tell about the mice?'

'Lice? Oh, surely not. Nina would never allow it. No, no, the man was hunting for mice, not lice. I don't know why. A Persian would have fared better.'

'A Persian?' Lestrade's suspicions were aroused. Time and time again on this case, he kept coming back to Moslems. `

'Or a Manx. But they in turn are so difficult to catch, aren't they? No tails, you see.'

Lestrade felt the conversation wandering. 'Do you say your prayers, ma'am? Before getting into bed, I mean.'

'Well,' said Her Royal Highness, 'in that every bedroom I have ever known is at the top of the house, I perforce *must* take the stairs. What a strange question. How long did you say you have been a policeman?'

'Thirty years, ma'am. Man and boy.'

169

'Humph,' snorted the Duchess, tapping Lestrade with her lorgnette, 'high time you retired.'

Lestrade flicked out his half-hunter. Nearly midnight. 'Indeed it is, ma'am.'

'Well.' Her Royal Highness swept to her feet. 'It must be nearly midnight. I should have been asleep five hours ago. I hope you have more luck with your traps than Whatsisface had with his.'

A strange light dawned in Lestrade's eyes. 'Thank you, ma'am,' he said. 'I'm sure I will.'

To everything there is a season. It was a time to plot and a time to plan. Lestrade ascertained from Lady Glamis where Her Royal Highness was to sleep and promptly changed the room. No one, except Lestrade, Lady Glamis and arguably, the old girl herself, was to know. As a safety measure, Lestrade sought out Alistair Sphagnum.

'Stand guard?' he whispered, adjusting his clothing as he came out of an old Scottish privy.

'Sshh!' Lestrade held his finger to his lips.

'Why?' breathed Sphagnum, wrapping an elegant smoking jacket around him.

'Because I fear for Her Royal Highness's life.'

'Come on, Lestrade. Bandicoot's story of assassination attempts has put the wind up you. McAskill is just one of those red herrings in the creel, that's a'.'

'No, he isn't,' Lestrade told him. 'Are you armed?'

'I have Major Weir's trusty staff strapped to the Quadrant.'

'Get it. The old girl's in the Green Room.'

'Aye, one hell of an actress,' grinned Sphagnum.

'Station yourself nearby. I think you'll find a small alcove to the right of the door. Can you stay awake?'

'Does a baby say ignominy?' Sphagnum raised a proud eyebrow. 'By the way, who am I to expect?'

'Everybody,' said Lestrade, 'and nobody. Keep your stick handy, though. If it's me, I'll whistle.'

'What?'

'What?'

'What will you whistle? "Bonnie Dundee"? "Annie Laurie"?'

170

'I'll just whistle,' said Lestrade. 'The chances of *two* of us whistling in the dark tonight – me and the murderer – are fairly remote, Sphagnum.'

'Stranger things have happened.' Sphagnum clicked his tongue. 'Where will you be?'

'Never mind. It's better you don't know.'

'Now, look, Lestrade. I'll admit I didn't exactly put all ma cards on the wee table before and I owe you one for that crack on the heed; but if this has to do with MacKinnon's secret formula . . .?'

'Ah, but that's just it, Alistair, ma bonnie.' Lestrade pinched the Scotman's cheek playfully. 'It doesn't.'

'What?'

'Get your staff, man. And stay alert. Remember,' he was reminded of the graffiti in the Yard Lavatories For Inspectors And Above, 'Britain needs lerts,' and he was gone.

Like Allan Ramsay, Gordon Bennett, the Bowes-Lyons' butler, was the soul of discretion. Loyal, upright, distinguished, he shambled into Lestrade's presence with a wild, rolling eye. That was the right one. The left one didn't move at all. Not that is until he took it out and polished it thoughtfully in his handkerchief.

'This,' he held the gleaming glass ball up to Lestrade, 'I show to see if there's a seat on the top of an omnibus. I throw it up in th' air to see if there are any spaces. Drink?'

'No, thank you,' said Lestrade.

'Nay, I mean d'you have a drink on ye? Don't talk to me about teetotallers, pal,' and he waved a waving finger vaguely in Lestrade's direction. 'I was one mysen until tonight.'

Lestrade liked a man who could hold his liquor, but from the aura of Bennett, he'd been at the boot polish below stairs. 'Tell me about Dougal McAskill,' he said.

'Ah, weel . . .' The butler lolled backwards, his collar suddenly pinging upright around his neck. 'He's dead, y'ken. Had a cousin who works in the Meteorological Office.'

'Yes,' said Lestrade, leaning forward in an effort to force the man to focus. 'I ken. That's why I'm asking you about him. Would you like some black coffee?' Lestrade rummaged in the vast cupboards in Glamis' kitchen, ferreting among the rows of gleaming copper and brass.

Bennett raised his head. 'I never touch the stuff,' he slurred.

'Well, then,' Lestrade gave the idea up as a bad job, 'Dougal McAskill.'

'Er . . . no,' the butler corrected him, 'I'm Gordon Bennett. It's the dead man who's Dougal McAskill.'

The last three people Lestrade had spoken to, with the arguable exception of Alistair Sphagnum, had all been idiots. Still, it went with the job. 'What kind of man was he?'

'A pervert,' said Bennett.

'Oh?'

'Kept getting his twinkie out in front of the ladies.'

'His . . .?'

'Twinkie,' Bennett said solemnly.

'Didn't Lady Glarms object?' Lestrade asked.

'Och, man, she didn't know anything about it.' His eye filled with tears. 'They're a lovely, lovely family, y'ken, the Bowes-Lyons. He . . . he's a perfect gentleman. She . . . she's a perfect lady. Right on doon to Miss Elizabeth and little David . . . They're perfect little children.'

'And Dougal McAskill?'

'A perfect bastard. I'll tell you, if someone hadn't done away with the old degenerate, I'd have had to give him his marching orders. Dinna tell his lordship. He's so bloody nice, it'd kill him.'

'Who killed McAskill?'

Bennett leaned forward so that Lestrade reeled in the fumes. 'Have you seen the biceps on Mrs Comfrey?' he asked.

Lestrade had.

'Well, there y'are.'

'The cook did it?'

'Well, it wasna the bloody second under-butler, I can tell you.'

'When did you discover Mr McAskill's little peccadillo?'

'Och, noo, I speak as I find. I didna care for the man, but his peccadillo was a fair size. At least, that's what Morag told me.'

'Morag?'

'The upstairs maid. West wing.'

'Yes, we've met.'

'That's how I first heard about it. His lordship and I had interviewed for the post of second under-butler and McAskill looked quite promising. Mind you, that was with his trousers on.'

'And then?'

'It must have been three or four days after he started. I went into the scullery, looking for the boot polish . . .'

Lestrade was not surprised.

'. . . There was McAskill completely out of kilter.'

'Out of . . .?'

'Bollock-naked. At least, from the waist down.'

'Where was Morag?'

'At the far side of the room, whispering, "Help, help."'

'What did you do?'

'I had it out with McAskill.'

'Really?'

'I did. I told him straight. I said, "Look, you," I said. Never one to mince words, me.'

'What did he say?'

'Came out with some rubbish about his braces snapping simultaneously and wasn't it embarrassing. "Not as embarrassing as it's going to be," I told him. I said if he did it again, I'd tie a bloody knot in it.'

'His kilter?'

'His twinkie.'

'Ah, yes. But he did it again?'

'Och, aye. It was a little bit of a compulsive thing with him. None of the serving gels was safe. Mind you, for some of 'em, it was clearly the biggest thrill of their lives.'

'Not reason to kill a man, then?'

Bennett sighed deeply. 'As I said,' he said, 'Mrs Comfrey's your man. D'ye know, I once saw her wrestle a full-grown Tamworth pig to the ground?'

'Really?' Lestrade was impressed.

'Mind you, the thing was dead at the time.'

'Oh, well.' Lestrade's impressedness left him.

'Aye, but who d'ye think killed it in the first place?' Bennett leaned back, clearly resting his case.

'Single man, was he, McAskill?'

'Aye,' Bennett told him, 'like a bloody malt.'

'Tell me, did any of the men tackle him over the frequent appearance of his tackle?'

'Rumour has it that Morag's young man gave him a good hiding once or twice. Certainly, McAskill had a black eye or two a while back. Unlike mine, which I keep immaculately polished.'

'How did he explain those?' Lestrade asked.

'Usual thing,' said Bennett. 'Walked into a sheep dip.'

Lestrade nodded. Clearly, usual things north of the border were rather unusual in his native patch. 'Well, thank you, Mr Bennett. I'm sure, late as it is, that you have many duties to perform.'

'Aye, indeed,' sighed Bennett. 'What's that wee rhyme? "I slept and dreamt that life was duty, I woke and found that life was duty." Or something like that. Good-night to ye, Superintendent.'

'Good-night. Oh, by the way, I almost forgot. A message from Lady Glarms. Her Royal Highness has insisted on sleeping in the Red Room again tonight. I've moved McAskill. Will you see to it that the staff know?'

'Leave it wi' me.' Bennett tapped the side of his nose nearest the glass eye and walked into the door on his way out.

The Red Room looked surprisingly black at night. Actually, it was the early hours of the morning, but this far north, there was no sign of the dawn. Lestrade lay on the Duchess of Argyll's bed listening to the mice scampering in the wainscoting. Perhaps some silly old spinster would write stories about that one day, he pondered.

He had let himself in with the only key to the room and checked the body again before going to bed. He wiped the blood smears from the head of the cold corpse and what he saw there *perhaps* confirmed his theory. One blow only. Was the murderer disturbed? In more ways than one? The weapon seemed the same. But the number of blows far fewer. Was this attack less frenzied than the others? Perhaps the murderer was not in the mood? Or perhaps he'd got the wrong man?

Lestrade had read for a while, to give credence to the fact that the room was occupied, and for a while his candle burned on the bedside table. The only book in the room was one of Scottish lyric ballads: not the favourite reading of a flatfoot from Pimlico, but there was one stanza of one poem that echoed like a ghost in his mind:

> For I ha' dreamed a dreary dream,
> Beyond the Isle of Skye.
> I saw a dead man win a fight,
> An' I think that man was I.

He glanced down at the under-butler, soon to meet the under-taker, and patted him on the head, stiff with congealed brain. 'Well, dead man,' he said, 'are you going to win the fight for me?'

And now he sat, his back to the wall in the darkness. He'd drawn back the curtains around the bed and likewise those over the window. Even so, the dour Scots night permitted not one chink of light. The snow lay thick on the ground, coating grass and gravel, but up here near the roof with the well-drained leads below the latticed glass, the snow had gone and there was no reflection. So Lestrade waited in total darkness with only McAskill and the mice for company.

He must have dozed off and something must have woken him. He focused his eyes on the door, expecting a candle flame to glimmer beneath it. Nothing. He heard the knob turn and the lock click. His hand tightened on the brass knuckles in his jacket pocket. He'd never felt the castle so cold before and a rush of even colder air hit him. He heard the door yawn open to its fullest extent and heard a shuffling tread. Unless there was another surprise on the guest list, it couldn't be Edward VII. That certainly narrowed the field down. The tread was getting closer, and Lestrade was aware of a blackness, darker than the rest, between him and the door.

The matches and the candle lay to his right. If he rolled off the bed, away from McAskill, he might be able to reach them both before he hit the floor. But that would give his visitor time either to reach the door or to plunge something sharp into his vitals. Alternatively, more in keeping with the man's practice, time to half demolish his skull. On the other hand, he wasn't sure he could tackle whoever it was in such inky blackness.

And talking of that, how could whoever it was see without light? There again, Mrs Comfrey, if it were she, was a dab hand at pig-wrestling. A mere superintendent wouldn't cause her to break her stride.

Then he heard the breathing start. Heavier than the tread. It was now or never. Ever the man of action, Lestrade felt the curtains shiver aside. Whoever it was was practically standing on Dougal McAskill.

'Who's there?' he shouted.

The breathing stopped. There was a thud. Whoever it was had fallen over Dougal McAskill. Now was Lestrade's chance. He flung himself sideways, snatching matches and candle as he went down. Unfortunately he caught the bedside table as well and it raised an instant purple weal across his cheek. He crouched in the darkness, fumbling with the matches. His hand was shaking so much that he couldn't get the head on the sulphur pad. These lucifers were useless. He struck blindly, the flame suddenly lighting up the room, and there, for an instant in the panicking flare, he saw the largest man he had ever seen, his head black with a shaggy mane and beard, his eyes wild in the fire.

Both men stared at each other, horrified. Then the giant let out a diabolical moan and fled. The pain hit Lestrade's fingers simultaneously and he dropped the match. The inevitable creeping damp of the castle extinguished it immediately and Lestrade set to again to light the candle. By the time he'd reached the door, whoever it was had gone. The passage off the Clock Landing stood gloomy and bare and Lestrade was alone save for the ticking of the clock and the thud of his own heart, slowly descending from his mouth. He padded north and south as far as the corridor would take him. Nothing. No sound. No movement. It was as though Glamis had swallowed up his visitor whole.

He locked the door of the Red Room again and tiptoed through the sleeping castle. In the great, gloomy, ghastly place, only three people should have been awake – Lestrade, his visitor and, he hoped, Alistair Sphagnum. But as Lestrade rounded the corner by the Green Room, the doughty detective wasn't there. Lestrade cursed noiselessly. Suddenly, there was a screech of metal to his left and an icy cold caught Lestrade around the throat, yanking him backwards against the wall.

'I thought we agreed you'd be whistling,' he heard Sphagnum say and felt the cold, strangulating grip lessen. He pulled away and found himself staring at a suit of armour.

'I've always wanted to do this.' The Scotsman raised his visor. 'But you must admit, it's not every day you get the opportunity.'

'Well, it's certainly subtle,' fumed Lestrade.

'I thought I'd blend into the background. Quite fetching this, isn't it? Made for the Tilt about 1580, unless my history lets me down. Designed at Augsburg by Helmschmeidt the Younger for the Run of the Disappearing Shield.'

'I'm more interested in the disappearing giant,' whispered Lestrade.

'Oh?' Sphagnum's visor slammed shut on him. 'Damn.' He raised it again. 'What giant's that?'

'The one in the Red Room a moment ago.'

'The Red Room? So *that*'s where you were. Hoping the murderer would return to the scene of the crime eh? They don't really do that, do they?'

'This one did. He was the size of a house.'

'Was he?' Sphagnum began to unbuckle his gauntlets. 'What did he look like?'

'Well, I only saw him for a second. He had thick black hair and beard. Tall as a fir tree. But it was his eyes . . .'

'Terrifying?'

'Not terrifying, no.' Lestrade thought about it. 'Not to a man whose dad once spent all night in the Chamber of Horrors at Madame Tussaud's. More terrified, I'd say.'

'You know, of course,' Sphagnum said, 'who you've seen, don't you?'

Lestrade waited.

'Earl Beardie,' he whispered. 'The Devil Himself. You didn't play cards with him, did you?'

'No.' Lestrade told him. 'Sadly there wasn't time.'

'Well, at least your soul's safe.'

'Oh, good,' said Lestrade. 'Actually, it was more my head I was worried about. Anything untoward here?'

'No, no,' Sphagnum chirped. 'All clear. I must confess, I dozed off once.'

'Tsk, tsk.'

'That's not quite all. The clock striking three woke me up and I'm man enough to admit, I wet myself. It's at times like these that you really appreciate a Knight's Friend.'

'A what?'

'A little something I rigged up, remembering my days as an engineering student,' and Sphagnum reached behind him to handle a long piece of tubing that ran from his rather outrageous codpiece to a handy firebucket in the nearest alcove.

'Ingenious,' smiled Lestrade, 'but the bucket's full. Let's hope you have no mishaps on the second shift.'

'The what?'

Lestrade turned to the man dressed for the Run of the Disappearing Shield. 'That Lady in there is the auntie of our King, God Bless Him. And you, Sphagnum, are all that stands between her and a ghastly, brutal death at the hands of a madman. Good-night.'

11

Lestrade was in no mood to be messed about. For the second
time at least on this case, he had come within an ace of losing
his life. He wanted answers and he wanted them now.

Accordingly, he tapped on the door of Harry and Letitia
Bandicoot's room a little after dawn.

'Sholto?' It was a bleary-eyed Bandicoot who opened to him.
'What time is it?'

'It's a little after dawn. I need a favour. Lord Glarms has been
called to one of his cottages. Something agricultural. That's
probably just as well. I'm not sure he'd agree to my request
anyway.'

'What request?'

'Get yourself dressed, Letitia.' She had joined her husband in
the doorway. 'There is danger here. I wouldn't normally ask it
of you, but someone's life is at stake.'

'Whose?' Letitia was tying the cords of her dressing-gown,
shaking herself awake.

'Hot water, m'm? Sir?' Morag, still red-eyed and purple-
nosed from the events of the previous night, stood at Lestrade's
elbow with a steaming pitcher.

'No.' Lestrade spoke for them. 'But you can show Mr Bandicoot the way to the laundry room.'

'Laundry room?' Morag and Bandicoot chorused.

'You're looking for hankies, Harry; and towels and sheets
and pillow cases and fol-de-rols of all descriptions. Make sure
you aren't spotted by any of the Bowes-Lyons and get back here
on the double. Got it?'

'Er . . . I think so.' Bandicoot toyed with pinching himself.
Perhaps this was some mad nightmare as a result of having his

179

pyjama cord too tight. As he flopped off in his slippers in Morag's shuffling wake, he was confident he'd wake up in a minute.

'Letitia.' Lestrade bustled her inside and closed the door. 'I want you to find Lady Glarms. What time is breakfast?'

'Er . . . eight thirty, usually,' she told him. 'Sholto, what *is* this all about?'

'Before they built Scotland Yard,' he told her, 'before they set up the Criminal Investigation Department, before the Detective Branch, do you know how policemen solved crimes?'

'No,' Letitia confessed, sitting at the dressing-table and brushing her ringlets.

'They looked for needles in haystacks. And that's precisely what we're doing this morning. Except that I suspect that Lord Glarms wouldn't even let us start looking if he knew.'

'So it's a sort of hunt the thimble?' she asked, still wide-eyed.

'Exactly. Your part in it all is to keep Lady Glarms occupied. Now. Find some excuse. I'll leave that to you. Suggest you take breakfast together in her room. That way she won't notice the absence of us menfolk at the table.'

'You menfolk? How many of you are involved? And what are you involved in?'

He patted her hand. 'I told you, Letitia. We're looking for a thimble.'

She frowned at him, but he only smiled and was gone.

'No,' she said when the door had closed, 'that's what *I* told you.'

They met, according to Lestrade's instructions, back in the Bandicoots' room. Letitia had gone to waylay Nina Bowes-Lyon and Harry had struggled up five flights of stairs, some of them spiral, carrying an enormous wicker basket, overflowing with linen. All in all, very unobtrusive. Alistair Sphagnum had tin-openered himself out of the suit of armour and had returned it to its stand outside the Green Room. Having been awake in the thing all night, he was suffering from a certain amount of metal fatigue, but he shrugged it off. Robert McAlpine had been packing to leave and stood on Bandicoot's carpet like an ox in the furrow, as bewildered by Lestrade's cryptic message as the others.

'Let's get this straight, Lestrade,' he said. 'You want us a' to play hunt the bloody thimble? Man, it's clear to me that not all your stanchions are in the water.'

'Humour me,' said Lestrade. 'Mr McAlpine, you've been in the castle for a couple of weeks now. You know its layout. How many rooms are there?'

'Er . . . let me see. Including the Great Hall and excluding the usual offices . . . sixty-eight.'

'Wrong,' said Lestrade. 'There are at least sixty-nine. Possibly as many as seventy-three.'

'Sholto . . .' Harry, as Lestrade's old friend, thought it was time he had a word. After all, umpteen blows to the head were bound, in the end, to take their toll. And Lestrade *was* at a funny age.

'Trust me,' said Lestrade, 'I'm a policeman. Last night, as Mr Sphagnum will testify – should it come to that – I slept in the Red Room. Well, perhaps "slept" isn't quite the right word. Anyway, I had a visitor.'

'The murderer!' shouted Bandicoot.

'I don't think so, Harry, but I'm leaving no stone unturned. Which is precisely where Mr McAlpine comes in. I take it you've noticed no hidden passageways? No secret doors?'

'Come off it, Lestrade,' McAlpine tutted, 'that's the stuff of fiction. Have you any idea of the complexities of excavating load-bearing walls?'

'There *are* such things as Covenanters' passages,' Sphagnum assured the builder.

'Och, aye, but that's mostly between their buttocks. Take ma word for it. Only us Victorians could manage an engineering feat of that enormity.'

'All right,' said Lestrade, who simply didn't have the time to get involved in any more stress factors for one morning, 'is there one part of the castle that is particularly Victorian?'

'Aye,' McAlpine told him, 'the West Wing, by and large.'

'That's where we'll start. Gentlemen, help yourselves to as much linen as you can carry. Go into every room on the first floor, Harry. Mr McAlpine, you take the second. Sphagnum, the third. I'll take the roof. Tie something from your linen to a window frame.'

'I see,' said Sphagnum. 'You want us to count windows.'

'Exactly,' said Lestrade. 'A quicker way would be to ask Lord Glarms, but I don't think he'd tell us.'

'Man, what *is* this all aboot?' McAlpine was still confused.

'We're looking for Earl Beardie,' said Lestrade and, grabbing a pile of Bowes-Lyon bedlinen, was gone.

The Duchess of Argyll snored, rather like one of those Tamworths Mrs Comfrey kept going ten rounds with. Lestrade heard the cooks bustling with breakfast below as he slid quietly into the old girl's room and he waited in the darkness. A fragile sun was illuminating the frost on the window panes, but the Duchess's thick curtains kept it firmly out.

Lestrade locked the door behind him and pocketed the key. Ideally, he'd have liked to have left a sentinel outside the door and another two under the bed, but he didn't have the manpower. He couldn't expect servants to carry out these bizarre acts and anyway, any one of them might be planning that very morning to stave in the skull of the Duchess of Argyll.

Just as Lestrade reached the window and flicked aside the heavy curtains, the lady stirred in her sleep, her snore jarring and her blubbery lips smacking. She turned over. 'Is that you, Dukee?' she asked.

Lestrade stood riveted to the spot. He had been in ladies' boudoirs before, often uninvited, always in the course of his duty, but explanations were complicated and magistrates seldom understanding. Besides, what did the Duke of Argyll sound like? Could he fool the man's wife with an impersonation of a man he had never met?

'Dukee?' she called again.

If she woke up now, to see a man in a winding sheet, it might be the end of her. On the other hand, this woman was daughter to a Queen. It might be the end of him. He took a risk and squeaked.

She frowned, pursing her lips. Obviously, not very realisitic, Lestrade thought. 'Well, bugger off, then,' he heard the old lady mutter, 'I'm not sleeping with you any more. I told you that fourteen years ago,' and she rolled over to snore again.

Lestrade saw his chance. He flicked the window catch and hooked his leg over the sill, clambering out gingerly on to the leads. He closed the leaded pane behind him and stood there, the Angus countryside white and beautiful beyond the avenue of trees. He felt his feet slither on the ridges. It was like a skating rink up here and his hands were full of linen. Somehow, he made it to the next window and peered in. Empty. He wrapped his fist in a coverlet and smashed the glass as noiselessly as he could; then swung out the window and catapulted himself less than gracefully on to the bed. Before he left the room, he tied a hanky to the window catch and began working his way along the corridor.

It had been a good time to choose. Many rooms in this part of the castle were empty anyway, the furniture covered in ghostly druggets, and the smaller servants' rooms were vacated because their occupants were elsewhere, beginning the day. In minutes, Lestrade had exhausted his supply of material and bolted down the stairs, nearly colliding with Alistair Sphagnum on the way.

'All done?' he asked.

'I think so,' said Sphagnum. 'You?'

'Let's find out.'

Robert McAlpine was the last to reach the ground and the four of them ran back, racing and bobbing through the oriental garden to get a better view. It was an odd sight that early morning: the entire West Wing of Glamis Castle with white material flapping in the breeze from every window.

Every window?

'No, by God!' Sphagnum saw it first. 'There, Lestrade. Beyond that gargoyle that looks like Arthur Balfour.'

The Scottish detective was right. It did look like Arthur Balfour; but more to the point, to the right of it stood two windows, small and barred, that carried no cloths at all.

'What the deuce is going on?' an irate voice called from the first floor. It was Lord Glamis, thrusting his head out of a window and shaking a tea towel at them.

'Which floor is that? Sphagnum, it's yours. The third. Come on,' shouted Lestrade.

Even as they dashed for the door, Lord Glamis's army of servants were scurrying in and out of rooms, ripping sheets and untying knots. Soon, only a few feeble flaps remained.

'Damn,' growled Sphagnum, leaning out of windows as he tried room after room. 'Bloody Glamis has had them all taken down. I've completely lost ma bearings.'

'Look for Arthur Balfour,' Lestrade reminded him.

'Dammit!' cursed Sphagnum. 'Glamis must have bought a job lot. They all look like Arthur Balfour on this floor.'

The four of them were just about to try again along the corridor, when they came face to face with Lord and Lady Glamis. Everybody stopped running around.

'Harry,' said Nina, 'Mr Lestrade, Mr Sphagnum, Mr McAlpine. What is the meaning of this?'

Silence.

'Well, George?' Glamis said to Harry. His moustache bristled. Mild man he was; loving father to his children; dutiful husband to his wife; perfect Lord Lieutenant to the County; but when that moustache bristled . . .

'I think explanations are in order,' said Lestrade.

'Indeed, they are,' growled Glamis.

'No, I meant from you, my lord.'

'Eh?' Bowes-Lyon turned a shade more carmine.

'Now, Claudie.' Lady Glamis held his arm. 'Remember your blood pressure.'

A figure in white hurtled round the corner. 'I'm sorry, Sholto, she got away . . . oh.'

'Thank you, Letitia,' Lestrade smiled. 'You did your best.'

'Letitia,' said Lady Glamis, more than a little crestfallen, 'how could you?'

'If you must blame someone, Lady Glarms,' Lestrade said, 'blame me. This whole thing was my idea.'

'Charades, Lestrade?' Glamis demanded to know.

'You tell me, sir.' The superintendent stood his ground. 'There is a murderer hiding somewhere in this castle. Somewhere on this floor, in fact. I think you owe it to us to tell us where.'

'Are you suggesting . . .?' Glamis was apoplectic.

'Claudie.' Lady Glamis patted his shoulder. She smiled at him. 'Perhaps you should.'

Glamis looked at her, the loving eyes, the knowing smile. He patted her hand, then passed her an antimacassar. 'Very well, dearest,' he said and turned to face them. 'But only you, Lestrade.' The smile had vanished. 'The rest of you must go downstairs. Mrs Comfrey has excelled herself in terms of breakfast. Lestrade and I will join you later.'

They doubled back on themselves, the Master of Glamis and the superintendent. Then they doubled back again. At the third twist of the stairs, Lestrade was utterly lost.

'I want you to be very quiet from now on, Lestrade,' Bowes-Lyon whispered, 'and no sudden moves.'

'Where are we going?'

'You'll see,' and he stepped on the bottom step of a sharply angled spiral. 'I want your word, Lestrade, that what you see here today will go no further.'

'I can't promise that, my lord,' the superintendent said. 'This is a murder enquiry.'

Glamis smiled a sad smile. 'No,' he said, '*this* isn't.' He pressed a stone above Lestrade's head and the wall swung away. 'Careful now. Mind your footing.'

He led the Yard man through a gloomy labyrinth of passages, hung with faded tapestries and little-known portraits of the late Queen. After a while, the paintings stopped and the rough-hewn stone was garlanded with children's pictures. There was a cat, a horse, a thing with purple ears.

'Elizabeth's work?' Lestrade asked.

Glamis shook his head. 'No,' he said. 'Some of these are more than forty years old. This one', he pointed to a line of trees in red and yellow, 'was executed only last week.'

Glamis fumbled in his pocket and produced a single, brass key. He brushed aside a dusty curtain and slipped the key into the lock of the heavy door that lay behind it.

'John?' he called softly. 'John? It's Claudie.'

Lestrade froze in the doorway, his fist closing instinctively around the brass knuckles. Out of the gloom beyond the door emerged the huge, shaggy-haired thing he had encountered briefly by the light of a match some hours ago. The room's occupant sensed Lestrade's unease, perhaps recognized him too from the same encounter, and drew back, the eyes wild and rolling.

'No, John,' said Glamis raising his hand slowly. 'This is Mr Lestrade. He's a friend. He's not going to hurt you.' He took Lestrade's hand in his own and led him into the room. It was dimly lit with one or two candles and the only window was high and small with bars across it.

'This is a cell,' Lestrade murmured.

'No,' said Glamis softly, 'it's a sanctuary. John . . .' He sat down carefully on an old sofa. 'Show Mr Lestrade your latest painting.'

John was standing with his back to the wall. The shirt he was wearing was stained with paint and the morning egg.

'I'd like to see it, John,' Lestrade said.

Slowly, like a figure in a dream, the giant lumbered across the little room. He picked up from the clutter on the bedside table a crumpled piece of paper and showed it shyly to Lestrade. It was not the usual postcard scenes that Lestrade had seen along the passgeway outside. It showed a Highlander in a kilt, swinging a broadsword in two hands. But there was no battle-field, no distant line of blue, remembered hills. Instead, there was a bed and a little man crouching, as though at his prayers.

'That's very good, John,' said Lestrade. 'May I borrow this? There's someone I want to show it to. I promise you can have it back.'

'He doesn't speak, Lestrade,' Glamis said. 'And he can't see too well, either. That's why he has soft lights. Anything brighter than a candle hurts his eyes. John, can Mr Lestrade borrow your painting?'

The giant blinked, kneeling as he was now on the floor in front of them. He looked at Glamis. He looked at Lestrade, Something like a smile flitted across his pale, sad face. He gave the paper to Lestrade.

'Thank you,' said the superintendent and rose to go.

The giant's hand caught him on the sleeve, a weak, feeble grip, and Lestrade sat back again. From his pocket, John produced a grubby set of playing cards, four in all.

'He wants you to play, Lestrade,' Glamis told him. 'Find the queen.'

The giant spread out the four cards on the carpet – the ace, the king, the jack, the queen. He was grunting with excitement. Then he turned them over, his huge hands like shovels. He moved them about, changing the order. Then he looked up at Lestrade.

'That one.' Lestrade pointed to the left-hand card. John turned it over – the jack. He grinned. He moved the cards again. Again, Lestrade chose. The king. A third time. And a fourth. And each time, Lestrade missed his quarry. Then the giant flicked over a card and the guttural 'Mama' rose in a harsh whisper from somewhere deep in his throat.

'Yes, John.' Glamis patted the tousled head. 'Mama,' and he and Lestrade saw themselves out.

They walked without speaking through the gloomy passage, back past the paintings and the portraits to the spiral stair.

'Who is he, my lord?' Lestrade asked.

'We just call him John,' said Glamis, 'and he told you who he is. He called the queen Mama.'

Lestrade stopped on the stone step. 'You mean . . .?'

Glamis nodded. 'That's Earl Beardie,' he said. 'The monster that stalks Glamis Castle. Oh, this old place is full of legends, Lestrade. Except that Beardie is real enough. He has the run of those four rooms, but he's not locked in. He can reach various parts of the house, but he never goes outside. Outside is too big. Space frightens him. His mother was Victoria, Queen-Empress, by the Grace of God. His father was a drunken old ghillie called John Brown.'

'My God.' Lestrade sank down on the step. Glamis joined him. 'Who else knows of this?'

'Pat, my eldest. Nina has a shrewd idea, but we never talk of it. No one else, Lestrade. Pat and I take it in turns to sit with John, bath him, see to his comforts.'

'How . . .?'

'How did it all happen? Well, you're nudging fifty, surely. I assume you have the rudiments of the birds and the bees.'

'I think I'm getting the hang of it,' Lestrade was big enough to admit.

'Well, it was all a little before my time, of course, as Master of Glamis, I mean. My father was Master then. After the death of Prince Albert, the old Queen went into mourning. Hardly stirred beyond the portals of Windsor, Osborne and Balmoral. But there were rumours of all kinds . . .'

'So I believe,' nodded Lestrade.

'Rumours that she and Brown had gone through a form of marriage.'

'Did they?'

'Who knows? All I know is that "Mrs John Brown" had a son, christened John after his father. He was born about 1863, I think. Unfortunately, there were complications. The world thought that the old girl was not prominent at her eldest son's wedding because of her grief over Albert. In fact, she was still recovering after a very difficult birth. I don't fully understand these women's matters, Lestrade – what man does? She was too old, I think, or Brown too whisky-soaked. Anyway, the boy was not normal. He was totally blind until he was three and has only spoken that one word – Mama – all his life. The problem was that the scandal, of course, must not be allowed to get out. They were Republican days, Lestrade, the 'sixties. There were demands for the Queen's abdication as it was. Imagine the stink if little John were common knowledge.'

'Hmm.' Lestrade nodded.

'Well, Balmoral was too small and too public. The Queen-Empress took my father into her confidence and asked him to have the child here. At first, Papa tried to make the boy part of the family, but it was hopeless. He was terrified of everyone and everything. In the end, he set aside the rooms you've just seen for him. I like to think he's happy.'

'And occasionally he wanders?'

'Oh, yes. Especially at night. As I say, the odd guest has woken up with the ab dabs, but you've seen him, Lestrade. I assure you he's more afraid of them than they are of him. You see, he has the mind of a child. To him, Glamis is some sort of giant doll's house. He plays with his paints and the one game of cards he knows. And I dare say he'll go on doing that until the day he dies.'

Lestrade nodded again.

'You can't think *he* murdered Alex Hastie and Dougal McAskill?' Glamis said.

Lestrade looked at the tense face, the pleading eyes. 'No,' he said. 'For all his size, Earl Beardie is as weak as a kitten. I sensed that when he grabbed my sleeve. No,' he sighed, 'I shall have to look elsewhere for my killer.'

Glamis visibly wilted with relief. 'Lestrade,' he said, 'you must understand my motives for not revealing John to you before. Outside this castle, he does not – and cannot – exist. Not even the late Queen's legitimate children know of him. It is vital we keep it that way.'

'Yes,' said Lestrade, 'it is.'

Glamis got to his feet. 'Why did you want that painting?' he asked. 'I must admit, it's rather a departure from John's usual stuff.'

'This?' Lestrade stood up too. 'Ah well, Lord Glamis, this is better than a photograph.'

'It is?' Glamis squinted at it sideways. 'Well, that's nice, Lestrade,' he smiled. 'That's very nice. Breakfast?'

As they walked past the Green Room, there was a thunderous hammering on the door.

'Ah,' said Lestrade, 'do you have a stout crowbar? I think you'll find that the Duchess of Argyll is locked in, rather tetchy, and I've gone and dropped the key to her room. And would you mind, you and Lady Glarms, staying close to her today? I fear her life may be in danger.'

Despite the cold and the danger to HRH, Lestrade braved the elements a little before luncheon and wandered by yon bonnie banks and by yon bonnie braes to the home of Ned 'The Laird' Chapman. There were some questions to which he needed vital answers, for time was short. And by the time he'd got those answers the Hebridean night had rolled in on dark snow-filled clouds and he trudged back.

In all the commotion, Lord and Lady Glamis had neglected to tell the superintendent that that was the night of the Annual Ghillies' Ball. By the time Lestrade dragged himself, snow-capped, into the hall, the festivities were well under way and the band was in full quadrille.

Lestrade looked a trifle dowdy in his wet Donegal as the pride of Angus rushed past him in a flurry of tartan and diamond-cut buttons and flashing cairngorms. Even Harry and Letitia had borrowed a local tartan and were whirling around the ballroom like things possessed, shrieking and whooping as they went. As ever, the Old Etonian and his lady looked every inch the part.

'Come on, Sholto.' Letitia grabbed Lestrade's hands. 'Join the reel.'

And before he could say 'Strathspey', he found his head whirling along with his two left feet and the Donegal flying out in lieu of a plaid. Once or twice, he collided with Alistair Sphagnum, wearing a perfectly obnoxious tartan which Lestrade assumed was probably dress Sphagnum and somebody else's doublet.

'You're in the wrong set, Lestrade,' the Scottish detective shouted above the whooping and the appalling skirl of the pipes.

'That's the story of my life, Sphagnum,' the English detective told him. 'I'm all right on the Roger de Coverley. You know where you are with the Roger de Coverley.'

'Wait till we get on to the salmon dance,' Sphagnum called the next time around. 'That'll have you leaping.'

And the tide of battle carried them apart again, Lestrade desperately trying to scan the faces of the wallflowers around the perimeter of the vast room. He saw Lord Glamis nodding time, elbow to elbow with the Duchess of Argyll who was reluctantly wearing her husband's tartan and trying to pick up the beat with her good ear. He saw the ghillies of the estate and their guests from the north, Laidlaws elder and younger, turning crimson in the face with the effort of forcing noise out of their goat-skin bags. He saw little Elizabeth, all curls and bright eyes, twirling round with little David, trying to make him swirl with the sets. Then Lestrade collided again. 'Sholto,' said Bandicoot, 'are you *supposed* to be dancing with me?'

'Oh, all right,' sighed Lestrade, 'if you think people will talk,' and he pranced away to be buffeted by a large lady whose frontage resembled the Grampians.

It was a grateful superintendent who spun for the last time as the piping came to an end and found himself bowing ceremoniously to a pillar. He consoled himself with the observation that at least the damned thing didn't have any feet he could fall over.

He mingled with the ghillies and helped himself to a glass of punch. Then, as unobtrusively as possible, he crept silently away . . .

'Who is it?' a voice called from behind him.

Lestrade turned to the figure silhouetted in the doorway. 'It's you, Mr Ramsay,' he said.

'Mr Lestrade? What are you doing, pray, in my rooms?'

'Looking for this.' Lestrade held up an envelope whose careful seal had been broken. The seal of the MacKinnons. 'Fancy all that being in every drop of The Drink That Satisfies.'

Ramsay closed the door behind him. The place was ransacked, in an efficient, Scotland Yardly sort of way, and there were clothes and belongings everywhere.

'How did you know?' he asked.

'I didn't,' said Lestrade, 'until this afternoon, that is. But I'm sure you don't want a lecture on logic at this hour of the night.'

'I'd like to know where I went wrong,' said Ramsay, 'so that I don't make the same mistake again.'

Lestrade smiled. 'But there's no need is there?' he said, holding up the envelope again. 'You've got what you want. The secret formula of The Drink That Satisfies. The legacy of Bonnie Prince Charlie. Tell me, if I hadn't come along to your room tonight, what were you going to call the new drink?'

'Drambuie,' said Ramsay. 'A shortened form of the Gaelic, so that even you Sassenachs could pronounce it. Now, for my own peace of mind, how did you get on to me?'

'Basically, your plan was flawed.' Lestrade sat himself down on the sofa. 'Take my advice – as one who's seen this before. If you're going to hide one victim among many, make sure that that one victim is the same as the others – the same sex, the same social class. That way, you blur the evidence, fudge the lines of distinction.'

'And who was my one victim?' Ramsay had not moved.

'Dick MacKinnon, of course. There were, before you – and now, me – only two men in the world who knew the secret ingredient of your Drambuie: the MacKinnon and his eldest son. Tell me, did you toy with killing the old man too?'

'There didn't seem much point. He never leaves Skye these

days and has an army of his revolting Highland family all round him wherever he goes.'

'But Dick was easier? More mobile?'

Ramsay nodded.

'But you wanted to disguise him, didn't you? To throw the local police off the scent. Well, that might have worked with McNab. He was stupid or indifferent enough to call your first murder – Amy Macpherson – suicide. What you didn't bargain for was the Duke of Connaught calling in, albeit unofficially, the Yard. Hence that clumsy mess with Acheson.'

'Aye,' Ramsay said, stony-faced. 'How was I to know the superstitious old salesman would change rooms? I called at the hotel and found the room you were in – Twelve. I knew from Prince Arthur that you were on your way. The normal route would be via Edinburgh so I could time your arrival fairly closely. I only had to try three hotels before I found you.'

'When did you realize you had the wrong man?'

'As soon as I'd done it,' Ramsay said. 'Unless there were things about a Scotland Yard detective it's best not to know, I'd just caved in the skull of a man travelling in ladies' underwear.'

'So you set fire to the place?'

'I had to. I couldn't risk you finding that Acheson and Amy Macpherson had died by the same hand. Whereas an accidental fire would look harmless enough.'

'But once embarked on that course . . .'

'I had to finish it. Hastie was a drunk. As a boy, I used to visit Glamis often. No one found it surprising that I was here from time to time. I'm always welcome here, in the servants' quarters and above stairs on account of my legendary finnan haddies.'

Lestrade raised an eyebrow. He glanced his man up and down and could not see what all the fuss was about.

'I merely told the groom whom I "happened" to meet at the stables that there was a wee bottle he would enjoy in the cellar. Then I waited for him and smashed his cranium. All very simple really.'

'Indeed,' nodded Lestrade, rising from the sofa. 'Then you took on MacKinnon. That's what I found out this afternoon. I asked Mr Chapman one question – where was he when he wrote to MacKinnon asking him down from Skye? He told me he was visiting Balmoral at the time. He told me more. He told me he was talking over his idea of unleashing wolves into the wild and that someone thought Skye would be an ideal place; and the person whose permission must be sought was Richard MacKinnon. The person who suggested that idea was the Steward of the Royal Household. Now isn't that a coincidence?'

'You don't know what it's like!' Ramsay's composure snapped at last. 'Skivvying day and night. "Yes, ma'am," "No, ma'am," "Three bags full, ma'am." Man, Balmoral's a living grave. Well, I wanted no more of it. With the contents of that envelope, Lestrade, I can retire anywhere I like in the world.'

'Indeed,' said Lestrade. 'How about the lime in the graveyard at Barlinnie? It has, I gather, an interesting south-facing aspect. Clever though, feigning your own near-death. But not clever enough. It was too dissimilar. Oh, I'll grant you for a while I had my money on Sir Harry Maclean. But you'd have done better bashing your head just a teensy bit, to make that one look convincing.'

'That was nothing to do with me, Lestrade,' Ramsay said. 'Someone really did try to kill me.'

'Come now, Mr Ramsay. There's no point in pandering to your own vanity at this late stage.'

'What happens now?' Ramsay asked.

'The formalities,' sighed Lestrade. 'Allan Ramsay,' he placed a hand on the steward's shoulder, 'I arrest you for . . .' but his words were cut off as Ramsay tapped his arm aside and brought a meat cleaver down with crippling force blunt side down on Lestrade's head. The Yard man staggered back to the sofa, his hairline streaming with blood. For all his mild manners and perfect courtesy, Allan Ramsay had an arm of iron. He came in for the attack again, but Lestrade was faster. This was no dim-witted servant girl, no drunken groom in the dark, no unsuspecting landowner out for an early morning stroll. The superintendent rolled sideways and thrust upwards, burying the switchblade up to its hilt in Ramsay's chest. The steward's eyes crossed and blood began to trickle from the corner of his gaping mouth.

Lestrade wrenched out the knife and both men lay still.

*

The superintendent staggered back along the landing, his head trickling blood, his hands shaking. It was over. Wasn't it? But why didn't Ramsay own up to the clumsy attempt with Maclean's castrator? He'd confessed to everything else. Lestrade stopped by the curtain with the arms of Bowes-Lyon embroidered on it, steadying himself against the waves of nausea he felt rushing over him. He toyed with sitting down for a moment and putting his head between his knees. But that would only make him bleed more and besides, he might never get up. If only Ramsay hadn't panicked, hadn't made his move when he did, he'd know more about Dougal McAskill. Why risk another chance of being caught by killing *another* false victim? Even in Lestrade's scrambled mind, it didn't make sense.

Somehow he found his room and plunged his head into the bowl of icy water there. He held a succession of towels to the wound until the bleeding stopped and lay down, fighting to stay conscious. He recited his tables, but the going got rough after five eights and he reverted to the old Scottish insomniac's answer of counting sheep. Contrary to the legend, that actually concentrates the mind rather than induces sleep. Particularly as in his nightmarish state, half real, half hell, all the sheep were wolves in sheep's clothing. He saw again the cold, yellow eyes of Romulus and the hideous toothless grin; he felt the hot, sweet breath. Then, in his delirium, he saw again the walking ghosts of Glamis – the little Black Boy sitting for ever outside the sitting-room; the tongueless woman screaming in silence as she chased him across the snow-laced lawns; he heard the scream of the *Bean-Nighe* and saw her washing the bloody linen at the burn, her eyes red with tears or blood. And he saw Earl Beardie, flashing the Devil's pack under a waning moon, and the ten-foot woman of the Stinking-Closs, laughing as time and time again Lestrade fell prey to Ramsay's steel blade . . .

He shook himself awake. The candle he had lit had dropped a little, but he could still hear the pipes and the whooping from the Hall, so the ball was at its height. He checked as well as he could in the mirror that there was no blood still visible. He didn't want to alarm the revellers. Then he slowly and carefully went downstairs to join them.

'Lestrade!' Sphagnum hailed him. 'Man, you've missed your chance with the sword dance just now.'

Wee Fingal held centre stage. He may not have been much of a hand with the broadsword, but he could certainly prance around one. Or two in fact. The blades were crossed on the floor between his feet as he pirouetted and jetéd like a Highland Nijinski to the admiring whoops and whistles of the watchers. The piping stopped and a rapturous applause struck up.

'Now, Sholto.' Letitia took his hands again. 'It's no good skulking off like that, you know. There's no escape.'

He raised an eyebrow in protest.

'No,' she said, 'I won't hear of it. I'm determined to dance with the second-handsomest man in the room.'

'That's kind of you,' beamed Sphagnum, as he stepped past between two pretty lasses, 'but a bit unfair on your husband, I feel.'

'I *meant* my husband,' Letitia told him. 'Don't worry, Sholto. This is a slow one. "Will ye no come back again?"'

'What's that?' Lestrade asked.

'A waltz, I think,' Letitia told him.

'Nay, laddie,' Sphagnum intervened. 'It's an ould Jacobite lament, addressed to the Bonnie Prince himself. When he left us after the '45, that's the question the clansmen asked – "Will ye no come back again?"'

'My God. That's it,' murmured Lestrade.

'Aye,' smiled Sphagnum. 'It brings a lump to the throat, doesn't it?'

'Or to the head,' said Lestrade. 'Letitia, I can't think of another lady in the world I'd like to dance with more than you, but there's a murderer in this room and I don't have time. Get over to Lady Glarms. I want you both to get Her Royal Highness back to the Green Room and keep her there. Sphagnum, you go with them. This time I want you on the inside of the room. No more nonsense with suits of armour.'

'Right you are,' said the Scotsman. 'Where will you be?'

'The same place I was last night – and for the same reason. I was trusting to instinct then, but now I know.'

'You do?' Sphagnum shook himself free of the lasses. 'Who is it, Lestrade? The murderer?'

'Of Amy Macpherson, Mr Acheson, Alex Hastie and Richard MacKinnon?'

'Of course.'

195

'Allan Ramsay.'

'By God. I'll get him.'

'It's too late.' Lestrade gripped his sleeve. 'You'll find Allan Ramsay with a knife wound in his heart, slumped across his sofa.'

Letitia gasped.

'He's not going anywhere,' Lestrade assured them.

'Then why . . .?' Sphagnum frowned. 'Wait a minute,' he said. 'Who killed Dougal McAskill?'

'"I, said the Sparrow,"' quoted Lestrade. 'Now, cut along, children. The grown-ups are busy.'

Lestrade crossed to the square bulk of Harry Bandicoot as the slow dance began. He tapped him on the shoulder.

'No, no.' Bandicoot coloured up. 'This isn't a policeman's excuse me.'

'I'm afraid it is,' Lestrade said and removed Bandicoot from his partner. 'Harry, something's afoot and this isn't a game. Do you know where the Red Room is?'

'I think so,' Bandicoot nodded. 'Off the Clock Landing, isn't it?'

'Right. Station yourself nearby. There's a little alcove to the right of the door.'

Bandicoot knew Lestrade of old. When the superintendent gave an order, even to civilians, you didn't stop to ask the reason why. 'Who am I expecting, Sholto?' he asked.

'I don't know, exactly,' Lestrade said, 'but watch yourself, Harry Bandicoot. I don't think our visitor is familiar with Eton boxing rules. Wait till he's in the room, then sneak up behind him . . . Not against your principles, I hope?'

'Sounds like Eton boxing rules to me, Sholto.' Bandicoot grinned and he was gone.

Lestrade saw the bewildered old Duchess of Argyll being shepherded away by Letitia and Lady Glamis. He noticed Letitia whispering animatedly to her and realized how pointless that was. She was walking on her earless side.

The superintendent crossed to Lord Glamis who was partaking of his umpteenth glass of punch. He whispered something in his ear, spoiled for choice as to which one to use, and sidled out of the Hall. As he reached the stairs, he heard Glamis stop the dancing and make the announcement he had asked him to make.

'Ladies and gentlemen, I'm sorry to break up the fun, but Her Royal Highness is leaving us tonight. She has been called away urgently. Hubris, McTavish, the horses if you please.'

Lestrade lay again in the dark of the Red Room. He had passed the tartan socks of Harry Bandicoot and flicked them with his toe so that the Old Etonian pressed himself further back into the shadows. This time there was no dead man for company. Only the mice. He lay with his thoughts and his aching head, watching, listening, hardly daring to breathe. Then, as the clock outside the room clanged twelve, he saw a glimmer of light under the door. A flickering candle. The door clicked once. Twice. Then swung open.

'Right on cue, Mr Laidlaw,' Lestrade said.

The huge Highlander froze in the doorway. Lestrade lit his own candle and sat upright on the bed, his head to the wall.

'I see,' Laidlaw said, closing the door behind him, fumbling with his left hand behind his back.

'There's no point in trying to lock it,' Lestrade held up the key. 'Here's one I had cut earlier.'

'A very clever plot,' said Laidlaw, 'for a Sassenach. So the old trout isn't leaving after a'?'

'Not tonight,' said Lestrade. 'And not from this room.'

'Where is she?' the Highlander snapped.

'Wherever she is, she's safe,' Lestrade told him, 'with three people with her. Tell me, what have you got against the old girl? Oh, she's a bit mutt, I'll grant you. But murder, Mr Laidlaw? That seems a little extreme.'

'Man, what would you know? It's a sacred trust I have. Me and mine.'

'Ah, yes,' Lestrade nodded. 'Wee Fingal.'

'Well,' Laidlaw sighed, 'I'm doing ma best to train him up, but he has no heart for it, I'm ashamed to say. Tell me, how did you know it was me?'

'I didn't,' said Lestrade. 'What threw me was that there were *two* murderers at Balmoral, not one. Allan Ramsay killed for gain, but you weren't part of that, were you?'

'What doth it profit a man if he gain the whole world and lose his soul?'

'Quite,' Lestrade nodded. 'Unfortunately, Dougal McAskill got in the way, didn't he?'

'The stupid lecherous ould bastard!' Laidlaw spat at the wainscoting, hitting a running mouse amidships. 'I knew the Duchess of Argyll retired early and I thought I saw her at prayer in the darkness. It was only when I'd clouted him I realized he had two ears and was a'together the wrong body.'

'What did you use on him?'

'My broadsword.' Laidlaw tapped the tasselled hilt on his hip. 'That's not *quite* what Allan Ramsay used, but it'd do.'

'Yes,' said Lestrade. 'How did you work things with Ramsay?'

'That pound-worshipping bastard!' Laidlaw spat again, his eyebrow rising in profound emotion. 'He was on tae me, but I was on tae him. When he killed poor wee Amy, man, I a'most cut him in half. Then I realized, wait a minute, this *could* work to ma advantage. We had a wee chat, what you poncey Southerners call a frank exchange of views. I'd keep quiet about his murders, show him how to disembowel Richard MacKinnon to make it look like a wolf attack, generally cover his tracks. He of course thought I was being a thoroughly guid Scotch egg or maybe I wanted a cut of his bloody Drink That Satisfies. In fact, I was waiting ma chance tae hit the Duchess and I could do it by using *his* methods – the guid old repeated blows to the head. I knew once you were called in you'd get him. And I'd get awa' scot-free, as it were, while he faced his Maker at the end of a length of rope.'

'What was the point of Maclean's camel castrator?'

'Just tae muddy the waters a bit,' said Laidlaw, placing the candle down on the sideboard. 'And to put the frighteners on wee Ramsay. It worked a treat. Confused you and had him shittin' hissen.'

'Just tell me one more thing,' Lestrade said. 'Why?'

'Och, you're a clever wee bastard, Lestrade,' Laidlaw said. 'You tell me.'

'All right,' said Lestrade. 'The Jacobite Cause. Guid ould Bonnie Prince Charlie. Am I getting warm?'

'Go on.'

'If my Scottish history serves me right, the Young Pretender left these shores in 1746, never to return.'

'"Yet ere the sword cool in the sheath,"' recited Laidlaw, '"Charlie will come agin."'

'Exactly,' said Lestrade, 'with a little help from his friends. People like you, Mr Laidlaw.'

'"Ye Jacobites by name",' Laidlaw said.

'You're a living link with the '45, Laidlaw. You gave yourself away twice. The second time was that touching little toast of Wee Fingal's – or rather your over-reaction to it – "The little gentleman in velvet".'

'Och aye?'

'Aye. I went over to Mr Chapman's earlier today. Really there was something I had to confirm about Allan Ramsay, but in passing I asked him about the little gentleman, because it had been nagging at the back of my mind. It's a mole, he said. An old Jacobite toast to the mole that killed Dutch William, the boring old fart from the flat country who had defeated James II. His horse stepped into a mole-hill in 1701 and the king broke his neck.'

'Glorious day!' shouted Laidlaw.

'Yes, indeed. The first time you gave yourself away was denouncing Wee Fingal to me. You told me he was always writing to pen pals in France. Now that's a pretty peculiar thing to do, Mr Laidlaw, even for a man who is not quite as other ghillies. Those pen pals are the descendants, are they not, of the exiled Stuarts? The heirs of Bonnie Prince Charlie?'

'Right enough,' Lestrade nodded. 'We're pledged, body and soul, to bring back the rightful kings of Scotland and England. And we won't rest until it's done.'

'We? You mean you and Fingal?'

'Fingal be buggered. I won't have you fingering Fingal. He's not worth the rope to hang him wi'. You don't imagine this is all there is to it?'

'Er . . .'

'Who d'ye think arranged for the horses to bolt all those years ago when the Duchess of Argyll was dragged from her sleigh? We only got her ear then. Now is the time to get the rest of her heed.'

'I see.'

'No you don't. Man, this thing is bigger than both of us. I won't bore you with the history lesson – George II getting his at stool in his closet; his noxious wee son Fred bein' killed by a cricket ball – a neat bit of bodyline bowling by a Jacobite. Most of the doctors workin' on mad old George III were slippin' him slow poison over the years. Let's just concentrate on the recent past. O' course, that bastard John Brown was the weak link. Och, he despatched Prince Albert all right, but then the stupid ould soak fell in love wi' Victoria. We had to get other people to try her. Unfortunately, one of them was mad, two o' them had empty guns and another was only four feet tall. He had to stand on tiptoe to look the old girl in the face. Only one o' them was a Scotsman.'

'Roderick Maclean.'

'That's right, but bloody Brown was always there, savin' her life.'

'Not on that occasion,' Lestrade said. 'It was actually the man outside the door, Harry Bandicoot. He saved the Queen's life then. Just as he's about to save mine now.' He raised his voice so that Harry could hear his cue.

'Och aye.' Laidlaw didn't move. 'That's when he wakes up.'

'What?' Lestrade started.

'Don't move, Lestrade,' Laidlaw warned him. 'Even in this light, I can snap your neck without really trying. Don't worry. Wee Bandicoot will just have a headache come the morning. Sadly, you won't be there tae see it. Did you think I'd be telling you all this if I thought there was the remotest chance you'd be telling somebody else?'

'Well then,' Lestrade leaned back, 'humour me a while longer. It didn't end with Albert.'

'Och, no. Four of her bastard children went the way of all usurpers. Not to mention that degenerate the Duke of Clarence.'

'The heir presumptive?'

'Aye.'

'What of the King?'

'Bertie? Well, we've had a few goes at him already. But I haven't tried ma hand yet. I'll probably get to him by about 1910.'

'It's a slow business, then,' Lestrade commented.

'Och aye. We've bided our time for a hundred and fifty years. Each generation of us longs for the time when we can wear the Stuart tartan again and the lion rampant flies from Buckingham Palace and the Stone of Scone is back in Scotland. But we're prepared to wait. Slow and sure, but we'll get it right.'

'How many of you are there?'

'Enough,' said Laidlaw. 'Now, I've got a wee date wi' the Duchess of Argyll. I really cannot stay any longer.'

'There's one problem.' Lestrade swallowed as Laidlaw deliberately drew his sword.

'Och, there are lots,' said the Highlander, 'but none that are insurmountable. Cover your face, Lestrade. I'll make this as quick and as clean as I can. That's 'cause I'm a reasonable human bein'. And think yoursel' lucky – many Scotsmen haven't forgiven you bastard English for Wully Wallace yet.'

'The problem', said Lestrade quickly, 'is that you can't pin my death or the Duchess of Argyll's on Allan Ramsay. Allan Ramsay is dead.'

It was the flicker Lestrade hoped for. The merest flash of a second when Laidlaw was caught off guard. The blade was up, but it wavered in mid-air. Long enough for Lestrade's left boot to lash out and catch the Highlander in whatever he wore under his kilt. Lestrade rolled off the bed as the broadsword flashed and crunched into the headboard and pillow, sending a cloud of feathers into the air. Lestrade kicked over both candles and the room lay in total darkness.

'Shame it's so dark,' whispered Lestrade.

There was a whistle and a thud as Laidlaw's blade scythed and missed him again.

'Because I have here in my pocket a nice little picture of you.'

'Stand still, Lestrade,' Laidlaw growled. 'Fight like a man.'

'It's a charming picture of you in the act of killing Dougal McAskill. Not a bad likeness, come to think of it.'

'What are you talking about?'

'You were seen, Mr Laidlaw. Even if that toothpick of yours gets me tonight, there's an eyewitness who saw you commit murder.'

'Who's that?' Laidlaw grunted, then swung forward again. His blade hissed past Lestrade's left ear and the superintendent whipped out the brass knuckles and pinned the sword to the bed.

'Earl Beardie,' Lestrade growled and brought the knuckles snaking backwards, raking across Laidlaw's jaw and sending him sprawling against the door. There was confusion and stumbling around in the blackness. When Lestrade found a candle again, the Highlander had gone, but at least he'd left his sword behind.

The superintendent leapt out of the room, checking the fallen Bandicoot as he went, and ran in search of his quarry.

Policemen are like Highlanders in one respect. They can both stalk game. Especially when the game was hurt and dripping blood. But Lestrade was hurt too. The exertion had opened his wound anew and blood was trickling crimson down his face. The spots of Laidlaw's spoor took him groping by candlelight to the first floor, where he lost it for a while, then to the ground. The superintendent ran past the straggling revellers, who looked aghast at a second bleeding man rushing past them.

Through to the kitchens Lestrade ran, where horrified skivvies pointed dumbly to the open door through which Laidlaw had just hurtled.

'A drop more cock-a-leekie, Mr Lestrade,' Mrs Comfrey called, 'afore ye go?'

Lestrade felt the freezing night air hit him like a wall. Away from the lights of the castle, his candle was snuffed out and he stood like a bloodhound, sniffing the wind.

'Over here!' a voice called.

He crossed to the corner, out of the icy blast, and saw a figure in duster coat, gauntlets and goggles standing next to a twin-engined machine, throbbing quietly in the night.

'Sphagnum!' said Lestrade. 'Did you see anybody come this way?'

'Aye,' Sphagnum shouted through his muffler. 'Get on.'

Lestrade grabbed the rim of the red sidecar and Sphagnum straddled the beast and kicked it into action. They roared through the drifted snow, past the avenue of limes, gaunt and bare against the night sky, and up towards the babbling waters of the Dean.

Here, Sphagnum jammed on the brakes and Lestrade somersaulted neatly over his feet to land face down in the snow. He sat up sharply to see Sphagnum towering over him. The words of the Duchess of Argyll came to his mind. 'Stay away from waterfalls,' she had said, and he glanced to his right where the river roared and rushed over the icy, black rocks. 'And don't accept lifts from strange men.'

Sphagnum hauled off the fur gauntlets. He opened the duster coat to reveal the kilt beneath. He tore off the goggles and Angus Laidlaw stood there, his dirk in his hand.

'Well, well,' said Lestrade, 'a very neat disguise. I didn't realize you'd gone via Mr Sphagnum's rooms. Or that you could drive his infernal machine.'

'Needs must when the Devil drives,' said Laidlaw. 'I canna promise your death will be as quick with this.' He raised the dirk. 'Anyway,' he wiped the blood from his swollen jaw, 'come to think of it, there's no reason why it should be. From now on, no more Mister Nice Person,' and he lunged for the sprawled superintendent. Lestrade caught the blade on his own, steel ringing on steel, and the two men grappled in the snow.

Laidlaw had it all on his side. Weight. Strength. The insanity of a cause. Lestrade found himself stumbling backwards in the snow, his head being slapped with Laidlaw's open hand, his groin being kicked by Laidlaw's open toes. He sank to his knees on the rim of the water and felt Laidlaw's fist come time and again into his face. The Highlander knelt above him, his foot firmly on Lestrade's wrist, the one that held the switchblade. He heard him grunt something in Gaelic, then shriek like the *Bean-Nighe* and raise the dirk in both hands above his head. Lestrade closed his eyes and waited for death.

It never came. At least, not on *that* hillside. Not by *that* waterfall. There was a crash and Laidlaw's body jerked forward, his chest peppered with dark spots. He writhed convulsively in the snow, his back torn to shreds with buckshot.

'Damn,' said a voice. 'Ma best coat too.'

Lestrade sat up, looking into the beaming face and smoking twelve-bore of Alistair Sphagnum. 'I think I owe you my life,' he gasped, fighting for breath. 'I'll say this for you, Sphagnum, your timing's impeccable.'

'Like everything else about me,' said Sphagnum, helping him up. He pulled Major Weir's staff, the one he had used to steady the gun for his aim, out of the snow. 'I told you,' he said.

'Magical properties. Without this, I'd have missed the wee bugger entirely.'

He kicked the dead man with his toe. 'Nobody steals my Quadrant,' he said. And he loaded Lestrade up and carried him back to the castle.

12

Lestrade took his leave the next morning. He'd tie up the paperwork later, but the Lord Lieutenant could be trusted to get the story straight. He said his goodbyes to Harry and Letitia, themselves packing to go home to their children – and his. He said goodbye to the Duchess of Argyll, who thanked him for arranging the music for last night's ball. She couldn't remember when she'd enjoyed herself more, but couldn't imagine what was keeping that nice Mr Ramsay.

At the castle gate, Lestrade looked up at the little iron-barred windows overhead, high near the battlements and the leads.

'Oh,' he said to Lord Glamis, 'I think this should be returned,' and he gave him the childish painting of a murderous Highlander, at work with his broadsword.

Glamis nodded.

'Mummy . . .' Little Elizabeth sat smiling in her mother's arms. 'That man still isn't deaded.'

Lestrade peered at her from under the bandage. 'Little lady,' he said, 'it's only a matter of time,' and he climbed aboard the Quadrant and was gone.

'So that, gentlemen,' said Lord Glamis, 'is the whole story. You will find the bodies of Mr Ramsay and Mr Laidlaw in the cellar. You'll no doubt wish to take them away.'

'Och, aye,' said Inspector McNab. 'My sergeant here will arrange a' that. We'd have got here sooner, my lord, but some bugger kicked the spokes out of our trap.'

He tipped his shapeless hat to Lord Glamis and he and Pond

trudged across the snow-rutted courtyard to the Forfar vehicle, with its refitted wheels.

'Well,' said Pond, 'what now?'

'Whisht,' said McNab. 'Lestrade's out of the way, now.'

'But he knows,' said Pond, looking carefully about him. 'He knows it all.'

'He doesn't know names,' McNab assured him. 'All he has is the word of a dead man that there's a conspiracy. Not the extent of it. We'll lie low for a month or two. Wee Fingal can explain things Over The Water. Between you and me, I always thought Laidlaw's methods were a trifle heavy-handed.'

He sensed the anxiety of his underling.

'Depend on it, Goldfish,' the inspector said, 'there'll be another time. Another place. Come on.'

There was a crunch of an Old Etonian foot on the gravel.

The Quadrant rattled into Princes Street that afternoon.

'Will you try for a train straight away? Or are you spending the night here?' Sphagnum asked.

'I'll get a train,' said Lestrade. 'You won't take it amiss when I say the sooner I'm at the Yard again the better. Time to see if I still have a job. Still, at least the Distillers will be pleased when you report to them. You can give them Allan Ramsay's head on a plate.'

'He was your collar, Lestrade,' Sphagnum said.

'After what you did for me last night, it's the least I can do,' the superintendent smiled. 'Now all the Distillers need worry about is the MacKinnons. Oh, by the way, I think I can trust you to burn this?'

He handed Sphagnum the envelope containing the ingredients of the Bonnie Prince.

'Good God,' said Sphagnum, 'so *that's* what's in it. As a chemistry student, of course, I had a suspicion . . .' and he lit the corner with a match. 'No, the Distillers will be all right, as long as Guinness doesn't try and take them over, that is.'

'Quite,' said Lestrade.

'Well.' Sphagnum extended a hand. 'The parting of the ways. I'm glad to have known you, Sholto Lestrade.'

'And I you, Alistair Sphagnum.'

'Tell me,' the Scottish detective said, 'will ye no come back again?'

Lestrade was silent for a moment. 'No,' he said, 'I don't think so.' His face said it all.

'Well, then,' grinned Sphagnum, 'lang may your rum leek, Lestrade,' and he roared off into the sunset. A moment later, he roared back. 'Forgot this,' he said. 'It came shortly before we left Glamis. Been rerouted from Balmoral. Luck to ye, Lestrade.'

Lestrade tore open the telegram. It said: HOW IS CASE GOING STOP BIT ALARMED BY EXPENSES STOP DON'T MEAN TO CARP STOP WAS MOTOR CAR PURCHASE NECESSARY STOP DID YOU NEED TO BUY A HOUSE AT COLDSTREAM STOP PLEASE EXPLAIN STOP CONNAUGHT

Expenses? mused Lestrade. Motor car? A house at Coldstream? Had Arthur of Connaught gone mad? He hadn't seen the Prince's chit to cover expenses since he last saw . . . Marshall and Snellgrove. A light of realization dawned in Lestrade's eyes. He rammed the telegram in his pocket, picked up the battered Gladstone and trudged doggedly round to Waverley Station, murder on his mind.

'A single to Coldstream,' he said to the ticket man, 'and make it snappy.'

'Are you Superintendent Lestrade?' the man snapped back in accordance with instructions.

'Perhaps yes and perhaps no.' Lestrade had learned to trust no one. Except Alistair Sphagnum. Harry and Letitia Bandicoot. Lord and Lady Glamis. One or two others.

'Well, if y'are,' the ticket attendant said, 'there's a telegram for you.'

'For me?'

'For Superintendent Lestrade,' the clerk said. 'I was told to look out for a funny wee, sleekit, cow'rin beastie with a bandage on his head.'

'Yes, that's me all right,' said Lestrade.

He tore open the telegram. It was from Harry Bandicoot. It said: OVERHEARD A VERY INTERESTING CONVERSATION IN THE COURTYARD AT GLAMIS THIS MORNING SOON AFTER YOU LEFT STOP CAN YOU COME BACK STOP SOMETHING YOU OUGHT TO KNOW ABOUT INSPECTOR MCNAB STOP

Lestrade gritted his teeth, took back the small change he'd

borrowed from Bandicoot, picked up the Gladstone and faced the north.

What was it Sphagnum had said? 'Lang may your lum reek'? Lestrade sighed. There really was no answer to that.